Evernight Publishing

www.evernightpublishing.com

WICKED FLOWER

DEDICATION

For Adrian

ACKNOWLEDGEMENTS

I was really touched during the writing of this book by some very special people who helped me with the research. A giant thanks to Josh "The Kentucky Gent" Johnson for being the visual of Will's tank tops which might seem like a small thing but to a writer, is huge. Smiles and fist bumps to a great bass player, Dino Villanueva, for happily taking time out of his busy schedule to answer a very long list of my bass playing questions. As always, thank you to my critique partners, Lynne and Kerri, my editor, JS Cook, and everyone at Evernight for continuing to support this series. All my love to my incredibly loving family. Most importantly, to you the reader, thank you from the bottom of my lucky little heart. Take it, it's yours. Enjoy. xoxo

WICKED FLOWER

WICKED FLOWER

A Sin Pointe Novel

Carlene Love Flores

Copyright © 2014

If you cannot be good, you should be the least bad you can be.

—Thomas More

Chapter One

Stefan could always tell when Will was about to lay one on him.

This should be fun.

He stared at the road ahead and waited while Will ran his usual course of fingers tapping his knees to hands tucking into his armpits and finally a mouthed "Oh shit." Will closed his eyes and fisted wads of his shorts into his hands. Stefan grinned and eased up on the gas before he took the next curve.

It was coming. Something good by the twist to his drummer's lips. Any second now…

"Have you ever had a girl go down on you while you were driving?" Will asked as they passed into the vicinity of Moonlight, Pennsylvania. "Because driving like a fricking maniac could kill any hopes of that ever happening and mangle your brand new baby too. Just sayin'. I know how much you love your new car."

Stefan flipped Will off. God, he loved this man.

But was Will kidding? Of course he had. It came with being Stefan Calderon. Will, of all people, shouldn't have had to ask.

Must be the outdoors. Or the insane amount of curves they'd flown through the last half hour.

Fresh air and curves, albeit not the ones found while driving, were known to have that effect on Sin Pointe members and the air didn't get much fresher through these old hills.

Since he was feeling kind, Stefan bit down to keep the answer to his friend's question to himself, even though something sweet and flowery in the air reminded him of the exact night the last time that very thing had indeed blown his mind. He'd enjoyed himself immensely. *Jasmine,* he thought. In a game of "Fuck truth, let's dare", the temptress had fair and square lost the right to tell him her name, but that scent made his mouth water. He took in a deep whiff and had to bite down even harder to spare Will the gory details.

With wind whipping through the convertible at all angles, Will secured the strip of mohawk he'd left unmoussed. It flogged him in the face as soon as he let go.

"Have you?" Stefan asked, wondering what his drummer would say. If Stefan had to guess, knowing Will like he did, he'd go with no. Check that. Will before Honey? Yes. Will after Honey? No. Love fucked men up. It was a mistake Stefan had yet to make like the rest of his bandmates.

"Nope, Honey was too shy for that kind of thing." Will's face was blank.

No big revelation there. Stefan knew his bandmates like he knew sex, music and breathing. In that order. In a few weeks, they'd be going back out on tour. Still the four original guys after all these years. Yeah, Stefan hadn't needed Will to confess his late wife's shyness and Will's devotion to her wasn't just written all over his stoic face, it was inked permanently around the drummer's wrist, over his heart, and across his ribs.

Stefan reached over and knocked Will's hand from the top of his head to lighten the mood, vowing to get Will back out there someday. The hair got sucked up into the wind again, bringing his mohawk back to life. Will adjusted his black-rimmed glasses, letting his hair fly. Clearly, his drummer was the most interesting bastard in the band. Stefan would gladly share his bedmates with Will but the man had yet to take him up on the offer. *Fucking love.*

Back to that blow job question. Stefan could tell the truth, but a lie seemed way nicer. "Nah, man. But that's fucking hot."

Will nodded his head and then let it fall back into the headrest while Stefan remembered a few years ago and the mess of red hair bobbing up and down in his lap as he sped down the 5. California had been bad but oh so good at times too. In an effort to save their souls, Jaxon had moved Sin Pointe out of the seedy streets of Los Angeles to the country loving arms of Nashville. Code for Jaxon and Marion had finally settled down and had their families with them so Stefan and Will needed to get with the program. Leave it to Jaxon to prove anything was possible. Stefan cleared his throat and Will threw him one quick look which he ignored.

"Oh, gas station sign. Twenty miles to the exit. Did you see it?" Will asked him, pointing.

"Food. Gas. Piss," Stefan said. "In that order."

"Gas. Piss. Food," Will echoed back at him. "In *that* order. Your new baby is almost on E."

This had been a long ass road trip and yes, his girl needed filling. But it looked like they were finally close to his mom's. There were truly beautiful green, lush trees everywhere. Tall ones that practically blacked out the sky in broad daylight. The hills went on forever. Stefan remembered the landscape well. Moonlight was close.

He blinked, but shadows from giant trees wouldn't hide Stefan's reluctance any more than closing his eyes to the past would. He wouldn't claim a fucked up childhood, just a confusing one.

More importantly, how was she doing? How was Mom going to look when he finally saw her? His seven year absence had been too long, he knew. Shit, the band had put out two records, even experimented with new sounds, and toured hundreds of cities since he'd last been here. Stefan closed his eyes tight, held them closed for several seconds, then cleared his throat again and playfully grabbed at Will's crotch as a diversion to his guilt and doubts about this return.

"Hey sexy, it's your turn to pump." He forced a grin out and Will punched his shoulder so hard it made the dog tags Will wore for his brother clink. Stefan rubbed the sting away and took in a deep breath of Pennsylvania air.

It had been so fucking long since he'd called this place home and trapped wasn't a good feeling for a grown man. Not one like him whose idea of ultimate happiness was to rip pleasure from life and its beautiful, willing creatures.

Reminders of his mistakes were not so appealing. Moonlight was full of them. He wiped at his brow and clenched the marbled toffee swirls of his lady's hard steering wheel tightly. *Forgetting why you left this place isn't as important as remembering why you're back now.*

His mom wasn't sick this time, but she was aging, it seemed faster than ever this last decade. Calling to wish her a happy seventieth had blown his mind. He'd promised himself then and there to visit more often, whether Mom welcomed it or not. Where had the time gone? If there was ever a time to show Mom she'd been wrong about him all those years ago and shouldn't be ashamed, it was now. "I have to show her," he muttered into the wind. His best friend graciously ignored him.

****

"God dammit," she said when her car lurched.

She'd seen that capital red "E" light up after leaving home but it hadn't seemed too important half an hour ago compared to the crappy morning she'd just had. When Dani could afford it, she was trading in her old gas guzzling Buick and getting herself one of those fancy new hybrids. Toyota or Honda, she couldn't decide, but one of them.

How far had she driven herself in her daze anyway? At this point, who the hell cared? It sure as shit wasn't far enough away. When she saw the sign for the truck stop, she sighed in relief. Far enough away from her bedroom and the damned email, but close enough if Mrs. C had an emergency.

Dani pushed her tongue against her cheek, feeling its heat, and debated cursing the Lord again or begging He let her at least make it to the next exit without stalling on the highway. Cursing the Lord wasn't cool and right now, He was undoubtedly the only good guy on her side. He was certainly the only man she cared to talk to after this morning.

"That's all I need," she said shaking her head. She pulled pieces of hair being whipped into her mouth back out but wasn't willing to roll up the windows to avoid it happening again and again and again. There'd be snarls to fight with later but she welcomed the perfect mix of cold and hot air while she could. A storm was due soon, the charcoal grey clouds pushing their way in and the battle between the cold and hot air all but guaranteed it. She, along with the rest of the town population, was out running errands before anything ugly hit. Just like they always did. Nothing new. She dreaded the lines and the familiar meddling faces. Especially today, a day when she just wanted to be left alone.

Even though her first instinct was to floor it to the truck stop when she saw the Pump-n-Go's billboard, she eased up on the gas pedal and came to a compromise on the tirade she'd been working on. "Thanks," she said under her breath.

What in the hell was she being punished for?

Wasn't she trying her best to do all the right things?

"Thanks for this damn messy day." Not only did she need to gas up, but her patience had been reduced to fumes.

How in the hell could he have done this to her? No, not the man upstairs, but Thom.

Dani's hand dropped to her stomach.

Her face was so tense she didn't feel the tears dripping down her cheeks until one streaked onto her forearm, making the soft dark hairs there even darker. She gripped the steering wheel tighter and stared up at the blue half of the sky where the sun poked through, trying to feel its warmth. Even with that, she drove on, tears and all.

As if crying over a guy who'd just shit all over her heart wasn't ridiculous enough, she'd be lucky not to disgrace herself before she got to the truck stop. Dani hated empty gas tanks and full bladders just about as much as she despised men right now. She hated it, but couldn't help but wonder if Thom was safe, even though he'd just emailed to say he had fallen in love with someone else.

Her fingers had hovered shakily over the keyboard but she wouldn't let herself type the words, I'M PREGNANT. Not yet. It would be a distraction to a man she somehow still managed to care about. Dani needed Thom to focus on his deployment and get himself home safe, even if it wasn't to her.

Soon it would be time for his mid-tour leave. She'd tell him then. That way he wouldn't be getting the news in a faraway country and war zone, away from his family. *Somewhere safe*, she thought, as her breath hitched and she sniffed her snot back in. "I'll tell him then, not in an *email*," she said and nodded her head.

And after that? Who the hell knew?

Right now, Dani was a bloated and confused mess, and she had to pee.

The only comfort, the one keeping her from sinking into this ugly grief, was knowing she was needed at home by Mrs. Calderon. Otherwise, she'd be a total wreck. Dani flashed her blinker and drove the rest of the way to the truck stop. When she pulled in, her phone flashed an incoming call.

"Shit."

The clinic.

She stopped in the lot just in time to answer. Except for her fingers were paralyzed and refused to move over the answer call button. Being dumped via email was settling in, stiffening up her joints and doing a number on her pride. Dani blew out then sucked air back in, exhaust-filled air that was heavy with hot diesel engine and rubber, several times. She wiped her cheeks dry and pushed in on her chin to stop the trembling. The old style telephone tone rang three more times and then finally she answered. It was just the automated reminder that she had her monthly OB check-up in a few days. Her fists squeezed and to calm them, she put her car back in drive, gripped the steering wheel as lightly as she could, and inched into the shortest line behind two other cars.

She'd be having her ultrasound at that appointment.

Alone.

Man, she felt like the most inadequate woman on the planet.

I don't know how in the hell we're going to do this, but it's just you and me now, baby.

A fresh storm of bumbling bees felt like they'd just landed in her lap. She felt one more tear fall while she rubbed the tiny rounded bump that was her belly. God, what if she'd have emailed Thom to let him know when she'd first found out she was pregnant? He probably would have never told her about his change of heart. She was glad she'd decided to wait. No way would she ever want a man to be with her out of obligation.

Dani rolled her window down to let the air blow through while she waited her turn in line. The car idling one pump over practically blinded her. Sitting inside the brilliant white convertible were two men. One wearing glasses, a tank top and tattoos thumped the dashboard madly with his fingers and the other, she couldn't see as well, but he could pass for a bearded Superman with the dark wavy hair and the strong arm draped over the steering wheel.

Talk about different and distracting.

She couldn't help but stare while she waited. Yep, she got a view of the hood emblem and it was a Mercedes. Must be nice. When they pulled forward in their pump's line, she saw the plates. Tennessee. *Definitely not from around here. Probably just passing through.* Dani had always wondered what that would feel like, but she'd never left the western half of Pennsylvania and in her current state, knew it wasn't an option. Besides, her Buick would never make it and men were just men, not super heroes.

   ****

  "Holy shit."

  "Yeah?" Will asked, clearly amused at Stefan's praise of the knock out getting gas in the next line. "Care to elaborate?" His friend rubbed a hand over the long, currently unbleached section of hair covering only the top of his head that had been whipped wild from the wind. With the mohawk now lying flat like that, Will did look slightly less sinfamous.

"Dude, why are you staring at me like that? You want some?" Will said teasingly.

  "Fuck you. I was just thinking it'll be nice not to be recognized out here. You know you almost pass for an upstanding citizen without your platinum spikes."

  "I could say the same for you, goat. That beard is temporary, right?" asked Will. "Jealous much? The ladies haven't had any complaints." Stefan threw back at his buddy but felt like shit as soon as he did, even though they were joking. Will didn't do women, not since losing his wife several years ago and he also had a practical reason for his mohawk. He'd been burned in the apartment fire that stole Honey from him and hair no longer grew in some patches on his scalp. Stefan didn't pretend to understand how Will went without—that was some serious devotion—but his good friend had become immune to most of his comments. Stefan eyed the dark haired woman across the way again who kicked at her gas pump.

Will hiked up one eyebrow. "You've only had that face rug for a few weeks. How many ladies are we talking about with no complaints? On second thought, maybe I don't wanna know. You slut." Will grinned at the end. The man was entirely too gracious to him. To all his band mates. It was why Stefan loved Will like a true brother and knew he'd eventually be okay in Nashville. Stefan? Not so sure of himself yet.

The truth was Stefan had only slept with one woman in that time Will just asked about. It had been three weeks now. The Tennessee beauty liked his stubble, but again, Stefan would keep those details to himself. It wasn't his fault the agent helping him find a place in Nashville was a triple threat and had liked his face rough, among other things. Funny though how Stefan hadn't been as into it as normal. Too much on his mind with coming home, he supposed, and finally showing up to Mom's with his big idea that she return to Nashville with him. Reminders that he might still be an embarrassment to her gnawed at his gut.

"Not my fault. She was a triple red. Not like I had a choice in the matter," he said eyeballing pump five some more and accepting Will would just have to deal with Stefan as-is. Her stance was so rigid, her shoulder blades showed through the back of her yellow hoodie. Someone or something had her pissed. Memorial Day gas prices maybe? He rubbed his lip and watched past Will.

Will waved a hand in front of Stefan's face to get his attention. "Triple red? Do I even wanna know?" he asked, his other brow hiked now.

"Hair. Lips. Thong." Stefan tossed Will his wallet. "Like I said, your turn to pump." He climbed out of the driver seat, much more slowly so he could take more of *her* in. She turned to see something behind her, giving him just enough of a glimpse before she was back at her stare down with the pump.

Full lips, probably too full for the average guy who wouldn't know how to appreciate them. But he would. Long legs. A round ass that the snug tracksuit she wore couldn't hide. He liked how her black hair looked hanging against the bright yellow color and Stefan wasn't the only one gawking. Two other dudes at pumps were checking her out too. *Keep your dicks in your pants, assholes.* That sharp stare focused on her pump's number ticker told him she could give a shit about her admirers and might just be ready to kick at something again. Probably didn't even realize anyone was interested, which made her all the more interesting. "Nothing. Just need to stretch my legs," Stefan said to Will and rubbed at his chest between his pecs. Will would see right through that lie.

"Pump five? Predictable. She's gorgeous in a next door gorgeous kind of way. Not your type, though."

Stefan just grinned and did his best to mess up Will's mohawk hanging limply to one side.

"Says who? She's hot. She's my type."

"Three words. Black, as in her hair, it's not red. Sober, as in she's not drunk therefore not falling all over you. And employed, as in…"

"Wait, how can you tell she's employed?" Stefan asked, eager to hear this one and ticked that Will insinuated he only got laid when alcohol was involved. Sober sex ranked right up there with safe sex. Both must haves.

"Well, she has a car and she's paying for her own gas. And uh, her shoes. The only woman I've ever seen in a pair like that was my dental hygienist."

What could Stefan say?

Sin Pointe men knew women and although Will didn't touch, perhaps he did more looking than Stefan was aware of.

Rather than argue the mountain of other explanations for those fine points, Stefan conceded. Sort of. Will deserved a little teasing. "Yeah, yeah, yeah. I get it. She's got a job which would seriously get in the way of all those late nights…"

But he stopped there.

Something about the way she looked like she'd love nothing more than to kick the shit out of the gas pump some more and strangle someone with the fuel hose killed the playful vibe of his chatter with Will. Something told Stefan she could really hurt a man. And hell, now that thought piqued him too.

"Hey, you good to get the gas? I'm gonna head inside," Stefan said, remembering why he'd snatched his drummer up and dragged him on this trip. Neither one of them were doing so hot on their own at the moment with the band's recent move to Nashville, even though it had been a year. He could pretend all he wanted, but deep down Stefan knew it might be time to take settling down in the band's new hometown seriously. The thought of his mom's age creeping up year by year, her need for a live-in helper, it made him wonder how he could keep walking away from her. How many more times could he leave, stay gone and then just assume she'd still be there for the next sporadic visit? That's where the crazy idea of relocating her had come from. But, Stefan could also feel his mom's rejection were he to ask her to come with him, her shame for things he'd done in the past. Mom was a proud woman. Independent as shit. The brand new house he'd bought her, only a few miles away from her current home, probably sat empty as the day he'd brought her to it and she'd told him no thank you. The house was on his list of things to check out these next two weeks, especially if he got to Mom's and their reunion didn't go well.

Just as he turned to head toward the shop, he caught the voluptuous woman's eye as she finished pumping her gas. So brown they were practically black, she looked at him curtly. If it hadn't been for the complete lack of humor he saw in those eyes, their depth and fire would have turned him hard. But Stefan was a grown man and that didn't just happen on the fly anymore. The pride he saw in her was strong, though. A strong woman turned him on.

Some desperate fool whistled at her back, and it wasn't Stefan.

A few minutes later, Stefan watched her hurry past the dickwads as she approached him near where he now stood at the store entrance.

"Excuse me," she said without bothering to meet his stare. Her coldness shocked him. Maybe even hurt a little.

Ridiculous, he thought, of his reaction to this stranger.

Stefan held the door open wider and let her pass. The old him wouldn't have let her get away so easily, instead having some macho thing to prove. But something about the way she shoved past without so much as a flirty nod told him he should let her be. Too bad it also had him curious. So who was gonna go inside and follow after her? The old Stefan, or the new one?

He rubbed just under his lip, deciding.

Maybe it was time to leave the game. Or maybe there was just enough time left for one more round.

Something told him it would be up to the lady.

"I guess there's no better time than the present to find out," he said to himself and pushed his sunglasses up on top of his head.

Chapter Two

The sub shop's smells used to be some of Dani's favorites. Now she could do with less baked wheat and pepperoni and more of the peppermint mocha that crusted over the cappuccino machine's spout. But caffeine was off her list for the time being. She'd finished enough medical assistant classes before dropping out to know what she needed to avoid to give this kid its best shot at being born healthy. Dani headed to the cooler for a bottled water and then back tracked to the snack aisle.

Grape licorice called to her. She knew better but grabbed a package and a thing of peanut butter crackers. Not the healthiest choices but she needed comfort and the crackers had some protein. At least none of it would give the little one a buzz. Hurt feelings pounded from her heart, making her face tense which she could feel in the tight way she had her jaw clamped shut. Absentmindedly, she walked to the cashier line. Thom's email had been easy to memorize. It poked fun at her now as she tried to block it out.

Dani looked to her right at the crusted frosting and stray sprinkles where donuts had been squashed up against their glass case. They were all gone now. Wouldn't have been good choices for her anyway...

Truckers needed their sugar too, she guessed, and glanced around the always busy place.

She wished for about a dozen less people to be crowding around her as she stood squished between the travel-size toiletries and dusty bags of cat food and antacids. Her stomach rumbled and she nearly cried again. The reminder that she needed to eat better, that her stomach wasn't exactly empty, forced her to fight for a grip.

But two seconds into that thought and she felt someone brush past her, only the guy made sure to graze her hip on the way by. She ignored it. Not in the mood, Dani simply pulled her arms in even closer to her sides and moved up one slot in the line. Unbelievably however, she heard a conversation taking place behind her that made her want to turn and slap someone. Instead she simply let out loud enough to be heard, "Grow up."

The guys behind her in line snorted but she'd had it with their snickering. Yes, her ass was big and yes, her lips too. It didn't matter what she wore, there was no way to hide all her *blessings,* as Mrs. C liked to say. Dani pulled down on her hoodie, as far as it would go. She'd have liked to have spun around and decked the two who she assumed were new-school truckers from their lack of manners, but she didn't. Biting into her tongue, Dani knew a truck stop brawl was not a good idea for a pregnant lady. She'd been ignoring taunts like that from guys her whole life, no need to stoop to their level now.

Not even in the state she was in.

Between blanking out through the donut case and these jerks, Thom's words crept back in.

Not sure how else to say this Dani, but I met someone over here. The connection is pretty fierce. You'd like her. Didn't want you to be surprised when I come back. Sorry. I understand if you're pissed. What you did for me before I left was incredible. I'll always appreciate that. I just...I really love this girl. You're great too and I didn't want to string you along. At least this way you know. Please take care of yourself, Thom.

The worst part? Dani knew Thom had done the right thing in telling her and that left her anger and hurt running rampant with nowhere to land. She had no idea what to do with it all. She caught the feel of her lip starting to quiver and took a moment for a few deep breaths. No way would she fall apart in this line. Dani had to focus on something else. Anything else.

Thom's dismissal had her on edge the same as it had that morning and that mixed with hormones the likes she'd never dealt with before egged her to a dangerous edge. A low, droning chatter filled the snack line. Dani turned to look at the intolerable guys behind her as the line took a collective step forward.

She started to lay into them, really let them have it, when a thick, deep, male voice pulsed out.

It vibrated. It was harsh and bold and full of taunt.

It stole the words right from her mouth.

"Shut your mouths, assholes."

It was the out-of-towner she'd pegged earlier whose bright white shirt stood out amongst the several darker, dingier truck stop varieties of the crowd. *A cursing Superman,* she thought and stared. Who would have known?

"She obviously doesn't want to hear it," he said. He touched a fine finger to a pair of expensive looking sunglasses sitting like a headband on top of his mass of dark waves. Up close, the curls were as thick as his voice and the exact reason Dani was pregnant.

Her whole life, his type of male was exactly her type and when she fell, she fell hard and fast. Her head ached as she closed her eyes and shoved the thoughts out where they wouldn't be so enticing. What would it take to learn her lesson?

The two smart mouths seemed at a loss for words now, Dani included. She opened her eyes, focused on getting her things and getting gone. But one glance and she was there again. Was it the intimidating height of the new guy or the unknown air he had of not being from around here? The way his clothes looked like they cost more than what she made in a month taking care of Mrs. C? When he folded his arms over his chest, she saw tattooed hands and forearms that worked to warn her of his danger just enough. Did she thank him for standing up to the two jerks? No. She knew better than to speak to him. Clearly, he was out of her league and would just blow her off anyway. *I'm probably his good deed for the day.* She was sure the ultra-rich did that, trying to get the balance right and all.

She just wanted out of there.

All she had to do was pay for her stuff, visit the restroom and then take the hell off. Dani righted herself to face the cashier counter head on and concentrated on the back of the man in front of her, studying the dates and locations of his concert t-shirt. But jerks one and two started up again and this time she didn't hear her rescuer piping up on her behalf. No, all she heard this time, still too close behind her, was more mean teasing. "I bet she thought we actually would have given her the time of day. Fuck her and her big ass. Busted out of those pants lately?"

Dani stood ramrod stiff, disbelieving their blatant cruelty. She couldn't turn and face them this time and hated the feeling that their stares were fixed on her ass as they let out their harsh taunts. She wanted out of there. Forget it. She dropped her snacks and water on a nearby shelf and abruptly left her place in line to go find solace in the bathroom. A hot tear managed its way down her cheek. Quickly, she wiped it away.

You'd like her... I really love this girl.

Dani opted to walk the length of the truck stop, squeezing her hands as she went, bypassing the busy bathroom closest to her, hopeful there was another one at the far end. Desperate, she picked up her pace. Hunger pangs rumbled around and her stomach growled but right now she needed a minute to regain her composure and hide.

Finally, she made it to the bathroom. It sounded quiet enough that it could be empty and she let herself hang limply over the sink for a moment. She stood there, hugging her face in her hands.

Honorable men, shallow men, rude men and kind men. What was wrong with her that she couldn't get on the same page with at least one of them? She was twenty-six years old. Why hadn't it happened yet? What was it about her that caught their attention at first until they got bored and then left? She hated her body in that moment. The fact that she attracted a certain type of attention, the kind that called to the wrong kind of man.

Worse?

That she fell every single time.

Her Thom, who she'd thought cared about her, was in love with some woman he was deployed with. How did Dani hate a female soldier out fighting for her freedom? Couldn't Thom at least have broken her heart with someone less heroic? Now Dani was left behind with his baby growing in her belly and guilt every time she tried to curse him for it. Four months along, four months since he'd deployed.

What you did for me before I left was incredible.

Dani's head now slumped as she gripped the sides of the sink. She turned on the faucet and let the cold water cool her skin. She'd been so dumb, sleeping with him the one time, the night before he left. Just in case he didn't come home. Her idea, her insistence. Stupid, stupid, stupid.

"Why? Why? I don't understand. What is wrong with me?" she let out in frustration. Her head swam with insecurity. Thank God she was alone. Surely this was an ugly sight and she didn't want to be seen.

****

Stefan had to pee in the worst way. Finally, he found a toilet that wasn't closed for cleaning. As he rounded the entrance to the men's, he caught the reflection of a bright yellow pant leg poking out from the women's. The ill-placed mirror probably got lots of complaints from ladies wanting their privacy but he could kiss whoever had screwed up and placed it so perfectly. There she stood, at the sink.

Fuck my luck.

Normally he didn't make it his habit to stalk women at truck stops, but he'd recognize the bright yellow outfit and those shiny, colorful snakeskin clogs for a long time to come. Man, she'd gotten a few deadly kicks in on that gas pump earlier in them. Reminded him not to ever be on the receiving end. At least not unprepared. She had a definite fire inside. He should be preparing to see his mom and everything that entailed, not picking up on pump five's vibes, but they were impossible to ignore. This peek was the most excitement he'd felt on his and Will's road trip. Slowly, he scraped his teeth against his bottom lip, deciding.

At least he didn't have to wonder about one particular burning question anymore. This is where his mystery woman had gone to. He'd had to leave her earlier while she'd been in line because that's all he needed was to make a scene and bitch slap those two dildos who'd teased her. His hand had been seconds away from the taller one's face. Hopefully they'd heard his warning loud and clear and left her alone. He'd bent down in the next aisle over to grab some gum and find some other cashier and when he'd looked back up, she'd disappeared.

He was contemplating going in there and checking on her right now, crazy as that sounded. She'd stolen his attention right from the jump.

Stefan stood, glancing around, grateful no one had followed him. He was rarely this lucky. He thought about the dark eyes and the angry kicks. How she'd treated him just like any other stranger, unaffected by him, but so obviously affected by something.

He'd pee and then if she was still in there, he didn't know what exactly then, but a friendly gesture of checking in on her didn't seem so wrong. It's what Trista would have expected him to do and he loved Tris like a sister. He and the rest of the guys still missed the hell out of her now that she was no longer the sheriff that kept their asses in line on a daily basis. Better known to the rest of the world as a personal assistant. But after the trauma she'd gone through for them, Stefan was happy Trista had made her exit when she did. Now she was in Tennessee too, married to Jaxon's cousin. Maybe it really was the kinder, gentler place where LA's bad boys went to become good men. And women.

Stefan pissed, then washed his hands and dried them using the super blower.

Trying not to be noticed or taken for a perv, he glanced back at the mirror but didn't see the yellow pant leg again and the colorful shoe.

He ducked in the entrance more and hunched over to see if any legs occupied the stalls. Maybe she was a clean freak and liked to wash before and after doing her business.

There, in the first stall. She appeared to be the only one. He poked his head in further, knowing Will was most likely taking his time in the gift shop. Stefan had a few minutes just to make sure this one was okay. He half expected to find her kicking something.

"Hey," he snuck in and tapped on the stall door. "Hey, sweetheart, in the yellow."

At first there was just silence.

"This is the women's," she called out. The edge in her voice was hard to miss and even harder to ignore.

"I know, I saw you in line earlier. Are you okay?"

"What? Who? What are you doing in here?" she snapped back. He was close enough to see her squint at him through the crack in the metal doors. Definitely pissed. But like a moth to the flame as the saying went...

"I know this is crazy, but I just wanted to make sure you're okay. Those assholes in line were just clueless losers." Why was he in here doing this? Trying to join that scumbag club he'd just mentioned? His charms didn't seem to be working and wouldn't the guys love a "perv in the women's restroom stalking incident" headline splashed all over the trash magazines if she reported him.

"You should leave," she said, but some of the bite was gone and he was sure he heard a sniffle.

Ah man, not tears, he thought. He didn't do well with those.

"Yeah, you're probably right. So, I guess that's what I wanted to tell you, sweetheart. Don't listen to pricks like that. They don't know what the fuck they're talking about." Stefan waited but this time she didn't respond. He waited another few seconds. "All right, well I'll let you, uh, finish up. Won't bother you anymore."

"Wait," came her soft, shaken sounding voice.

All he could picture were the fleshy plump lips that would have formed that one word. And in true old him form, his mouth watered at the vision she'd left him at the pump and again in line. A woman who didn't want to be messed with who he couldn't seem to leave alone.

The stall door opened and she held a wad of toilet paper up to her nose then tossed it in the trash. She had been crying. Those douche bags must have kept at it when he'd left. Maybe he didn't care about making a scene if it meant satisfying his odd need to do right by her.

"Hey sweetheart, what's a matter?" he asked. No woman should be left alone, crying. Stefan had no doubt in his ability to cheer her up. If she'd let him, he'd take her to a very happy place right alongside him.

"Men," she said, obviously trying to be strong in front of him with her throat clearing and tall neck. "Not a big fan of them right now."

He fought to keep himself from grinning. She was serious, he should be too. Stefan found that he liked her too much to piss that away.

"Me neither," he said. "They can be such dicks."

He thought that would have made her laugh but she just launched into a painful set of tears that made him shift from his eyes to his feet. Stefan hated seeing women cry or be hurt. He worshipped them way too much for that shit. It was uncomfortable and he needed to make it stop.

"Hey, don't cry. Come here." He wished he knew her name. Who in their right mind would insult such a beauty? Jackasses. The thing was she'd kicked that pump like a hot-blooded woman, not some delicate flower who'd crumble because of a few slimy words.

That being said, something had happened to bring on the waterworks. He tucked her into his arm and led her back into the stall, sensing she wouldn't want to be seen like this by anyone. He closed them into the cramped space.

Oh fuck, big mistake. His cock leapt to attention faster than he'd expected.

"What's wrong with me?" she asked him blankly, distracting him from her tense, hot shoulders and the way he wanted to surround her with his. She was curvy but he was still much larger than her. It was a huge turn on and a call to the way he wanted to dominate her.

Should she be letting him get this close?

It only took him a second to guess that could be her problem. He'd seen it a thousand times. The tougher the girl, the more fragile the self-esteem. Those girls— women, he corrected after glancing down her voluptuous body. Those women got hurt the worst. He had to back off this one, now. If not now, as soon as he cheered her up. Someone had already been here and done that as far as causing pain went.

"Who says there's anything wrong with you, sweetheart? Not me." He pardoned himself for the lie. Kind of like he did on a regular basis with Will. He might have broken a few hearts in his time, but Stefan didn't go around hurting people if he could help it. That's why it had always bugged him that his Mom could think him capable of it.

"You don't have to say that."

Shit, he wished he might have been wrong but that rang of low self-esteem.

Stefan rubbed at the whiskers covering his jaw allowing him anonymity. She trusted him, or was jacked up enough to be letting him close for now. If Stefan Calderon of Sin Pointe had shown up, he could guarantee this would have played out much differently. It always did. For some reason, he didn't want to be that guy with this girl. His attraction to her lingered thickly between their bodies.

"Look, I don't know what assholes you've been listening to, but they're not worth your time if that's why you're in here crying. You're a beautiful young woman."

He didn't have to tilt her chin with his fingers to make her see him.

On her own, she looked at him, rather fiercely, and her dark brown eyes held him. She wore desperation like night old makeup. Maybe that's all this was. Stefan understood intense, depraved need better than most.

"Now you sound like my ex," she said and continued to pin him with those eyes.

Bingo. The asshole who'd hurt her. "How ex are we talking about?" he asked.

Her mouth worked like it wasn't something she wanted to share. She held up her hands and her shoulders hiked. "This morning," she said, then let her shoulders fall limp.

Hell. What kind of...? "Dumb ass motherfucker," he said, finishing his thought out loud.

She shrugged again, like it was just one of those things and he shouldn't be surprised. Then her shoulders began to really shake. "I hate him most of all because he's a good guy."

In other words, she hadn't seen it coming. Fuck, how many times had he pulled that shit?

And right now, her grace was right up there alongside Will's. She should be cursing this so called good guy to go bald or for his dick to shrink. Most women he knew fresh off a breakup would have been doing at least that. Her hand went to her stomach and she rubbed it like she was trying to soothe hunger pains.

"Hey, if I run out real quick, do you promise to be here when I get back?" he asked, an idea brewing in his head.

"Um, I don't know," she said with fresh wrinkles from where she frowned so cutely. He wished he hadn't used the word promise and he couldn't get over how hot it was that she continuously blew him off. "How long?"

31

she asked. He caught a trace of fear slide from the corner of her eye when she looked sideways. "How long?" she said again.

"I'll be right back. Just wait."

Stefan left—something told him she'd stay—and made his way to a secondary, smaller snack area near their end of the truck stop. Thankfully he found what he was looking for quickly and there was a cashier manning the register. He paid for her treat, something she'd had in her hands when he'd seen her in line, and made his way back to her stall, grateful no one seemed to have found out about their secret hideaway. He took a look at his phone. No text from Will yet.

"You still in there?" he asked as he tapped his knuckles gently against the metal door. But he knew she was because the kaleidoscope of colors on her snakeskin clogs stood out. "It's me." He nearly spit out his name but held back. When a woman didn't ask for it, they almost always had their reasons. He didn't blame the ones not caring who he was, only wanting sex, because sometimes that's all he wanted too.

The door made a metallic sounding groan as she opened it and let him back in.

"Here," he said. "For you."

Stefan started to hand her the package of grape licorice but when her face lit up, he pulled it back. Curious that such a simple thing pleased her so much, he didn't mean to tease her, but couldn't help it. Until she frowned.

He wouldn't be mean for long but he craved her strange reactions to him. Stefan bit a corner of the plastic wrapping off and pulled out one piece. Would she tell him to grow up or insist she didn't like being teased? The sweet, distinct smell overpowered their small space. He held the purple candy stick out to her and rather than furthering the play by taking his offering into her mouth, she tugged it from him with her fingers and then fed it to herself. Which, fuck, was even hotter. He just smiled, hiding the heat exploding under his skin.

    "Listen, you're not just beautiful," he told her as she chewed and then took another piece when he held out the package. "And this ex of yours might be good, but..." She wouldn't be pleased if Stefan insulted this guy, no matter that her heart was broken. He could sense that much. "He's obviously not too bright. You're fucking sexy as hell, and yeah it's an old cliché, but any guy would be lucky to have you." He pinned her with a stare and waited to see how she'd take that last bit. Damn, he must really want in her pants because even Stefan knew he was laying it on thick. She took out another piece of licorice but to his surprise, she offered it to him instead of eating it herself. The smell was way too sweet—not his particular liking—so he smiled, showed her the gum he was chewing between his teeth and offered the licorice back to her. Now if she'd have offered to let him eat it from her mouth, he'd have downed the whole package, no matter how nasty the sweet grape would have made his cinnamon gum.

    She shook her head and wiped her nose. The cute but reddened tip of it rose and she said, "Prove it."

    Come again?

    Had he heard her right?

    His cock had, crystal clear. Stefan shifted, trying to find a comfortable spot for his junk. Damn, it wasn't happening and her eyeing him only taunted and grew him more.

    "Prove it?" he asked, his voice rumbled in his throat, not quite the growl he could have let out but close.

    A sniffle sounded when she breathed in. She dared him with her eyes.

Fuck, Will probably had his pizza by now and who knew what other gift shop oddities. But no way could he leave her after what she'd just said. Old him, new him. In the middle him. This was about her.

Self-esteem wasn't her problem.

She had a wild streak, and she'd just dared the wrong man. He stared, hard and direct, committing to take her on with each second that ticked by between them. The package of licorice fell to the floor. Heat made everything smell sweeter in their four by four metal box.

"You don't mean that," he said into her face, allowing her the time to back off and recant if she'd just been fooling with him. If all she'd wanted were the words of praise he'd already given her and nothing else. More often than not, the good ones did that, no matter how curious they were about him. He knew he gave off a strong sexual aura. Intimidating to some, he hadn't always been like this.

He waited, ready to play but expecting her to call game over any second now.

Chapter Three

Prove it.

In her head, Dani had thought those two words would have been the things to send Sinister Superman running. But here he was, inching closer. The four metal stall walls absorbed nothing. Not his smell that splashed itself on her skin like expensive cologne and none of his sensual intensity that scorched her throat. What had she gotten herself into with this one? She licked her teeth, hoping they weren't purple with licorice bits stuck in the cracks.

"I meant it," she said, not letting herself chicken out now that he'd pulled her in with those sexy but tender eyes and the candy gesture. Thom might not want what she had to offer, but something told Dani this guy did. That he'd take it greedily and not apologize afterward. But then his eyes narrowed like he didn't believe her. If he was rich like she suspected, that unrepentant air shouldn't come as a surprise.

"You want proof?" he asked. He took his aviator sunglasses from that crown of dark waves on top of his head and coolly set them down on top of the toilet paper dispenser. Dani followed his hands as he did so, admiring his movements and the crisp precision of his tattoos. "You sure about that?" The way he looked down at her caused Dani's skin to shiver.

He was giving her an out, wasn't he? He went so far as to back away from where he'd been standing over her and leaned against the furthest stall wall, still only a foot away. This close up, she could see the stitched detail of his white shirt, the tiny little squares making a mesh-like pattern over a thicker under layer. There wasn't a smudge on it anywhere but it clearly showed the muscles of his chest where he was broad, and then it was loose near his waist where he was undoubtedly narrower. He held up his colorful hands as if saying she could pass by him freely and she noticed a small black cross on his palm at the base of his thumb. She hoped it was a sign that he feared God or at least had faith in something. At this point, she didn't think he would hurt her although to be honest, what did she know about men? But something told her his gesture of letting her pass was genuine and maybe his biggest flaw was that he was simply horny. If she was having a change of heart, she'd better do it now because each slow blink of his eyes with those long dark lashes reminded her of the time ticking by. Something about him and this crazy situation fired her already heightened hormones to life.

I can't lie to you ... I understand if you're pissed.
Thom had no idea.

Neither did this guy ... she almost asked him his name but realized quickly she didn't want it. Not knowing was better. He would simply be known to her as Superman.

And, if the dark intense man locked in this stall, breathing the same air lied to her, it wouldn't matter. There would be nothing for her to understand and no reason for her to be pissed. No email to cry over. Just the feeling any woman wanted, once in a while at least, to be cherished.

Should she touch him? His tanned neck and dark gaze called her to do it. She felt her fingers curl but forced them to stay relaxed and instead squeezed her toes. He couldn't see those. They were hidden and he wouldn't know her reaction to him was so strong. Not yet.

No, he had to make the first move. What would be the point then? Otherwise, he wasn't proving anything. If she was sexy, desirable as he'd said, let him show her.

"Whatever happens right now, don't make me any promises," she said, her eyes falling victim to the shiny silver metal of the toilet to their side. But just as quickly she brought her eyes back up and locked them on him. "And be convincing." Yes, it was bold. But they had to get this right, no screw ups, so she could at least have this one moment. And when she saw Thom around town with his love, she'd have this one memory to fall back on. From here on out, it would be all about her baby. Dani blew out.

His black eyebrows hiked up at that and in the center of his chin she could see the cleft area where his whiskers pooled in the small circular dent and became even darker. She had the urge to set her fingertip over the dimple where it looked like it would fit perfectly but she didn't, still needing him to make contact first.

He reached out one long arm and tilted her chin up with no more than the crook of his tattooed finger.

She wanted to let her head loll back. To sink to the floor before him. She stood tall and focused on anything she could not to get lost so easily, so fast.

The inked patterns so precise, this man hadn't gotten them just anywhere. He had to have paid good money for the intricacy. No doubts about it. He wasn't from here. He was just passing through and would be long gone once he pulled out, in his expensive, white European luxury car on his way to some place like New York City. Those things made him perfect for right now. The one clear thing ... his gaze was burning a hole through her chest each time he failed to keep his eyes raised. Those dark eyes drifted again.

"I promise," he said, chasing the words she'd asked him not to use with a definite grin. His cockiness sealed her decision to do this and promised, like he'd just said, to follow through and to do it well enough to leave her with no doubts.

At least you know up front what this is. You can move on with no strings.

All she needed was a passionate kiss and some rough hands. Both of which dark-eyed, tatted Superman, seemed perfectly capable of providing.

"Fine," she said and straightened her spine when she realized she'd let herself slip a few notches with his gaze and the erotic things it promised.

The air became wicked and hot as she took her next breath and he eyed her ominously.

Carnally.

He wrapped his arm around her back and then pressed her against the wall with his manly chest. His body heat was as intense as his stare. Her head clunked at the metal but her masses of thick hair shielded her from the pain.

"Sorry," he said.

She didn't care. Hadn't really felt it. The pain that was. Wouldn't have stopped him if she had.

He hooked a finger into her mouth, enough to wet it, and then pressed and swiped it over her bottom lip. In response, he licked his own. The rawness he just shared unlocked something inside her, the pain she needed to dull with whatever passion she had left. Continuing, she bit down on his finger until he gasped.

"Ouch," he said, his naughty intentions clear in those gorgeous brown eyes and throaty voice. "Kiss that," he told her. His kissable lips barely moved with the sexy, bossy demand.

She did. Her heart pounded at this recklessness and at something else. Something hid in his eyes, darkening them. Like he needed this too? She was delirious and didn't care.

As soon as Dani followed that one command, he let loose on her. Like he'd been a coil of repentance just waiting to be given the okay to spring forth and indulge again.

His hands moved to her shoulders and pressed them back and held her there then it was his lips. Like time was precious to him, he didn't waste a single second of it debating. He was all forward motion and deliberate action. Whether she was prepared or not, Dani had his kiss, his taste, his hot breath with no breaks for breathing or thinking. His mouth adored her face and neck, leaving them wet.

"Why do you taste so good to me, sweetheart?" he whispered, so deep it felt like his words reached all the way into her lungs. It was understood he didn't want an answer. He ran his tongue along the ridge of her upper teeth like they'd been doing this for months. She had the sudden and fierce urge to bite down again. For all the women—surely there had been a few who had come before her—trapped in his cinnamon tasting mouth, and the ones who would undoubtedly come after this little tryst was over. But no, this wasn't for those other women. He was Dani's right now. God, she prayed he didn't have someone currently.

She nearly lost her nerve at the thought.

She would ask but he was no one to her. No names, not his, not hers, not anyone who might be his.

This was for her.

And it would never happen again.

She would be a mom soon and not just a woman licking her wounds.

"It's not me, it's the licorice," she let out and found the courage to offer him the tip of her tongue. He took it hungrily, nibbling it and then sucking her into his mouth. Every angle he took this kiss to let his dark whiskers scrape against her cheeks. Then he ran a thumb over the angried skin as if he was trying to soothe it. The callous of his fingers was just as tough. She didn't care. At least he tried.

No, no forgiveness allowed.

"It is you, if I say so." He had no idea the thrill his territorial words gave to her fractured ego.

"Cinnamon." Her voice was all hot breath under the onslaught of his tongue.

"That's me. You like how I taste too, sweetheart." He showed her his gum then swallowed it and gave her more just then, letting his tongue slide next to hers with a long slow lick. He planted a soft kiss that got lost inside her mouth. He pushed his hands without any calculation against the sides of her face, capturing hair in uneven handfuls she could feel between the pressure of his fingers and her skin. It pulled a little. She didn't care because somehow she knew he hadn't meant it. He was simply into what he was doing to her. That's what she was after.

She nodded to answer him. Yes, his spicy taste carried her to someplace else. She liked it. Too much.

He sucked more of her lips into his mouth then and she didn't know how long she could last with him. They were merely kissing and her tummy was already swirling, her legs already weak. Blankly she remembered they were in a truck stop bathroom so this couldn't last long. Somewhere, he had a life to get back to, the same as her.

With time seeming to both stand still and tick by at extraordinary speed, Dani accepted this could all be

over before she was ready for it to end. Before she'd
proved to herself Thom was wrong.

"Make the most of it," she said, barely making
sense.

He pulled his face back the second the words left
her mouth but still cupped her ear on the one side and jaw
on the other in his warm and tattooed, calloused hands.
Everything else she'd noted about him seemed so refined,
except for those callouses. She wondered what a well-off
guy like him did with his hands for a living but refused to
ask. It wouldn't matter. Pressure from his thumbs rubbed
tiny circles that served to both relax and electrify her. He
was so good with those hands, maybe he was a
millionaire masseuse.

Dark chocolate brown eyes, so deep she nearly
missed the gold flecks mixed in, dared her to make
another slip like that.

"You don't know what you're asking,
sweetheart." His sincerity gave her a chill.

Clearly he was right. But right now, she didn't
care.

****

She had no idea what she was dangling in front of
him right now.

Every second she stuck it out, he could bet she
was daring herself. He'd have to be a dumbass not to
know this meant something to her. Her determination,
that amping up she had to be doing to have stayed in here
with him, kept her skin hot and smelled so fucking good.

Stefan leaned into her, testing space and need.

She was no petite little thing. The areas he liked
smaller were deadly so, like her wrists and her waist. The
others, where he liked a woman ample, she promised to
be plenty. Her thighs kept distracting the shit out of him.

Fuck it that they were in a goddamned public shitter.

He gave her more of his weight and pressed his chest to hers. She should know he was all man and she should have at least a few seconds to decide if this was what she really wanted. Her back arched, her hips moved. Shit, *he* needed a few seconds, which wasn't the norm.

"Yes, I do know. Wouldn't be here if I didn't," she said to him. "Just don't squeeze me."

Everyone had their pet peeves. He didn't particularly like that ultra-sticky lip gloss women wore nowadays. He would remember hers. "No squeezing," he told her. Then her hands reached around and dipped to his ass. Her breasts had nowhere to go but to press into his chest. She rolled her rib cage just then and angled her neck, granting him complete access. Okay, maybe she did know what she wanted. Didn't mean he wasn't gonna make her say it.

"Tell me what you want, sweetheart. Exactly," he said into her mouth, nibbling some of that plump decadent lip between his teeth. "What you want … and I promise I'll do it for you." Then he whispered his long-standing caveat. "If you've changed your mind and we're done, then we're done. No harm, no foul." He caressed her cheek softly, knowing she wouldn't leave. Her need to be touched flamed between them. His cock thickened at that display of need she couldn't help or hide.

She breathed out and the rest of his body tensed, ready to take and claim and satisfy her.

"Whoever you are, make me feel like I'm the only one."

There was only one way Stefan knew how to do that.

He let both hands drop to her waist and then followed the curve back out to her hips. "Make you feel it here?" He rubbed the soft lemon velour covering her ass cheeks and then slid his hands under the material, bypassing the panties she wore as they were short on time. Her skin was soft and filled his hands as he squeezed. "Sorry, you said no squeezing," he let out. Hers might have fluttered closed but keeping his eyes open and on her face was essential. He'd know the exact moment he crossed a line.

"There is okay," she said with more breath than voice. Her eyes were half hooded, a sign he was doing a good job, as he kept one hand on her supple cheek and moved the other around to caress her hip. The warm skin and womanly bone pleased him. What he wouldn't give to have her naked and mounted on all fours.

She leaned forward and whimpered into his shoulder. "I just want to forget."

Fuck, why did that make his chest tighten? But it was all he needed to keep going. He watched her get lost when his one hand trailed up the zipper line of her hoodie and then back down to her pants' drawstring.

His body primed to provide for her. He relented and finally let his cock become completely full and hard. What he wouldn't give to be naked with her too, enjoying her gifts.

She blinked a couple quick times as he came to life against her thigh.

"Fuck sweetheart, if I had more time, this would be so much better." His hand left her ass cheek and tugged her hair gently from behind then pushed her head to his so he could kiss her.

"I believe you," she let out as they kissed slower now. Less like complete strangers, more like new lovers.

With his other hand, he found her moist and warm as he stroked the outside front of her panties. She rubbed his hip over his pants with the backs of her knuckles.

"Mmm, I like that." He bit her lip and then kissed it in case he'd hurt her. "Sweetheart," he whispered into her mouth. His brain failed him when he told her the rest, "I want to fuck you."

"I don't do that with strangers," she said, but her voice lied. Yes she would. With him at least. Maybe it was just the words she didn't like. At any rate, he was glad she'd said it. Imagining her doing this with anyone but him pissed him off.

But this wasn't making love. He wouldn't be a dick and lie to her.

"What about this?" he asked and kissed down her neck until he found the hollow of her throat. He circled the area with his tongue, over and over, wanting to make up for his crude comment, until he felt her nails gouge into his back. He didn't stop and she whimpered.

"Please, you can't give me an orgasm," she said quickly like it was a stipulation she'd failed to mention.

"I assure you, I can. If that's what you want."

"No, that's not what I mean," she said and pulled her neck away.

All of a sudden, Stefan's arms felt oddly heavy. What was he doing to this girl? How was this good for her? And what exactly did she want from him?

But then her fingers left his hip bone and a second later he felt them cup him. Her grasp started soft and then became harder, firmer. "Just be nice. Okay?" she asked, killing him with her game. How did he fuck her and not make her come? There was something he wasn't getting.

"I promise," he said, but decided in that second that being nice to her meant something else. Something the new him decided to risk and try out. Clearly the air out here had affected him, not just Will. What he was about to do was crazy, especially when all he wanted was to hold and fuck and please her.

He kept his mouth on hers while he dug his hands into his pockets. She was going to have to understand, well learn fast anyway, that he cherished a woman's body like he did breathing air. This stall was too cramped for the ways he'd like to adore her and he was short on time right this second but he was in town for two weeks and would like to see her again. "Have dinner with me," he said into her ear, taking a small break from their kiss.

Shit. She didn't answer. Stefan grabbed for his cell phone which was wedged tight against his wallet in his back pocket. He wasn't willing to give up yet.

He nearly had it out when she unbuttoned the first button of his fly and tried to wedge her hand down the front of his pants but it was too tight, filled with his cock she'd left throbbing.

"Dinner? I, I don't know." She moaned more deeply now. The sex dripping sound surprised him and his wallet fell to the ground with his phone. Was she really saying yes to crazy hot bathroom sex but no to dinner with him?

Shit, that was smooth.

Distracted, he reached down to pick them up but she had the same idea. Being shorter, she was closer and got to his wallet first.

The damn wallet was old and worn and barely held anything anymore. He'd bought it from an inflight magazine once on the advice of a flirtatious flight attendant. It was supposed to have lasted forever. His driver's license fell out and she grabbed that for him too. She handed him the wallet and the phone but held onto his ID. That was fine. He didn't have anything to hide from her.

"Yes, dinner. And if you still want that proof, that too," he said and kissed her cheek. "I actually have a house not too far from here. It's uh, in Moonlight. We could eat, talk. Have amazing sex." He ran his fingers up the back of her neck and massaged. "Whatever you want." Why was his heart pounding so hard and why did she look like she'd like to disappear right now? Her face lost its pretty pink wash of passion from minutes ago. She'd really wanted him to pound her in here?

The look in her eyes a second later branded him. She'd obviously been ripped out of their zone. Dammit, and new-him was the ripper. Fuck.

"Stefan Calderon?" she asked.

His license fell from her hands to the ground. The kitten was out of the bag and the pussy did not look happy.

She ran smooth, lightly tanned fingers over her black hair and her fleshy lips, like she was trying to wipe away his touch.

That had never happened before. And damn, it didn't feel good.

"Yes, that's me," he said. He'd give a million dollars to know what she was thinking and a few more to be told why.

She backed out of the bathroom stall so fast, she literally became a bright yellow blur.

What the hell? It was all he could think at her abrupt reaction.

"Hey, wait," he called after her and leaned down to pick up his license, reading his name and wondering why it had been so offensive to her. Did she have a thing against musicians? Read one too many articles about the dick lead singer of Sin Pointe? Been just toying with him this whole time? Until just then, he was sure she really hadn't known who he was.

Just like that, she was gone.

His lips were swollen from their kiss, no doubt he'd left hers just the same. She'd wanted it, been into it as much as him. He picked up their uneaten licorice and his shades.

At a total loss, Stefan left the bathroom as a girls basketball team filed in. Half of them eyed him suspiciously but the others gave him flirty looks he'd rather not have seen on such young faces.

Stefan kept his eyes alert, searching out the bright yellow but nothing matched her as he passed through the crowd. He ran into Will whose hands were full of food and drink and a thin plastic bag that looked to be filled with CD's and DVD's. He sat on a giant silk flower planter with all his goods.

"Hey man, sorry it took me so long but the pizza crew were fans. They wanted pics and asked me to sign a few things. They gave me way more pizza than I can eat alone. So, you're welcome. And, we should probably get going."

Stefan glazed over most of what Will had just said. "Did you see that girl in yellow from pump five come through here?" He should have gotten her name.

"Nah man. Why?"

Stefan looked around some more as they walked out the truck stop doors to where Will had parked the car.

"You hooked up with her, didn't you? Where? In the bathroom?"

"Not exactly." Stefan wished. "Something spooked her."

"Shit man, maybe stranger danger? Smart girl after all."

"No, it was more than that. We were vibing. I actually asked her to dinner. Then she just left."

Will's eyebrows shot up. "She bolted on your dinner invitation? What did you do to her before that? Had to be something, man."

"Nothing. She saw my driver's license, said my name, then took off."

It didn't make sense and he couldn't shake the feeling that he'd left her worse off than when he'd found her. The feeling sank into the pit of his stomach and brought up memories of how he'd been forced to leave things with his teenage girlfriend twenty years ago. Mom had jumped so fast to believing Amanda's parents over him. No matter how much he'd tried to stand up for himself and get Mom to believe the truth, Mom never took his side. From the moment the Coopers accused him of getting their daughter pregnant and then not taking responsibility, Mom's eyes had never seen him the same way.

"Hey, it just wasn't meant to be. She wasn't your type anyway. What's gotten into you?"

Will got his attention back but he was wrong. That one, that woman could have been exactly his type. He'd never felt that way. Unfortunately, now he'd never know. "Nothing," he said. "I guess you're right, it was nothing."

With her taste still in his mouth, Stefan climbed into his car and pulled out of the lot toward his mom's house, clenching the steering wheel and picturing what might have been if he hadn't tried to be something he sucked at. Noble. Let Jaxon and Marion and Will be the good ones. All good had gotten him just now was gone.

"You gonna eat that?" Will asked and pointed at the package of licorice setting on Stefan's lap. "Grape. Never had that before. Is it any good?"

Will's small talk shouldn't surprise Stefan. He'd never given Will any reason to believe that one single woman could affect him like this.

"I don't know, I guess," Stefan said, sad for the absence of *her*. Why did he feel like this? "Shit. I'm so screwed."

"What?" Will asked with a mouth full of *her* candy, *her* taste, *her* smell.

"Nothing. It was nothing."

"Yeah, you said that already."

Stefan's foot hit the gas pedal hard.

On to the next hurdle. Mom's.

Chapter Four

Dani sat in her car, pissing off the horn-happy Volvo owner who wanted her parking space. They honked again and she continued to ignore them. It was warm out and her tracksuit had already absorbed too much sweat today.

At some point she'd have to go inside the drugstore and get the stuff she needed for Mrs. Calderon.

The name made her head throb and she grabbed it with both hands and rubbed.

How in the world had she not put two and two together? Granted, she'd never seen him live and in person as a grown man. Which was really strange considering her mom and his mom had been best friends. Hard as she tried, no memories of him came to mind. What surprised her was that she couldn't even remember overhearing the moms talk about Stefan. There were a handful of pictures he'd been in from when she was a very little girl and the high school graduation photo that hung on the wall at his mom's, but those looked nothing like the lethally sensuous bear of a man she'd just encountered.

"I'm such a dummy." Mrs. C's well-off son was due to visit, in drives a ritzy Mercedes from Tennessee, and her first thought wasn't Stefan Calderon has shown up? Her scalp stretched to its limits and even her ears felt the tension.

She shook her head at her thickness.

Well he'd arrived to one hell of a welcoming committee. Dani sighed and finger massaged her temples.

Making out with him in a public bathroom? There was no point in lying to herself ... she'd have had sex with him. Not to the point of climaxing but close enough. *If*, she thought. If she hadn't just found out he was Mrs. C's son. She wouldn't now that the chaotic situation had slapped some sense back into her. Or some embarrassment and humility. But back there, in the stall? It would have happened, even in the face of all the reasons it would have been the worst mistake.

He was a musician who was never home. Dani was his mom's caretaker in his absence. She didn't know much more about him but that was enough.

Her feelings about that were mixed to call it lightly. How many times had she thought lowly of him for not coming around more? For financing his mom's care but not caring enough to come home more often? But that uncommitted jerk didn't sound like the man she'd just spent time with.

Real, significant problems began to mount the more implications she thought of.

She'd never finished her medical assistant degree because she'd quit school to care for her own mother. And then Mom had passed and Mrs. C had fallen, breaking her arm and needing surgery. The natural option had brought the both of them together. Gina Calderon needed someone to help her around the house. Her son had sent word that he was going to hire a live-in caretaker, basically a nanny for seniors. Gina had responded that she would put his money to good use and hire someone reliable. Two weeks of post-surgery help around the house had turned into two years and a permanent live-in situation. One Dani cherished with all her heart.

Oh this was not good.

It hit her hard just then. The money Mrs. C paid Dani came from her son.

Dani hunched onto the steering wheel and rolled her forehead over its hard plastic, begging her headache to subside.

Mrs. C's son, the one I just degraded myself in front of, pays my bills, buys my food, puts gas in my car.

Any sense of "sexy" she'd run away with from their encounter turned quickly to "dirty".

As a final reminder of what a fool she'd just been, Dani's hands fell to her stomach. The money she saved by not having to pay rent went directly to the hospital for the self-pay birthing plan she qualified for.

Someone honked long and loud and then sped past, presumably to find another spot. Finally, Dani found the wits to ease her foot off the brake. Her ankle cramped as she stretched it out and prepared to drag herself into the pharmacy. It hit her just then as she rummaged for and found Mrs. C's list of prescriptions to be picked up.

She would come face to face with him again. Very likely tonight if Mrs. C's was his first stop. She felt dizzy. He could be there now.

I actually have a house not too far from here. It's uh, in Moonlight. We could eat, talk. Have amazing sex. Whatever you want.

What had she done?

More importantly, where could she go?

Not there. Definitely, not there.

Too bad she didn't have a choice. She dug Mrs. C's list out of her pocket and began smoothing her tangled hair.

Chapter Five

"Mom?" he called after opening the front door. A gust of wind helped blow it open even further and he caught the slab of wood just in time before it crashed against the inside wall. That should be locked, he made a mental note. "Hello, Ama?" he said, switching without thought to the Spanish his father had taught him as a boy. "Mom?" he went back to, realizing she might not appreciate a reminder of his dad.

Will walked up behind Stefan with his one bag strapped across his shoulders. "Anyone home?" he asked. A boom of thunder pounded loudly and dark clouds creeping across the blue parts of the sky reminded him of the frequent childhood storms that had fascinated him but kept him inside too often.

"Not sure. Door was unlocked so I'm assuming."

"This is where we're staying, right?"

Stefan searched the entryway to the house which hadn't changed in all these years. Same wood painted a creamy brown color and the key rack still carved with a "C" hung as soon as you entered. "That's the plan," he said. The whole point was to try and make up for times past and get right with his mom once and for all. He hated that it had taken her last fall to wake his ass up. Staying at his empty house nearby would have been the asshole move to make. But he wouldn't lie. He was glad to have it as a backup.

"Hey brother, take a breath," said Will quietly with his hand on Stefan's shoulder. Stefan did and felt his shoulders relax.

Until he saw her in the next second.

His heart sank to the pit of his stomach.

Coming slowly down the stairs, she was shorter and her hair that had still been mostly blonde seven years ago was now all white.

"Ven paca." *Come here.*

She hadn't forgotten Dad's teachings either, what surprised Stefan was that she used them. Thrown off by that, he set his bags down, wiped at his mustache which he forgot he had grown, and went to her. She stayed on the last step which made her taller but not nearly enough. He leaned over like he did when he was hugging Jaxon's little daughter back in Nashville. "Hello, son." She kissed his cheek and waited. He couldn't move. Finally, she hugged him. Stefan made it a point to lose his rigid stance, and his shock. "You look well, Stefan." She patted the sides of his arms. "And your friend?"

If anyone should be complimenting the other on their looks, it should be him admiring his mom. For having just entered her seventies and making it through one of the harshest winters on record for the northeast, she looked amazingly better than what he'd envisioned. Still had a lot of her hair, it just wasn't thick like his anymore and she'd always been thin but seemed to have just enough meat on her bones. Her elbows poked out from the short sleeves of her fuzzy coffee colored robe. Stefan remembered she'd also asked about Will who cordially stood there smiling. God, what must his mom think about the two of them and the ungodly amount of tattoos? He'd meant to throw on a jacket like he always did the few times he'd visited, to spare her the view. He hadn't felt ashamed of himself or any of his friends in a long time, but Mom was different. She didn't see him like anyone else.

"Mom, this is my good friend, Will Cordero. Will, this is my mom, Gina."

"Will. It's nice to meet you," his mom said in her northeastern accent.

"Mrs. Calderon." Will dipped down for a hug before Stefan could warn that his mom wasn't the touchy feely type. But she embraced his friend and smiled. "It's great to finally meet one of my son's friends. Are you from California, Will?"

"Oh, no ma'am. I was born not too far from here, in Maryland actually. But I did meet Stefan in California."

"And Stefan tells me you live in Tennessee now. You boys really get around. How do you like it?"

"Very much, ma'am. It's nice seeing the seasons change again. Kind of like right now."

She smiled. Stefan didn't know if Will really loved their new hometown or if he was just trying to be convincing for Mom.

Stefan was comforted to know some of her strictness had mellowed and so far, it didn't look like he'd need to go hiding with his tail between his legs at the empty house. Even though she didn't go as far as to suggest Will call her Gina, there was a warmth about her Stefan didn't remember. Shit, maybe her added years and frail health had done that. Kind of like that looming fortieth birthday had his ass thinking about being a better son. She'd beat cancer in her sixties and this damn osteoporosis now had shrunk her but she was still standing. Truth be told, he'd been counting on her sternness to keep her going like it had when Dad left them. He hoped she hadn't softened up too much.

"Well, it's good to have you both here. Have you boys eaten?" she asked.

And just like that, it was as if he'd never been asked to leave.

Like Mom had never looked at him the same ashamed way she had his dad standing at the front door on their way out. Dad had left her for another woman. Two years later, she'd asked Stefan to leave because of a young girl who hadn't known how to deal with being fourteen and pregnant and had lied, throwing him under the bus, to save herself with her parents and get rid of a responsibility he would have shared in.

Stefan wasn't sure what he felt. It was going to take more than a few minutes to sort it all out. But food was always a good place to start.

He and Will answered on top of each other. "Starving." Apparently Will's pizza hadn't done much for his buddy's hunger. A sizzling memory of someone eating licorice made his own gut twist. He had to stop thinking of that young woman. He stretched his neck.

Stefan added, "I could cook you something, Mom. What would you like?"

"Oh no. Daniela prepares something every morning. I'll just take it out and we can reheat it."

"Daniela?" he asked, the name vaguely familiar.

His mom's eyebrows hiked ever so slightly at his question. Was that the live-in nurse? He'd wondered whether his mom had finally found someone compatible. He'd been sure to send her enough money to cover those costs, even though she insisted her pension could handle it. He hadn't pushed when she'd said she didn't need his help to find the right person. Mom might be old but she wasn't a pushover. She could handle her business and he knew better than to suggest otherwise.

"Yes," she said. "My helper. She's out right now picking up my prescriptions. Why don't you boys put your things away and I'll get plates out. We'll set one for Daniela, too."

"Yes ma'am," said Will.

Stefan nodded, unsure of the ease of the situation but glad his mom seemed at peace. Finally. Maybe he could do this. Maybe his plan would work and she'd say yes to him and the life he could give her in Nashville.

Upstairs Stefan motioned for Will to follow him. Mom wasn't the only thing that had shrunk in his absence. "Man, I remember this place being so much bigger." Will muttered something in agreement but Stefan knew Will's childhood had been spent in and out of extended family's homes, as close as a person could come to foster care. And then to have lost his only brother in combat. It fucking sucked. They passed his mom's upstairs room which he still thought was ridiculous and dangerous. If she'd have taken the house he'd bought her, she'd have a master suite downstairs and wouldn't have to force herself up and down the stairs every day. He'd read up on osteoporosis and knew the risks. Stefan trailed his fingers along the wall, remembering more things that made no sense to him. He'd always thought his parents had the perfect marriage until one day Dad sat him down and explained he'd be leaving them soon.

Just like that.

Dad had fallen out of love with Mom.

The kicker? Dad had stayed living with them until Mom finished her college degree. It sounded so kind. So benevolent. Well, it should have been messier. Angrier, in Stefan's opinion. Heart ache should hurt, right? There should have been fights with screaming and slamming doors. But no. Mom graduated college and then Dad had left quietly. Stefan shook his head, vaguely aware Will was speaking.

"So how long's it been since you were here?" Will asked him, standing near an old wedding photo of Mom's parents that hung in a polished brass frame that had hung there for forever.

If it had been anyone else asking, Stefan might not have answered truthfully. But this was Will and there was no need to lie. "I've been back a handful of times for Christmas and Mother's Day in the last twenty years. Not nearly enough, man." He wouldn't dredge up the reasons why.

"Didn't you take time off from the Play tour to come visit her? I distinctly remember feeling like a total ass for like three weeks straight that year." Will rubbed the bare sides of his head with his hands.

"What are you talking about?"

"You didn't tell any of us why you had to go home so I just remember being stoked to spend the time off with Honey. That was such a long ass tour. Then I found out like a year later why we'd gotten the break and felt like shit that it was because your mom had cancer."

"That was a long time ago. I can't believe you remember that stuff. You shouldn't feel bad."

Will shrugged and that characteristic sadness washed over his face right before he donned the same smile he always did to cover it up. Will's love for Honey scared the shit out of Stefan. The effect was never-ending and Will's wife had been gone a few years now.

Hell, his dad had been gone a little over twenty and Mom still carried the man's last name. She was either too proud, too stubborn, or even more hung up than Will. Or maybe like Stefan, she had no idea what to do with love.

"It's been too long. I'm an ass," he said, because it was the absolute truth.

"Hey, your mom looks good for her age. She could probably kick both our asses. Moms are like that. She'll be okay."

Stefan hoped so.

They passed by what used to be Stefan's room. He assumed from the purple, yellow and white daisy bedspread that this was where the home nurse was now staying. Made sense since it was right next door to Mom's. The delicate white and yellow flowers had him thinking about a certain yellow tracksuit he'd never see again. *Get over it,* he told himself.

"This is gonna be us," Stefan said, pausing at the third and final room of the modest house. They peeked in together. They both stared at the single bed. "Looks like you're finally gonna get your chance to cuddle with me, stud."

Will hit him hard. The guy had ridiculously strong hands, especially when they were balled into fists. At least Will didn't have his sticks. "Don't know what you're talking about. You know how many floors I've slept on? Toss me a pillow and blanket and I'm good."

Stefan could only guess. "Fuck you. You're not sleeping on the floor. I'll see if Mom has an air mattress and if not we'll buy one tomorrow." He'd go tonight but thunder had now joined the lightning which flashed in the bedroom window. If they lost power, his Mom shouldn't be alone and the nurse had yet to come back. He'd be sure Will slept on the bed tonight since it would be wasted on Stefan. Too much to digest for a good night's sleep tonight.

"Oh, a shopping trip. Sweet. You know I love me some Taggert's."

Stefan grinned, remembering the late night phone calls he often got from Will, always wanting an opinion on snacks, candle scents, sheet thread counts, and teeny bopper books. A thought hit him. Will spent a god-awful amount of time alone. "Hey man, you found a place yet?"

"In Nashville?"

"Yeah."

"Nah. Not yet. You?" Will asked.

"I'm close. I was having fun drawing it out and looking with Triple Red but I think I'm gonna get serious about it now. Find one big enough to hold us all," he let out at the end.

"Who? You and your harem?"

Will knew better than that. Stefan didn't have live-in girlfriends. Visitors, yes. He scratched his head. "Not exactly. I'm thinking about bringing my mom back with me. You know, maybe get a place with a house in back for her. Kind of like what Lucky and Tris did for Grace."

Out loud, the statement surprised him too.

While Mom should be the only woman on his mind right now, the troubled young lady he'd held a few hours ago wouldn't leave him. But that was crazy. He had to see that for what it was. Two paths crossing for a minute in time. A very hot moment in time but one that was gone now. He'd had lots of those to speak of over the years. So why couldn't he smile this one off like he always did and move on?

Fuck, I'm turning soft.

He looked over at Will who was sitting on the edge of the bed, thumbing through the DVD's he'd bought at the truck stop. A shrink-wrapped copy of "Road House" lay on top with some teeny bopper werewolf drama underneath it. What he'd love to let a "We need to find you a woman" rip, but he didn't.

"And my main man," he said instead. "Think about it. You, me, my mom. Good times to be had."

"And her nurse," Will added.

"Her nurse," he said and subtly wagged his eyebrows at Will who barely smiled. What had his mom said her name was? "Daniela." He said it with his father's Spanish accent.

"Sounds right up *your* alley," Will said, effectively dismissing Stefan's hint.

Will made a good point but not in the way he thought. Even having Mom living with him, Stefan would still need someone to be with her for the times he'd be gone. This new tour starting in a few weeks would be a long one. Probably a nine-monther. There was a lot he loved about being on the road but it was still something he had to gear up for. Get his head in the right place. Stefan cracked his neck from side to side.

Shit, them all living together had the makings of some crazy reality TV show, but Stefan loved Will like a brother and hoped his friend would take him up on the offer. Besides, he couldn't keep getting his usual gaming buddy, Ben, in trouble at home. Now that the band's webmaster had a woman, their late night Fall for Duty sessions had come crashing to an end. Love, the ultimate man-friend killer.

"We'll see," Will said and restacked the DVD's on the floor near the small TV in their room. "Road House" was now second to "Dirty Dancing" and the teen werewolf flick dropped to third. Looks like Will would be up all night watching his new Swayze stash. There had to be some way Stefan could get Will around someone new without his buddy knowing what he was up to. At least one of them needed to get laid.

"Yeah, I guess this visit will be a pretty good dry run with us all under the same roof." Stefan wouldn't push. He would unpack his clothes later and left his suitcase against one of the walls. For a second, he stood facing the mirrored closet door. "Hey, thanks for coming with. I appreciate it."

Will just nodded then said, "Let's go eat. I'm starving." He smoothed his hair down over the side of his head with the harsher scars.

"You're always starving." Not sure why he kept doing this to himself, Stefan's thoughts immediately went to how hungry he was for *her*.

"I know. Hey, out of curiosity, has your mom ever seen a picture of Sin Pointe?"

Stefan considered the fact that glancing around the walls as they'd made their way through the home so far and all pictures of him were the same childhood ones, probably not. "I don't think so. If you want I can dig one up and show her," Stefan said as they made their way back out of the room, down the hall and to the stairs. "I'm sure she'd be fascinated by the platinum spiky mohawk, leather and chains. Your piercing would go over really well." He pulled out his phone and mouthed "Let's see here, Google Image search Sexy Sin Pointe Drummer Will Cordero. Nipple Ring."

"Asshole. You wouldn't."

"I would but I won't. Besides I'd be outing myself too," Stefan said and rubbed his still growing beard.

"Oh, so mom's never seen her boy wearing eyeliner?"

"That's guy-liner and you wear it too."

God, he hoped Mom hadn't seen any of the band's magazine spreads. Sin Pointe's shoots were about being fast, easy and pleasing to the fan base. They'd once posed butt naked for some full body tat shots. All but ink-free Marion, who stood there dressed in what looked like a black apron, looking more like a butcher with his arms folded across his chest than their keyboardist. "Dude, you remember that shot that had Marion looking like our Dom Master?" Stefan asked.

"Yeah, all he needed was a whip. That was fucking funny until he slapped my ass," Will said, rubbing his butt. "That shit stung and left a welt. He's got a firm ass slap."

Stefan nearly cracked up. "Yeah, that was fucking funny … unless Mom saw that issue."

"Something tells me we're safe then. Mom doesn't strike me as a *Tat Master* subscriber."

Will had a point.

But worse would be the paparazzi rags they always stocked right there at the grocery checkout and the parade of bad shots with him and who knew how many different women.

They hovered near the last few steps and spoke over each other again.

"Agreed, no band pics for Mom."

"Something smells good. This Daniela must be a really good cook," Will said as he hopped down, skipping the last step. Stefan smiled, remembering doing that as a kid.

The more he heard the name, the more it bugged Stefan that she wasn't here with his mom. He'd give the lady credit, she kept a clean house. At least he hoped that was her doing and not Mom's. How many times had the babysitter made him do the chores when she'd been paid extra to do them? At least until Stefan was old enough to keep her occupied with other things. Mom had apparently never known about that or she'd have had even more to be ashamed about when it came to her only son.

His mind flashed to the new daisy bed in his old room but actual hunger brought him back to the here and now.

Will was right; something did smell good. But the flavors were all wrong. Mom had never been real big on Indian food. The spices had always wrinkled her nose whenever they'd gone into town and passed by the Tandoor Tavern. Dad had liked that place. Stefan regretted the even smaller amounts of time he'd spent with his dad. But with the new family, it was just easier to stay away. He had heard they lived in Idaho now. Stefan had never been.

"Why are you frowning? I bet you a hundred bucks there's some bad-ass Chicken Curry awaiting us," Will said as they approached the kitchen. "You love Indian."

"Yeah, but from what I remember, Mom doesn't."

Will gave him a look. "This Daniela must be a really good cook then, if she's eating it."

He raised his eyebrows. "Must be."

Was this woman the right person for Mom? Was she even listening to Mom? He could be pissed all he wanted at those thoughts but when it came down to it, if he'd moved Mom closer years ago, it wouldn't be an issue. He shook his head and led his friend to the kitchen and the rich fragrant smells of curry, ginger and onions. The garlic made his mouth water as surely as it probably churned Mom's stomach. He felt Will's hand on his shoulder.

"It'll be alright, Stef," said Will.

Yeah, well where the hell was this nurse? They needed to talk. Because the way he saw it right now, his idea of packing Mom up and moving her to Nashville with him was looking better by the second. He'd have to find a new caretaker, of course.

He saw his mom had served them plates and stood by the sink. She washed her hands then crossed herself, just like she always did before sitting down to eat. She turned to him while she patted her hands dry. "Ready to eat?" she asked the two of them.

Stefan didn't miss the grimace turning her mouth down. Yeah, she loved Indian food now his ass. "Let's eat," he said and leaned down to kiss her forehead. She didn't pull back. He was as grateful as he was surprised. "But tomorrow, I'm making breakfast. What would you like?" he asked as they followed Mom to the dining room table. Will stayed close behind.

"Oh, I don't know. Surprise me," she said, surprising him indeed with her spontaneity. If he hiked his eyebrows anymore tonight at the changes, he'd have a raging headache to go along with the raging hard-on once he was left alone and thinking about *her*. Not a good combination.

"What are we making?" Will asked with a smile. His head bopped to invisible drums. Man, some woman would find Will irresistible someday if he let her. Even Stefan could see that. It had to be the glasses.

Stefan thought about it for a second. "Pan-fucking-cakes," he said quietly over his shoulder so only Will would hear.

"Okay then. You sexy Latino men don't mess around when it comes to food, do you? Pancakes? I thought maybe we'd be having Huevos Rancheros or something." Will teased.

"No, we fucking don't mess around," he whispered, hoping his mom hadn't caught his cursing. It was like he was sixteen again and not nearing forty. "Mom can't stand all that spicy stuff." Both the Indian and Mexican food would just remind her of his dad. It was bad enough that Stefan's mere presence probably did it in spades. Mom was tolerating him well so far.

Will nodded. "Pancakes it is then."

They sat down and his mom stabbed at a bite of food. Stefan came this close to snatching her plate up and throwing it in the trash and cooking something fresh. Any other time, maybe he wouldn't have cared so much. But she was seventy fucking years old, deserved respect from all of them, nurse included, and this was unacceptable to him. If she wanted to eat fruit loops sprinkled over donuts, hadn't she earned that right? That was probably pushing it, but he was so damn angry with himself. When *Daniela* got back, he would clear this up. He took a bite. The damn food was delicious.

Dish duty was pretty entertaining with Will. When was the last time either of them had put on yellow rubber gloves? He'd washed. Will had rinsed. A mess had been made which they'd cleaned up. But Stefan was now irritated that the nurse still hadn't returned. The storm outside had cycled through a few times and rain and wind were now on the rise again. Summer was so close, just like he remembered as a kid.

He propped a pillow under his mom's feet and searched for a channel on her TV, settling on a legal drama. He sat on the edge of her bed, her frailty and acceptance of him punching him in the heart. Strangely, he found himself wanting to talk about Dad but that would be selfish and he'd learned a thing or two from Will. Selfish was bad. But he only had two weeks and there were things they had to talk about if he had any shot of getting her to return with him.

"Mom, can we talk?"

She propped herself more upright, even though it looked like some nerve somewhere was being pinched from the effort. "Sure we can, son."

Where did he begin? "Thank you for letting me stay here. And Will."

She nodded. "Of course."

They talked about her most recent doctors' appointments and the harsher than usual winter. He told her about his move to Tennessee and how he was still looking for a house.

"I've always heard Tennessee was lovely. Especially during the fall."

It would be cowardly not to use that comment as his lead-in.

"You know, Mom, I've been gone so long. Haven't been here for you. Regardless of anything else, I've felt really bad about that. And," he shook his lowered head, knowing this wasn't the heart of the matter and he was about to blow the lead-in she'd given him. "I've let the one thing I can honestly say I love keep me away."

"Oh Stefan, don't." Her hand rested on top of his. "Does your music make you happy?"

He nodded, shocked she'd grasped so quickly that his one love was his music. "Yes, most of the time."

"Listen to me. Whatever else has happened between us in the past, I have a son who has found success doing what he loves for a living. As your mother, that makes me happy. I'm the one who should apologize for not making sure you knew that. You're here with me now, son. And who knows? The day may still come that you find something you love more than your music."

She shouldn't count on that and wouldn't be proud if she knew everything he'd indulged in over the years. God, he hoped Mom hadn't followed his career that closely. If she'd ever stood in line at the grocery store ... The fear of her seeing his face splashed with a scandalous headline or two gouged him again. But what nearly had him doubling over was the shine in her eyes when she'd said the hopeful words. Fuck, he was a selfish bastard. He'd honestly never thought of how his finding someone would impact her.

There just wasn't anyway he could see marriage in his future. A girlfriend would be hard enough to manage. The couple times he'd tried, they hadn't been happy when the music took him away.

And especially not after that shit that had printed when Will lost his wife. Leave it to the idiots in the press not to have checked and made sure they had the right Sin Pointe member's face attached to the tasteless write up. Because it saved Will from more heartbreak, Stefan never said anything.

In any case, hearing his mom speak of being proud was a shock, especially under the circumstances of when he'd left home.

How did he tell Mom he hadn't just been out making music this whole time? What about the nightly debauchery, the countless women he'd slept with? The hearts he'd been careless with in order to protect his own? Potential daughters-in-law? Not likely.

He handed her the remote and gathered up his courage.

"Mom, have you ever thought about leaving Moonlight?"

She took a second to grasp the remote in her hand and frowned. "Moonlight's not for everyone, son. I understand that. But I want us to focus on the present. It's what's important."

Shit. She'd misunderstood him. "I understand."

That was supposed to have led to her saying she'd consider it and then him making his offer. Stefan let out his breath and accepted that Mom didn't want to talk about the past with him. He couldn't be selfish and push anymore. He'd also try his best not to bring up his dad who was clearly a part of the past she didn't want to discuss. Maybe she was like Will and the reason there'd been no raging fights when Dad left was because she'd suffered in silence.

"Have you heard from your nurse yet?" he asked her, needing something else to think about.

"No, not yet. But sometimes the pharmacy takes a long time. And there are bound to be long lines with this evening's bad weather."

"So, are there many nights like this, when she's not here?"

His mom looked at him and reached for his hand. Her blue eyes squinted. "No, not like that, son. She's a hard worker. She's a great help to me. Very dedicated. You must not remember her." Mom rubbed her hand over the tats covering his fingers and closed her eyes.

How could he? He'd never met the woman.

Stefan felt his sinuses pinch. He looked away and rubbed at them with his free hand. Only when he was back in control did he return his attention to Mom. "It just seems like she could be more attentive. And I don't say that lightly. I know I haven't been here…"

"Stefan, you've called me every year on Mother's Day, my birthday, Christmas. You visited me with the cancer and you're here now that I'm officially an old lady." She reiterated what she'd already assured him. She patted his hand again and then yawned. "That's what matters. It's early but I'm tired. I think I'm going to go to sleep. I'm sorry I didn't realize your friend was coming with you. The spare room isn't that big but Daniela made sure to put fresh linens on it before she left. Unfortunately with my old bones, making beds isn't something I'm supposed to be doing anymore."

It was hard to admit as he sat there soaking up her words, but Stefan wondered if his mom regretted asking him to leave all those years ago, even if she refused to talk about that past now. But that felt weak and it was ultimately his fault, his actions that had forced her to be ashamed. If he hadn't gotten Amanda pregnant in the first place, his integrity never would have been called into question. Amanda wouldn't have freaked out and lied to her parents about him saying he would never help her with the baby. All that on the heels of Dad leaving them. Maybe he'd have done the same thing in Mom's position. He wiped hands over his pants legs.

"It's fine. We fit just fine. I'll let you get some rest."

His mom reached up and touched her wrinkly fingers to his growing beard. She smiled. "Will you stay up until Daniela gets in?" she asked.

He cupped his hand over hers. "Of course." Because he had a few words for the woman.

"Okay, mi'jo. Good night and God bless you."

"You too, Mom. It's good to be here with you." He watched her eyes close. This time they stayed that way. The Spanish she used for his benefit, the smile, the last name she kept. The "C" on the key rack. They were reminders that had to bring up sad memories for her. Why did she keep them? For him, even though he knew he didn't deserve any of it? Stefan kissed her hand and then placed it at her side. "Thank you for loving me, no matter how awful I've been," he whispered.

If she didn't feel bad about believing everyone else over him when he'd needed her in his corner, so what. In her own way, she loved him. She just might be the only woman to ever do that. If things kept up this well, he'd ask her about Nashville in the morning.

Chapter Six

Half an hour later, there was a knock at the front door.

Stefan hopped up out of his mom's recliner and checked his watch. It was eight o'clock but had been dark the last hour now with the recurring storm fronts passing through. Maybe staying gone this long was the norm but if this was the wayward nurse, he intended to find out for sure and remind her she got paid to be here.

"I think my mom's nurse is finally here, man."

"Be nice," Will said and flipped the channel from the tattoo show to the one about Big Foot.

"Always."

Stefan opened the door, expecting to invite the woman in and then walk her straight back to the kitchen to sit and discuss his concerns.

Long black hair with sexy waves.

Full fleshy lips.

A bright yellow tracksuit.

What was *she* doing here?

Her arms were full, wearing grocery bags from her wrists to the crook of her elbows. Water droplets pinged from the plastic bags. Had she been out in the rain? Her dark eyes were huge, staring back at him. Not happy dark and not even surprised, but embarrassed?

Holy shit. *You have to be kidding me.*

He hadn't taken her for a fervent Sin Pointe fan at the truck stop. It was amazing how they found him sometimes.

No, he remembered she hadn't had a clue as to who he was. That's not what this was.

A crumpled, small, red and white bag with the letters Rx told him the truth.

He needed a second to accept the reality staring him in the face.

"Tell me you're not Daniela," he said, incredulous.

I told her I wanted to fuck her. I'm such an ass. He rubbed his face hard with his hands. The fingers he'd stroked over her panties stretched the skin of his chin downward as they streaked through his beard.

"Stefan," she said, blinking.

"What?" they said in unison.

She stuttered and lifted her chin but slumped under all the bags. He eyed her shoulders and could see the yellow track top was wet from the erratic rain. It was cloudy and dark outside behind her with only one street light a good hundred yards from Mom's. "I'm, I'm just here to drop this stuff off for Mrs. C. Here you go." She seemed frantic as she handed the bags over to him, letting some of them clunk to the wet ground in the doorway.

Stefan was still trying to process that this little heart thief of his from earlier was his mom's Daniela. And now that he had the name and her face together, he realized why he'd felt the odd connection. There was enough familiarity still there in the long black curls and the favored color of yellow she'd always worn as a younger girl. *Fuck, I bit her. Hell, she bit me.* She tried to turn and leave. "Wait," he said. "You're Daniela, Sandra's daughter?" Holy shit, he hadn't seen *that* girl in ages.

She stopped a few feet away from him and rocked back on her heels. "Yes," she said.

He caught himself before making the horrible mistake of asking how her mother, his mom's best friend, was doing. He remembered the short phone call from Mom two years ago that Sandra had passed away. Stefan had been rushing through an airport with poor reception, calling to wish Mom a Merry Christmas from the road. When he asked how everyone back home was, she'd broken the news.

"I'm sorry," he said, holding the bags she'd unloaded into his arms and picked up the couple that had dropped.

Her eyebrows plucked together at the center. He realized he'd made it sound like he was sorry she was her mother's daughter. "Where are you going?" he asked as she backed further away. She'd just gotten there and they were supposed to talk. Not sure whether it was his irritation or attraction that made him want to reach out and grab her arm frustrated him on a whole new level. *I never thought I'd see you again*, he thought to himself.

"To my car," she mumbled.

"Are there more bags?" Their strange connection seemed to be winning out. "I'll help you," he offered, finding it wasn't at all hard to be nice to her, even with the interrogation he'd planned.

"No," she said shortly and practically sprinted to the old blue Buick.

"Don't you live here?" he asked, regretting the sarcasm in his voice but not the edge. He had to shout for her to hear him from her car. Where in the hell was she going now?

He searched desperately for the last time he would have seen little Daniela but the only memory that chose to visit—which wasn't funny at all if the Big Guy was paying attention right now—was the first time they'd met.

She was one of the very few babies he'd ever held in his life. He'd been twelve. Dad hadn't left yet. That would be in another few years when he turned sixteen. Stefan's scalp itched and tingled. Holy shit.

"I do," she finally said.

"Then I'll ask again, where are you going?" His jaw hurt but if he didn't keep his mouth clamped shut, he'd say something he regretted. She heard him but only shook her head.

****

Where in the world could she go? Daisy's apartment, she supposed, but her baby sister had two roommates stuffed in the studio already and Dani wasn't ready for the third degree she'd get regarding Thom should she slip and confess. Let alone the Stefan fiasco of the last few hours. She could maybe afford a hotel room but the nearest one was at least an hour drive and she didn't want to be that far from Mrs. C. The May nighttime air was currently warm and humid, suggesting more storms were still in store for them. Shivers began inside her and made their way out, most noticeably from her chin. Fight or flight came to mind.

"I don't know. I—"

"Come inside," his voice commanded her like it had earlier. But it cut clearer now and he stood there with his arms folded over his chest. That cocky air about him and his fancy white car parked nearby and his fancy white shirt pulled tight over his massive chest were back. "It's dark and ugly out. You and I need to talk." He looked away from her at that last bit.

Dani closed her eyes and wished this all away. The whole damn day. But it didn't work. He still stood there like an unmovable pillar. His intense aura as effective as a red light.

"I'm not letting you leave until that happens." His chest seemed to expand, his arms bulged across it.

Great. But what had she thought was going to happen when she finally dragged her butt back here? She'd had two extra hours to think about it sitting in her car in the drug store lot. Envisioning showing her face and playing the fool hadn't prepared her at all for the real deal. She'd never quite gotten to the exact words to say either.

"Come on, *Daniela*." Was that caution or cockiness in his voice? She wouldn't lie and deny how much she liked that about him when they'd kissed.

"It's Dani. Just Dani."

He seemed irritated now and not at all like the man who'd come to her rescue earlier at the truck stop. Not at all like that protective yet playful man who'd kissed her senseless ... and told her of the thing he wanted to do to her. The vulgar word he'd used that had only sounded needful, raw and honest when he'd said it into her ear and her response to him that had been more of a gut reaction than the truth. Her chest, neck and face flamed at reliving those words here at Mrs. C's house.

But she did live here. Full time. This was her home now.

If she left, the back roads would be dark and hard to navigate. How close was the next round of storms? The thought of driving in lightning and hail stiffened her neck; her timing coming back just now had been pure luck. But how could she make herself stay, knowing what she'd almost done with Gina's son? Clearly, he didn't want her around now. Not scowling the way he was.

Her back ached, her stomach hated her, and she really needed to get inside to her stash of Tums and the bathroom. Apparently she'd have to get through Stefan Calderon to do it.

Could she?

Dani would have to forget, pretend like the truck stop had never happened.

She took a step forward, ignoring her body's idiotic thrill at being near him again. He waited, but eventually stepped back and then aside, giving her plenty of room to pass through, just as he had earlier at the truck stop.

When she was past that first hurdle, she only made it a few feet into the house and heard the door close behind her when she saw another man getting up from the couch. He was the man who'd been playing the Mercedes' dashboard like the drums.

"Hey, nice to meet you. I'm Will, um Stefan's friend." He offered her a hand and she saw his arms that rivaled Stefan's for tattoos, but Will's ended neatly at his wrists with what looked like lettered cuffs. "You're the nurse." His chin dipped and she could see a section of his head where his skin looked like it had been burned.

"Dani," she said back to the man who had an incredibly firm handshake and those same calloused hands. But his eyes, behind his glasses, they were a crisp blue and there was something unbelievably kind about them. A second into their handshake, humiliation swaddled her skin with its heat. Were Will and Stefan the kind of friends who told each other everything? Weren't all guys?

Before she could think about it any further, Will excused himself. "So I'm beat. Gonna go hit the sack. See you two in the morning."

Oh, he definitely knew something with that abrupt and presumptuous departure. The man practically flew up the stairs.

Why couldn't this day just end already?

"Looks like it's just you and me," said Stefan.

Oh God, the deep vibrations in his voice made it impossible to forget. She almost slipped back into the stall.

"Yep, looks that way," she said shortly, making her way past him to the kitchen for a glass of milk and antacids. "Is Mrs. C asleep?"

"Yes." He just stood there.

Who would break first?

He followed behind her when she took her first few steps, which she felt the whole way.

"So, about the truck stop," she couldn't help but say because apparently she was now a masochist.

In the open space of the kitchen, Dani realized just how massive he was. Mrs. C always made the refrigerator look huge when she stood near it, but her son was taller than the old thing and his shoulders just as solid.

"Yeah, about that," he said back and rubbed behind his neck.

Famous last words from the dumper to the dumpee. She'd heard it before.

It all sounded like one big, bad ass joke to Dani who had no idea how she'd gotten through the day but was ready for it to be over. She'd deal with Gina's famous rocker son tomorrow. Because right now, in all honesty, she couldn't take being one more person's regret. Her tears wouldn't do either one of them any good. Besides, he still hadn't changed back into her brown-eyed, albeit bad-ass Superman, able to lift spirits with a single kiss.

She sighed.

If she had anything left in the tank right now, she'd guess he had a bone to pick with her. So did the baby because Dani felt like throwing up. She rubbed her

stomach. Stefan's eyes followed. *Of course, because this day just won't end...*
****

"I have a bone to pick with you."

She rolled her eyes and walked right past him, faster than he'd expected. He knew better when a woman did that than to follow after her. Stefan was so mind-fucked right now that he wouldn't have followed that woman into paradise if she'd been naked and leading him with a collar. He let her pass as had become their apparent custom. But a second later he heard the distinct sound of retching.

Unsure about most things happening in his mom's house right now, he gave up and walked into the kitchen. He remembered Dani's day had started with being dumped. Contrary to what many might think, he did have a heart. He'd never been more sincere than when he'd invited her for dinner earlier.

From out of nowhere a very confusing image popped into his head. A paper heart. And a little girl with long black curly hair who handed the pink construction paper cutout card to him. No, come on, really? He rubbed his eyelids.

Another heave into the kitchen sink pulled his attention back.

"You okay in there?"

"No," she croaked out. "Don't." More heaving.

Stefan swallowed. Once he was at her side, he pulled her hair back, twirled it into a knot around his fingers and held it in a loose fist. "You're sick."

"I'm not sick. I'm pregnant. And I'll be fine."

Chapter Seven

Mind, blank.

Thoughts, gone.

Seconds, wasted.

Fuck, the number of times he'd heard the pregnancy line. But this was different. It hadn't been months since they'd hooked up. Shit, they hadn't even hooked up. Then, he realized.

"Oh sweetheart," he started but she held up her hand to stop him and shook her head. "Your ex?"

"Oh my God, I don't want to talk about it. Can't," she said coolly.

Her face said she was feeling beat down, to the bone. What the hell could he say to help?

"You know I was supposed to be pissed at my mom's live-in helper." He thought about the long, silky black curls in his hand and how amazing they would feel spilled over his chest. "You're not fighting fair," he said, leaning closer so only she could know this truth. "I don't think there's any way I could possibly yell at you now." Just like earlier, he found it impossible not to seal up the rest of the space between them. He laid his hand over hers where it was cemented to the kitchen sink ledge. Her shoulders kept hiking up with each breath. He wouldn't have yelled but she didn't know that. *Come on, just a tiny hint of a smile? Please?*

She twisted her head and glared with her eyebrows drawing in together. Didn't say anything though. A second later she twisted away again and turned on the faucet, cupped some water in her hands and rinsed her mouth. He let the fist of her hair loosen so that he was only holding the ends back for her. The lightly tanned skin of her neck moving as she swallowed a fresh handful of water got to him. If he let it, his body would harden and mock him while he spent the rest of the night fighting this insane need to be her proof again. No, it didn't help picturing her sleeping in his old bed. Maybe it would be better to be pissed at her over the stupid curry. Because what the hell was his other choice? He shouldn't bed his mother's caregiver. *Pregnant caregiver.* Fuck, it dawned on him that he paid this girl her salary. He didn't need anyone's genius brains to figure the rest out.

No wonder she'd run out on him earlier and hadn't been too keen on coming back just now.

"I'm glad you're here," she said in a monotonous voice. "Your mom's been looking forward to this. I hope you have a really good visit with her." With that, she pulled and reclaimed the last strands of her hair he'd been holding onto. A few strands stayed tied between his fingers. She then shuffled past him and disappeared from the kitchen.

He stood there leaning against the kitchen counter, at a loss, but aware she needed space.

Fifteen minutes later, she came down the stairs with a large duffel bag slung over her shoulder. Clearly she wasn't letting him get a word in edgewise. "Your mom has my cell number. If she needs anything, just call—"

"Really? That's it, you're leaving?"

They couldn't figure something better out? He also didn't like her carrying heavy shopping and duffel bags. "Give me your bag," he said. She did not like that. At. All.

She stalled and worked her lips with her teeth from the inside. "Your mom knows when she needs her meds but it's written on the refrigerator too. Don't let her miss the blood pressure pills. There are dishes in the freezer for the next few days. The plain, heart healthy stuff I've been making her is getting old so I've got a few tastier things I'm trying out. Anyway, the laundry is done." She was looking in his direction but speaking right through him, as if he didn't exist as a flesh and blood man, hanging on her every word. He felt like a total piece of shit, not to mention a fool. "Let me know a day or so before you leave town and I'll come back. Like I said, enjoy your time." She set her bag down on the small kitchen table and pulled out an unsealed envelope, pushing it toward him. "And here."

"What's this?" Obviously it was a wad of cash but…

"It's two weeks' worth of wages for home care for your mom."

"Come on, Dani. You're killing me. Is this necessary?" And then the five hundredth ball of their short time together dropped. She had no idea he wanted to take his mom back to Nashville. No idea she'd be out of a job if he did that. *Fuck the living shit out of me*, he silently cursed and closed his eyes hard. *She has a baby on the way.*

"What do you think?" she asked and then turned to leave.

This time how could he not put his hands on her? "You think I'm really letting you walk out that door?" he asked and grabbed the bend of her elbow.

"Yeah, I do. Don't touch me again." She looked down.

The steam in her voice acted like a bolt cutter and he let her go in an instant. He'd never held a woman against her will and wasn't starting now. Funny that was exactly what every fiber of his being demanded he do. "All right, no touching." He held his hands up.

She left the room.

After a few heartbeats, he followed, still unable to just let her be. He wouldn't lie either, she had the uncanny ability to walk away from him and it drove him crazy.

"Wherever you're going, is it far?" He hated using the mom card but Dani was leaving him no choice. "In case my mom needs something and I can't take care of it for her." It became abundantly clear that he had no idea what this might be. Mom had looked pretty stable but she needed a live-in nurse for a reason and Stefan hadn't as much as babysat for Jaxon. His repertoire of caring for someone included rubbing oil over a lover's skin fresh from a bath not being a steadying hand as his mom got in and out of the shower. He'd do it if needed but could guarantee he'd fail miserably. Not to mention how Mom would feel about it.

He watched Dani's head dip forward and from behind all he could see was that her hands went up to rub at her temples. "She does get dizzy some days. But that's usually when they adjust her blood pressure dosage. Just keep an eye on her near the stairs and when she's showering. And no lifting things or reaching over her bed. The stress is too much on her bones."

"Please stay, Dani. My mom obviously needs you here. A lot more than she needs me."

She shook her head. "I'll be at my sister's. Mrs. C knows Daisy's address in case of an emergency."

If her intention was to make him feel distant, she'd done it.

She opened the front door to the house and closed it behind her without making a sound. He hated that shit worst of all.

The hell she was heading out into the dark out here in the hills and woods, pregnant. He'd chase her down and yell at her for being so damn stubborn if he had to.

"Will," he called.

Will ducked his head out at the top of the stairs. "Yeah man?"

"You okay with my mom for a bit? I fucked up and Dani's taking off."

"I thought you were gonna be nice. But yeah, I'm good with Mom. Go get your nurse."

"That's the plan," Stefan said then grabbed his keys out of his jeans pocket and went out quickly. Luckily she'd had to let her old car warm up before taking off. His brilliant plan was to follow her taillights to wherever she went and convince her to come back. However loudly he had to do it. She'd hear him out and get her ass back here. He sucked in some air and then forced it back out, unaccustomed to this kind of chase.

"Damn, less than twenty-four fricking hours I've been home," he muttered to himself as his engine purred to life and he turned the wipers to full blast. "And it ain't even over. Not by a long shot." He couldn't help but think things would have been better had he stayed gone.

Chapter Eight

Dani pulled into the Walton's Drug Store parking lot which had begun to feel like her home away from home after today. The lot was lit. The store was open twenty-four hours. And the best part … it was quiet. And Stefan-free.

Just a peaceful rain breaking through the night sky at the moment. A crackle of lightning sparked every now and then in the distant mountains.

With the windows up, she let the fan run while the engine idled, hoping the air wouldn't become stagnant as soon as she turned off the car. Five minutes later and that's exactly what happened. Her stomach also chose to gurgle, sounding even more dramatic out in the quiet night.

"Let's see if we can find you something good for a change, little one."

Dani touched her window, tracing a stream of raindrops and grabbed her coat. Obviously, this was all being done as a distraction to the scene she'd just left behind. She bundled herself up and then rubbed at her belly. She made her way inside to the small refrigerated section of the drug store and pulled out a small jug of whole milk and a package of string cheese. She started to make her way to the front of the store to the checkout area but decided she had some time to kill since she was in no way heading back to Mrs. C's anytime soon. Two weeks he'd be there, she reminded herself. But really, she had no idea how she'd stay gone that long. She loved Gina like a mom. She'd call Daisy in the morning to see about shacking up for now and figure the rest out later. Yeah, her pain and humiliation was that bad.

"Congratulations May 25th. You won. Now please leave me alone," she grumbled out. An employee straightening shelves hiked his eyebrows at her.

Dani twisted her mouth, ignored him, and found the magazines. She never bought any of this stuff because let's face it, she didn't have money to waste, especially after the self-imposed pay cut she'd just given herself. But her browsing always began at hairstyles, then fashion and without fail, ended on the manly fitness magazines with the buffed-out, cut-steel physiques of male body builders. But tucked behind the *Glazmo* issues, she spied the heading for *Guitar Freak*s and the unmistakable jagged heart of the Sin Pointe logo. She grabbed it out of pure curiosity.

Stefan Calderon's deep, dark honey gaze, made all the more intense rimmed by smudged black liner, tormented her like the silly magazine cover had magical powers. In his hands, he held of all things, a white guitar. A bass, she supposed, since that's what the article title said. The thumb and pointer finger of his right hand rested over two of the lower strings while his left cupped it at the top near the neck by a pearly butterfly logo. Clearly, he loved his instrument by the way he gazed down at his hands on it.

She knew the feeling of those hands. That gaze. Those rough fingertips.

Dani nearly dropped the magazine and went to put it back down but couldn't. This was a part of him she didn't know anything about. She read the cover headline again. It said there was an interview with "A rare breed, the bass playing lead singer."

Eager to find out more, she thumbed to Stefan's article where a few of his statements had been set apart from the rest of the text. Her eyes went to those first.

"The trick is to sing melodies that are in rhythm with the bass. Once you figure that out, it's not too hard to sing and play. Nah, that's a lie. It's still hard as shit but it's my thing so I practice. A lot."

He was a hard worker and cared about something. She could have guessed at that.

"No idea where that one got started. There are plenty of better places I can think of to do that than on a bean bag."

Oh, she was going to have to read this entire article and find out what that snippet was about. But before she folded it closed, she saw this last one.

"I guess I am famous for saying that. Shit, we all have regrets, right?"

The glossy magazine cost as much as her milk but this was going to be her distraction for the next few hours. And even though she knew that man, intimately in a way, she didn't recognize him at all. Dressed head to toe in tight white clothing that showed every contour of every muscle on his long body, his dark waves she knew to be soft to the touch looked more like wild barbed wire. This Stefan Calderon seemed unreal. But his words, those were unmistakably human.

Dani left her money on the counter and then paid for her snacks and distractions. Paid for them dearly. The baby needed the milk yet she was lactose intolerant. Her mind needed a clean break from men, yet she couldn't wait to sit down in her car and stare into those wicked, absorbing eyes. She was also Stefan Calderon intolerant, that much was for damn sure. Maybe when she asked for a calcium supplement at her OB check-up, she'd see if there was anything they could give her to combat her Superman problem.

Dodging raindrops that had picked up in size and intensity during her shopping excursion, she quickly climbed into the Buick, turned on the engine and let the wipers clear her windshield. Turning sideways in her seat and tucking her legs as best she could, she pulled the interview out of the bag and found Stefan's pages. It was too dark to read easily but she squinted and found a spot illuminated just enough by one of the parking lot lights. She should at least call Daisy but the drive over would be total crap right now. It would have to wait until morning. She hunkered down in her front seat.

She read a few lines then glanced at the close-up of his black-rimmed, chocolate eyes.

Then a few more and the zoomed in shot of his white bass, a *Fodera,* which she mistook for the word Fedora at first, strung at hip level and his fingers falling naturally against the wiry strings.

Headlights nearly blinded her through the front window and she lost her place.

If she didn't know any better, she'd swear a white Mercedes was pulling forward. The Tennessee plates confirmed that. It stopped beside her.

Her muscles tightened and it took all she had not to start sobbing.

"You won, I said you won," she whimpered, leaving the magazine on the seat.

****

What was this one's game?

Once he figured that out, he'd be okay. Did she want him? Did she hate him? Was it both? What did every person who'd ever played a game want to know?

The rules?

Sure, those would be nice but not necessary. He wanted to know the end result.

Was this winnable? No hearts, no strings. Just the peace of the moment they could have together. No hurt feelings.

Dani sat where he preferred her for the moment, safely inside her car. Stefan's confidence leaped. Because she wasn't on the outside, affecting him and saying no to him, tormenting him. She couldn't walk away from him in there. She'd already tested his very last limit. Was he a fool to think the thin glass was really going to keep him safe from her? Wait, who needed safe-keeping?

With her there, he was in control. He was the one who could call the shots and act like this was simply a game of attraction. So what if that was complete bullshit? Stefan wished his band brothers were there with him now. He could really use a well meant kick in the ass and the reminder that life could be very real.

Will would tell him love is the one thing you don't keep hidden in the dark.

The band's brilliant webmaster, Benny, and his patience that Stefan was so fucking jealous of, would remind him to ease up and play it cool.

Good ole Marion would take him out for a beer and some pool. Problem solved.

Jaxon. Man, Jaxon who had survived so much crap the last twenty years they'd been in the band together. Tragic shit. The Aussie still battled his demons but he smiled most every day now. Stefan knew Jaxon's wife and daughter, his girls, did that for him.

Was Stefan ready to listen? Way back, like all the way back in his mind, he wondered if maybe it was time to consider quitting the game. There was something about seeing her in there, protecting what was hers.

One thing he couldn't do was stand out here all night. Rain soaked through his hair and began to do the same to his shirt.

He stepped up to her car, leaned in and tapped on her passenger side window but she clearly mouthed the word No.

Fine, he could be creative when he wanted something and felt bad for how he'd already treated her. He leaned closer and then wrote through the raindrops on the window with his finger, TALK.

Nothing.

He tried again. PLEASE.

Zilch.

His head dipped and he tried once more. If she didn't go for this one, he was done. This didn't mean anything to her and it shouldn't mean anything to him.

Instead of using his finger to write, he leaned down, and then pressed a kiss to the glass. The rain felt nice on his dry lips. He probably looked foolish but luckily he didn't care right now. He took a step back and waited. It took a few seconds, but the lock sounded with a pop. He tried the handle.

She'd let him in.

Exhilaration at the clear win spiked his pulse for a moment until he realized something.

They had to talk and he doubted Dani was going to like anything he had to say.

****

Stefan Calderon could do her a favor and let this day end. Like it should have a few hours ago. Why couldn't he have let her do her nightly puking and then gone to hide up in her bedroom? Why did he have to look at her the way he did? And the way he teased her, it was like he was the sour green apples and the damn delicious pie they turned into all within a moment's notice.

He was being cruel and adorable which she had learned the past twelve hours had to be the man's nature. It was hard to believe he was Gina's son. The finger writing reminded her how wet it was outside. Each time he stroked his finger to make a new letter on the glass, she had nowhere to go but crawling back to images of them in the bathroom stall and his magic hands. His warm, strong chest. The soft black curls topping his wicked angel's head. No, he was no angel.

She wasn't opening the door.

He should go home.

Back to his mom who rarely got excited but had smiled more than usual this past week. Then he leaned in and all she could see were his puckered lips, pressed against the glass.

Soft yet hard, cinnamon. Wet. Hungry lips. Alive and male, not just a photo in a magazine.

What did he want? To pick up where they'd left off?

He'd proven enough and made her feel incredibly sexy in those split seconds of their kiss and play, she'd decided that much. With recent events, that would have to be enough. Now she was left with the daunting reminder that he paid her paycheck. She couldn't get that out of her head no matter how hard she tried. She glanced down at the rock star on the page and then back up at the man standing out in the rain.

Which was he? Boss, friend, forbidden? Those waters were so murky, her head spun.

But this kiss print he'd left on her window meant something. She wasn't sure what or why. Lucky for him, Dani's heart wasn't in the business of hurting others, no matter how battered and bruised it was right now. In other words, she was a sucker for this man.

He wiped at his face as rain fell from his sleek black waves, made straighter from the water. God, his brooding brand of sexy killed her.

She pushed the unlock button and the doors popped open.

He quickly hopped inside and sat on her magazine before she could remove it. Maybe he hadn't seen it and she'd be spared the embarrassment. He dried his hands on the thighs of his jeans while she cringed, mentally crossing fingers he couldn't feel it under his ass.

"Thank you," he said.

She just nodded.

"Would it kill you to say you're welcome?" he asked.

She would have under different circumstances.

"So this lot. It's nice. If I was gonna be a stubborn pain in the ass, I'd have picked it too," he said, not giving up.

"You've got a lot of nerve," she finally let out.

"You don't deny it."

No, she didn't. He would have been more correct if he called her an irrational stubborn pain in the ass. But admitting that to him made her queasy. So did the way her body treated the man's presence like he was the gold standard of carrots and she the malnourished rabbit.

She tried not to look at him straight on but that didn't matter. It just sent her nose in search of his scent. Cinnamon, again. She would not think of how satisfying his taste was.

"You said you had a bone to pick with me. I'm assuming you're wanting to tell me that the truck stop incident this morning was a huge mistake. So here's where I tell you I already know that. And don't worry, you don't have to have dinner with me." Mistake or not, she still wanted him.

"The bone that needs picking has nothing to do with that, sweetheart." His chocolate brown gaze stripped her bare and stoked the need she was barely able to keep hidden.

So. Unfair. That word and the way it made her want to melt into his chest.

"It doesn't?" she asked, hearing her voice hike up at the end. She shouldn't let that happen again.

"No. Turns out that particular bone isn't as important as I thought."

"What? Why not?" She wanted to ask him why he'd chased her out here then if it wasn't to have this discussion. But oh no, it was just then that he ever so slightly lifted his ass and reached a hand down underneath it. She went bug-eyed, then blew out a breath and pretended to see something out her side window. She wouldn't look his way.

After a deafeningly silent minute, she heard him chuckle, low and dark. "Ahem. Read anything good lately?"

"You're mean."

"I know. Look at me," he said.

But Dani just kept her eyes trained on the rivulets of rain showering her window and what she could now hear gaining in intensity in the distance and see crackling over the tops of faraway hills. Thunder and lightning. Round four, five or six. She'd lost count.

"Well, we can talk about this fun magazine or there's always the time we got gas together and ended up…"

She cleared her throat and shot out the first question she could think of to keep him from going there. "What is it you're so famous for saying?" *Don't fidget. He's just another man.*

"Hmm. I thought for sure you'd want to know about the bean bags."

A tiny line of built up dust wedged in the cracks of the gear shift console caught her shifting eyes. It needed cleaning. Why had she never cleaned that before? She ran her fingernail over it, repeatedly trying to dislodge the bits. *Stop it.* She pulled her hand back into her lap.

"Fine, what's the deal with the bean bags?" she asked, refusing to look at him yet and desperate to hide how curious she was about the silly things as well. Her imagination brought fresh waves of color to her neck and face. If the man did what he did in a bathroom stall, lord only knew what he'd be willing to do on a bean bag. She imagined him folding her like a pretzel and licking the salt from her sweaty body.

"Jaxon once told some interviewer that I could play bass anywhere a man could have sex. And then jokingly said I often engaged in the two at the same time. Somehow bean bags got thrown into the mix."

She didn't want to give in but it was impossible. "So now you get asked about it."

"All the time."

"That must suck."

He let out a small laugh. "I could, in fact, perform both acts very well on bean bags but in case you were wondering, I don't."

"I wasn't curious," she lied through tight lips, her pretzel fantasy making her mouth dry.

Stefan was doing something with his tongue and his teeth inside his mouth, she just had no idea what. Outwardly, his cocky grin gave way to what she could only describe as sincerity.

"If you think you could stand to look at my ugly mug, I'd appreciate it." He laid a hand in her hair and without thought, she turned her head all the way. That was no ugly mug. He was more handsome than any other man she'd ever met. So much so that his good looks made her nervous. A drop of water fell from the wet skin of his wrist and landed on her collarbone. It reminded her of the tear that had fallen earlier today, before she'd met him. She fought to keep her breath even.

"Why do you hold your guitar so low? It doesn't look comfortable, at all."

Something she said made him grin.

"What's so funny?" she asked.

"Nothing. You're just very pretty. And I like the way you talk when you're nervous."

How dare he point that out right here in the face of all her nervousness? "So you're not going to answer me."

"It looks good in pictures. Now you. Why did you let me … kiss you today?" he asked.

Well that's one way of putting it.

"Why didn't you tell me who you were?" she shot back.

Their eyes locked on each other and their jaws worked in the same grinding way.

"I could ask you the same thing, Daniela."

She shook her head. "You didn't tell me what you're famous for saying and yes, I'd still rather talk about that than the other thing."

He muttered something she couldn't quite hear and she asked him to repeat himself.

"You, uh, you're not gonna like this. I believe the quote said I wasn't proud of it."

"It said you had regrets about it."

Great, now he knew how intently she'd read.

His chest rose, the pristine white shirt still showing off that broad, contoured appeal as he breathed in and out. He rubbed a hand over the muscled parts and Dani ached to lay her head there, right in the middle. She'd have imagined it even had she not been so exhausted and tried to decide if his chest was furry or bare. Did he have more tattoos? Would he let her pet him for hours on end?

He smirked and then ran his hands through his wet curls. He'd definitely let her have at those with as much as he touched his hair himself.

She should ask him just to get that smirk off his face but he spoke up instead.

"My usual response when people ask if I feel bad about shit I've done in the past, is the standard 'Unless you and I are fucking, you really shouldn't care.'"

After digesting his very concise and in-your-face words, Dani turned in her seat, touched. "And you regret saying that now? Because I kind of think you might have a point."

It was as if some invisible hypnotist snapped their fingers, causing both hers and Stefan's faces to relax. He even half-smiled.

"Did you feel that? I'm pretty sure a miracle just happened. You just agreed with me. Hey." His voice became tender, lower. "I wasn't hiding who I was from you today. You never asked me for my name and when you saw my license, I didn't bolt. Now you on the other hand, could have told me several things. You're Sandra's grown daughter, you're my mom's live-in nurse, you're having a baby." His voice gentled at that last part of his remark and his eyes went to her stomach.

She tried not to bristle at what felt like accusations and took a moment to close her eyes then open them again.

"I guess this is where we try to move on and forget about all those things. I'd sure as hell like to start the day over," she said.

"Yeah, about that. So what happened this morning? Because I was pretty flattered but I'm seriously worried if the woman taking care of my mother is out picking up dudes in truck stop toilets. Wanna talk about him?"

Not. If. Her. Life. Depended. On. It.

Chapter Nine

The problem with Stefan Calderon wasn't that he could have a woman out of her panties—anytime, anyplace—in under sixty seconds, it was that he had the same effect on Dani's thoughts. At this rate and with him this close, she was going to need a needle and thread for her mouth. More than she'd ever intended on sharing started spilling from her lips.

"You want to hear about how I was dumped?"

He nodded and ran his hands through his hair again. He had to stop doing that. But a curl, heavy and shiny black from the rain, fell halfway down his forehead and now it was her turn to smile inside. *Superman.* She pressed her lips, containing her slip. Why did she feel so safe around him?

If she didn't know better, she'd say Stefan knew exactly what she'd been looking at. And that half-quirked, devilish grin yelled he liked it.

His tongue slid along his lower lip and then it was hidden again. "Let's start with a name. What do we call this young man of questionable intelligence?" he asked with a straight face.

She laughed at the absurdity of her situation. "His name is Thom. You're gonna love this. He's a soldier and his specialty is the intelligence field. And before you crack a joke on him, he's currently deployed to Afghanistan so…"

"So he's supposed to be hero material," Stefan said gently.

"He is. Just not mine." Her lip quivered. Dammit.

"How sure are you about that?" She felt the rough pad of his fingertip settle at the corner of her mouth. It helped, a little. "I find it hard to believe he'd let you go."

"As sure as the email he sent me this morning where he did the stand-up thing and was honest. He told me he fell in love over there. She's deployed with him and she's such a great person that he knows I'd like her too."

"But uh, assuming you're the good girl I suspect, except for when faced with your one weakness that is— truck stop johns—you don't strike me as the type to sleep around. So this guy is your baby's father?"

"For the record, I'm not the only one with that weakness."

He dipped his head at that and pressed his lips together. She wished they could kiss again but knew it would only feel good while they were here. Once they returned to her house, scratch that, his and his mom's house, all the wrongness of what they were doing would come flooding back.

Mrs. C would never approve.

Relationships were sacred. Not to be taken lightly and only when you were sure the person would love you back forever. They'd had a few mother-daughter-like talks when Dani's mom had passed and Gina had taken her in. Mrs. C's adamancy about committed loving relationships was why Dani hadn't said anything about Thom and the pregnancy yet. Those would be strikes one and two. Inappropriate relations with Stefan would be three. And Dani began to realize now, she should have kept her big mouth shut rather than spill everything to Stefan. Her wrist bones cracked as she rotated them tightly. What if her secret got out before she was ready? When would she be ready? Pretty soon she wouldn't be able to hide it. Never or right now, either way, her stomach flip-flopped.

"So Thom? He's the father?" Stefan asked her, sounding quite thoughtful. There wasn't a drop of his playful sarcasm in the question. His warm, heavy hand stopped on her wrists, just like he'd done to her quivering lip a moment ago. "Stop that," he said, the deep baritone vibrating, again undoing her but centering her as well.

"Yeah. Yes, I mean. Yes he is. Definitely the father."

"And what does he think about that?"

She stilled for a long couple of breaths. "I don't know." She looked at him like she was searching for something. "Care if I turn this around on you? You could actually be helpful to me."

Playful Stefan smirked. "Bring it on, sweetheart. Shoot." He stretched in a way that undid all the careful ties she'd bound her desire with. They were too close and secluded. Everything about him was masculine from his cocky attitude to his strong whiskered jaw to that mouth-watering cinnamon flavor he gave off when he gave out his bossy demands. Not to mention the way he sat with his legs spread like his lap was made for seating women day and night. His arm rested up against the Buick's roof, bent at the elbow, and muscles hinted at where the white sleeve bunched. She could have reached over and ran her fingers over his shirt-covered ribs. An inch of tanned skin near his waist poked from where his shirt hiked up from the stretch. The nighttime made it dark. She wanted to strain to see him better. Even if it was just that inch in the shadows. Why had she stopped him earlier? This was painful. Maybe it was for him too because he brought his arm back down and rotated his shoulder.

She smiled but it wasn't real and returned to serious in the next heartbeat. "What would you do if the girl you'd been dating for a few weeks before you deployed told you she was having your baby after you'd just declared you'd found your soul mate and were moving on?"

His left brow rose, in true comic-book hero fashion, and he rubbed his lips together. Dani was so distracted by that simple deed that she barely heard his next words. "Can I think about that for a second and ask you something else first?" he said.

"Sure." She wanted to blow out all the air quadrupling in her lungs but practiced neat, even breaths all the while taking him in. The more they talked, the harder it became to call him arrogant and thoughtless. Friend didn't seem that far a stretch to make.

"This in no way is meant to sound judgy, but how did you get pregnant?" he asked, looking her over quite directly. Her body responded to those dark eyes. Her body would send her off a cliff if she didn't get a handle on it. She ignored the warming and tingling and tensing, barely.

His face told her he was being serious for once. Her face blanked and then she frowned with her brow, her eyes, her twisted lips. "Um, the normal way. Semen exchange."

"Oo, sexy talk. You can be very funny, and cute by the way, when you try." He smiled and she nearly smiled back but held it in because something in his eyes when he looked at her like that and flirted the way he did promised things she now knew she couldn't have. He swallowed and smiled again. Dani needed to look away but couldn't. "I meant did you use protection and if not, why not?" he asked.

She couldn't believe she was having a birds and the bees conversation with Stefan Calderon, Mr. Sinfamous himself, according to *Guitar Freak*. And now she was embarrassed to admit how careless she'd been that one night with Thom.

"Don't be embarrassed, Dani." And then his voice buried her in its deepness. "I've wanted it bad like that before. Many times."

How could she not be self-conscious with him staring at her like that? She felt a ramble coming on.

"He took me to the movies three times before he even kissed me. I felt safe with Thom, like he wasn't just trying to get laid. On our fourth date, he came over and made me and your mom dinner. Then he told me he was deploying. He's younger than me. He never said it, but I could tell he was worried about possibly not coming back. So that night I slept with him." Dani's hands clapped together and then she rubbed her palms in small circles. Stefan kept watch over her closely. "It was just one of those things where we thought about protection but it would have meant stopping and a trip to the store. It was stupid. But what's done is done. It was my fault. I practically seduced him. I kept pushing, knowing he wouldn't be able to stop." She told Stefan the story, aware it was pretty dry and lacked passion.

Stefan rubbed his hands together now, concentrating on the tops of his knuckles. He shifted in his seat and she reacted accordingly.

"For the record, and you may not believe this, but if I had been in bed with you, I would have stopped and gone to the store for you." All the joking left his voice.

"For some reason, I believe you."

Although she didn't want to entertain it, she couldn't help but to wonder if Stefan was more motivated by being safe or getting sex. It had to be the first, right? Because the man could get any woman he wanted. "Stefan, can I ask you something else?"

"If you insist," his eyes twinkled when he grinned, the cocky flirt back by her side.

"Why do you think I let what happened between us this morning get so far?" she asked, curious to know what he thought. Stefan had probably seen all there was to see in the world. Maybe he had an answer for something that left her baffled.

He considered her for a long moment. "Honestly?"

She nodded, readying herself for his harmless teasing that shouldn't excite and unnerve her but did.

"I think you were hurt and needed a friend."

It was not what she'd expected to come out of those beautiful full lips of his. "You're being too kind. Which is weird because I think I like it better when you're teasing." She couldn't allow herself to take too much from his words. She shouldn't be this close, confined again, feeling the chaos his nearness brought to her nerves and flesh. She rubbed at the side of her neck.

"Why? Because I'm right this time? Hey, there's no shame in needing a hug when life kicks you in the balls. Or a quick, hot fuck at the Pump-n-Go." His boyish grin shattered any modesty she might have faked at that. He said the craziest things to her yet she loved it.

They shared a good chuckle after a couple seconds of holding it in.

"You know, I was totally ready to give you a hard time about this whole needing a special friend theory, but…" She considered her words very carefully first, wondering if she truly believed them. Funny enough, even if it was the most unrealistic thought she'd had all day, she did. "I think you and I could be friends. Good friends."

This time when he grinned it turned softer at the edges. "I see some promise there. You could help me understand all those angsty shows the kids are so into nowadays and I could school you in all sorts of worldly adult interests." The grin was once again wicked and so unfair.

"Stefan, are you ever serious?"

"Always."

But wait. Did he just look away from her? What did Stefan Calderon have to be nervous about?

He didn't need her upping his cool factor. But it was nice of him to pretend. They needed to keep talking because otherwise, her breath hitched at the other option.

She tried to tease him back. "Okay, that 'worldly adult interests' sounded kind of creepy. I am most definitely an adult and you're not that much older than me. Are you?" she asked.

Did he just blush?

No, this man was not a blusher.

He'd probably gotten some sun from his fancy convertible. But was that a nervous twitch over his left eye? Checking out his face so much, she began to see how he wasn't chiseled from stone, perfected to perfection. Stefan's nose was just a little crooked near the top of the bridge which made him look tough and he had a little dent near his eyebrow, maybe from a chicken pox episode. When his mouth was relaxed like it was now rather than grinning, his top lip was fuller than most men. Dani bet he'd been teased about that in school just the same as she'd been. She tried to remember his school photo hanging on Mrs. C's wall and didn't think his shoulders had quite the size they did now. Much smaller than his full grown man self, Dani wondered if he'd been picked on and if he'd fought? The more little quirks she discovered about him, the more human he became. She smiled for no apparent reason.

"God, you're gonna love this. When you were born, your mom brought you to the house to show you off. I, uh, I held you. I was knee deep into the sixth grade."

"Ten, eleven years then? That's not so bad. You don't look it. You definitely don't act it. I was trying to figure it out today and I thought you were older, maybe in your forties."

"Try twelve. Not forty yet but not too far off, sweetheart." He scratched his head. "How did you not recognize me this morning? Honestly? You really had no idea who I was?"

She made a face like she was still just as clueless. "Well, I'm not really a fan. I mean, that's not what I meant. Not that I don't like your band's music ... I'm sure it's really good. I've heard about your fans." She'd heard some of Sin Pointe's bigger hits on the radio over the years. "I just ... I mostly listen to country. Your mom talks about you, but not the band stuff and the only pictures around her house are from when you were little. When I saw your name on your license, it wasn't the whole 'band' thing that got me." Her gaze dropped with her air quotes.

"What? You have to tell me now, after that little look."

The band angle would be a cop out right now when the real shocker had been that she'd nearly hooked up with the man who paid her paycheck. Who called Gina Calderon mom. It would be blatant disrespect for Mrs. C. But she went with something she hoped he'd appreciate more. She'd been so attracted to him. Still was. Her heart raced a little as she remembered her fingers stroking his face. "Your beard. You look more like one of those rugged Alaskan mountain man calendar guys than a punk rocker."

Had she offended him? What was that eye roll about?

"Sin Pointe isn't punk rock."

"But you wear eyeliner and your drummer has a mohawk." Things she'd learned just moments ago in that magazine.

"And all that being true, does not make us punk."

She must not look like she believed him. At all.

"Well, whatever. Hey, everything being what it is, I had a shitty day. I'm sure yours has been mixed. I feel a lot better and I really appreciate … this." She held her hands up, realizing there was no gesture for the distraction he'd provided her. They fell awkwardly back into her lap, grazing her tiny baby bulge as she went. "You've been surprisingly easy to talk to on a day when I really did need a non-judgy friend."

"Ouch." His face took on a hurt look but she couldn't tell if he was sincere or just bluffing to get his way as he seemed so capable of doing.

"What?" she asked, afraid she'd actually hurt his feelings.

He rubbed at his chin and she watched his dark whiskers slide along his fingers. "Surprisingly easy to talk to," he echoed. "You may as well add that I've got a great personality."

Dani felt the immediate need to explain. "Usually I'm not real big on surprises, case in point my being dumped this morning. And being easy to talk to is a good thing." God, had no one ever told him that? She supposed in his rock star life, that was a big possibility. She felt very bad for him if that were the case.

He rubbed her hand and she wished she hadn't just been thinking about her attraction to him. But even when she was thinking of how nice it was to talk to

Stefan, she was at the same time wishing they were wrapped around each other, no matter who he was.

"So let me get this straight," he began. "You woke up to Thom Clueless-Pants' email, then there were those assholes in line who I nearly assaulted, by the way, and then there was me."

"And then there was you."

"Man, I'm really glad I didn't fuck things up for myself. I was this close to joining those losers."

"Oh yeah, maybe it's not too late. You were saying you had something to yell at me about? Don't think I forgot about that."

Stefan's jaw worked. His eyes flashed an intense dark before he blinked and they reverted back to the deep chocolate brown again. "Because you're feeding my mom Indian food and she hates it." For the first time, he took one quick glance down before pinning her again with the confidence and assuredness of a man used to getting what he wanted.

She smiled then hiked up her eyebrows. "Yeah, I think I would have kicked your ass if you'd have come at me with that tonight."

"I'm sorry now for even thinking it. And uh, that's not even the real issue I have with you, anyway."

"I didn't realize you had an issue with me," she said. "What's the real issue, Stefan?"

Chapter Ten

This could either go really well, or really really bad. Stefan could only handle being locked in this car with her for so much longer. Her softness even smelled good to him. Whatever the fuck that smelled like.

Shit, what was wrong with him?

And there were only so many sitting positions he could switch between before she knew his mind wasn't solely on talking. He shifted from his side and pushed his legs forward until his knees locked. Big mistake. Oh well. She should know what they were both up against. The way he was holding himself in check for her benefit. He wouldn't put himself through this for just anyone. Why did he want her to come away from this knowing that?

"The issue is that I need you back at Mom's. *Mom* needs you back at Mom's. And I need you to use that gorgeous brain of yours and take your money back. I've only been home a few hours and I can already see how hard you work."

She shook her head. Okay, he hadn't insulted her with the not using her brains bit. But her pretty lips were drawn damn tight.

"What?" he asked. "Take your paycheck. It's yours; you've earned it. Don't let my dumbass get in the way of that." He looked down at her belly, something he couldn't keep himself from doing. He'd watched Trista morph through the stages of pregnancy. So beautiful. Hell, he'd even seen Jaxon's first wife, Vangie, soften from major bitch to motherly at times. But he'd never seen either of them the way he saw Dani right now. He'd never wanted to touch Tris or Vang. Never been drawn to their bodies this way. Good thing or he'd have had his ass kicked by Lucky and Jaxon. He'd seen the cousins fight each other and it wouldn't be pretty. And those men loved each other. It was shit the way the world had played this out. Dani deserved better. No matter what kind of crap he might give her, he had an enormous amount of respect for her. The kid would have a good woman in its corner. "You need to be thinking about that little guy, right?"

"Yes. But..."

"But what? You know the one thing I see ruin people all the time is their pride."

All these things he was saying, they came from his heart. It was a place he didn't normally speak from but this one, he couldn't stop himself around her. As badly as he wanted to be close to her again, he found he wanted to be honest. Even if it didn't get him what he wanted. And that shit was crazy. No one who knew him would believe it. He could barely make sense of it.

"I know, you're right." She shook her head back and forth.

"Tell me." He wasn't used to asking for so much and expecting so little in return. But for some reason, Stefan knew he'd be happy with a smile, the same as he'd be happy with a kiss. Of course, he'd be overjoyed if she gifted him her body. His mind flashed to the unoccupied house he owned not too far from here that Mom had said no to. It was furnished. They'd have their choice of beds, tubs, rugs by the fireplace. He'd picked out only the best. A quick stop by a store and he could even get food to cook her that dinner he'd offered.

"The minute I take that money from you..." She shook her head and her face turned down.

The instant she said it, he knew what she was referring to because he'd thought about that too and how it didn't matter to him but to her it was probably going to be a major sticking point.

Them. *Special* friends. It would work for him but not for her.

She wouldn't sleep with him if he was paying her in any capacity. He wouldn't lie, he wanted to sleep with her. But he also wanted to keep talking and teasing her. Kiss her again. Feed her. He shouldn't want it this badly but her fire had him hooked like a fiending moth. Was he willing to give up over something as mundane as money? Money meant shit to him. Fuck no, if that was her reason, he wasn't giving up. She'd thank him for his persistence, eventually. He wasn't imagining their connection. It was strong enough to have his ass out in a parking lot talking and not doing. Man, what an amazing two weeks they could have.

"I get it. Looks like there's only one solution to this problem," he said.

"Really? What's that?"

God, her hopeful cheer making those words come out high and clear gave him the dangerous go ahead. Would he take it?

Hell yeah he would.

"You're not gonna like me very much after I say this."

"You. Are. The. Worst. Tease." She stalled on each word, driving him insane.

"You like it and you know it." Conversation was so easy with this woman. He couldn't shut up around her. Could totally see himself talking to her in the middle of sex. Shouldn't be thinking of her back at his Nashville suite. He tried to think of anything else but her standing in his shower and him soaping up her curves. Will's

109

goofy ass in the shower was quite a riot because he was a bath product whore and loved a certain peppermint soap, even though it was so strong you could barely breathe when the steam mixed in with the stuff. How many times had Will got that crap in his eyes? Will's burning eye dance did the trick. Stefan backed safely away from wanting her at his suite in Nashville and got back in line with how hot it would be to have her here and now in Moonlight. "Man, I scare myself sometimes. This could actually work."

"I do like you're teasing." Dani grinned. "So stop being mean and tell me the solution," she said.

So she did want him to figure this out for them. "First you tell me why you're so eager to find out. If you're willing to do that, then I'll tell you."

Fuck, his dick was so hard right now. No surprise there. But his heart could take a break and stop scaring the shit out of him with all the pounding. He tried to explain it away with a mini-science lesson. She had him so turned on, his damn heart couldn't stop sending blood south.

She hemmed and hawed for a few seconds and then tightened up her posture and spit it out. "You made me feel like I was the only girl in the world this morning when everyone else made me feel like dog poo."

God, she was adorable. He'd guarantee there was a second half of that she was leaving off. He'd put it out there for her because he had no shame when it came to expressing his desires but before he could, she spoke up again.

"And." He smiled. She continued. "And fine, I'm woman enough to admit that I would hate for that to have been our only kiss." Then her smile was gone and instead, she frowned. "I shouldn't even be going there, but I can't *not* go there. You scare me just as much as you scare yourself."

He swallowed his grin at her sudden change in mood, trying to match it. But he couldn't deny what was happening between them. He waited a second, then took her hand in his, turned it palm side up and trailed his pointer finger down the thick pink crease that separated her thumb from the rest. She needed this physical release. The rush and cleansing that only sex could give a person. He knew it this morning as clearly as he knew it now.

"You're fired. Officially off the payroll for the next three hours." His finger worked a shiver from her and he watched her forearm muscle contract. She didn't pull back.

"You put some thought into this," she said. Her voice turned soft and he wanted to pull her in closer, not give her the chance to deny him again.

"Mm-hmm. After that you're rehired."

"So just for the next few hours…"

She was considering it. Considering him. The dark joy of taking from her and giving to her egged him on.

"Oh. You misunderstand. I plan to fire you for a few hours every day for the next two weeks." Fuck please don't let her slap him. He hated being slapped by women.

"Unbelievable Stefan Calderon. You are wicked."

"I know." Was she aware of how her smart reply turned him on?

"Here? Now?" she asked, surely paying him back for his constant teasing and aware the ball was in her court. All she had to do was say yes.

"It's just a kiss," he replied, hovering inches away from her mouth. "To start."

"It was almost more."

"Say yes and it *will* be more."

****

"I can't," she said, staring at his lips. Her throat went dry.

"You won't," he said back, hovering closer, baiting her.

"It would be wrong. Your mom would be very disappointed in me. In both of us."

Stefan reached over her from where he sat in her passenger side seat and turned the key in the ignition. Instantly the heater came to life, hissing and blowing air through the car. He rested his hand on her steering wheel, his arm long and curved like a protective cage keeping her where she sat. His tattooed fingers promised they'd play nicely too if she gave his lips the permission they craved.

Inches from Stefan's gorgeous lips, another thought crossed her mind.

Thom, you probably would not like him. But I do. I'm not sorry. And that's all I care about right now.

He didn't swallow, didn't take a deep breath, didn't even look her up and down, just stared into her eyes and waited. Honestly, his intensity scared the shit out of her. But she uttered the tiny yet powerful syllable anyway. It was the only thing she could say to this man. For three hours? And they weren't under Mrs. C's roof and technically, she wasn't on the payroll right now? To hell with everything else.

"Yes," she said.

His grin made her shudder as he pulled that full lip of his between his teeth.

Chapter Eleven

He couldn't stop talking to her. He couldn't take his lips off of hers either.

"You're squirming. A lot," he said, wondering why it was such a turn on. Secretly, he stole a moment to nuzzle up against the peach fuzz of her skin. There weren't many soft or sweet things he craved from a woman but Stefan was finding out the benefits of his newly grown facial hair. Will could call him goat all he wanted. That look, that little dip to the side of her head, when he scraped her with his whiskers, was worth it.

"Beard," she said so close to his mouth.

"I thought you like." He nudged her chin gently again with his whiskers.

"I do."

Oh shit.

He rubbed it harder until her breath caught, exciting him to the point of steel. Sex would be so good. "You do," he said and pulled himself closer to her using the steering wheel. He found her waist with his hand and pulled her forward until he had her nearly out of her seat. He stopped immediately when he felt her tongue abandon his.

"Okay?" he said low.

Her breath poured out and set fire to his cock. Yes, he'd have amazing sex with her, cherish all those irresistible womanly curves. Fuck, her body was magnificent, made to do exactly what it was doing. She'd made a baby and now held it warm and protected. It was raw and sexual and he'd never been with a woman carrying a child inside her. The unknown territory excited him. The curiosity he had for her body kept him glued to her every nuance.

How would she feel about that? Would she have really gone through with it earlier today? Would she now or was she just torturing him? *Shut up with all the thinking, Stefan.* But he couldn't forget when she'd told him not to make her come. It had been strange and contradicting to the need she was giving off. He never thought this much.

He took a deep breath in an effort to get away from his brain and sink back into her. "Dani? Sweetheart, are you okay?" Maybe once she answered him, he'd get back to being lost in all her soft supple curves and that salt he'd tasted on her skin. She'd busted her ass all day, he was sure of it, and even that thought of how hard she worked turned him on beyond normal.

"No, I'm dying over here," she let out. "Stop talking, I only have a couple more hours until I turn back into a toad. I can't believe I'm doing this." She shook her head but smiled and nibbled his lip.

"I'm no expert, but I think you mean a princess," he said then pulled down on her track suit zipper, only a couple inches, and laid a fingertip on her collar bone. He watched her skin dimple while he pressed down. Flesh colored lace peeked out from her bra.

"No, you're definitely no expert. And neither am I." She rubbed his arm. His muscles bunched. "I think the word we're both looking for is pumpkin."

The only fairy tales Stefan wanted to be tangled up in with Dani were the naughty kind. "Fine. Climb over here, pumpkin. But be careful."

That gearshift of hers was dangerous. If she lost her balance she could fall on top of it and land on her stomach. More questions and curiosities about her barely swollen body than his brain could currently handle throttled him into overdrive like she was his new toy. He knew his body's tendencies and cravings when it came to being with a woman but this need to possess and claim her—and her baby for that matter which was really fucking with his head right now—brought fire to his chest like he'd never felt before. This shit was intense. He wanted to hold her. Like she was his and only his.

He guided her clunky crawling with both his hands until she was out of her seat and hovering over him. "Don't be shy now." He reached down and found the lever to slide the seat back as far as it would go. "There we go." Then he caught two handfuls of her yellow velour and pulled her into him. He kissed her while her knees settled on the floorboard. What he'd die to do right now was feel her belly so he could gauge how pregnant she was. When she flattened the rest of her gorgeous body against him but protected her stomach, his sexual prowess wavered. Could he hurt the baby?

Her head tilted back. "What are you thinking about?" she asked and touched his cheek. He hummed inside.

"How can you tell I'm thinking?" Most women could care less what he was thinking about because admittedly, what he was *doing* to them was usually pretty damn amazing.

"Your kiss changes. You stop nibbling," she said.

"One would be crazy to stop nibbling. I'll try to stop thinking so much. You have me off my game." He toyed with her ear between his teeth as he said it. Stefan wanted to be on it like he'd invented it.

"I like that you're thoughtful. Another nice surprise."

Fuck. Did that mean she was not going to like when he settled down and went real on her? Maybe it was

115

one of those signs Jaxon was always talking about with his fruity karma shit. But why in the world would the universe want to put out his fire? Had he burned too many people? Fuck, he shouted in his mind. No more thinking. About anything.

He bit her lip, she gasped, and he held it between his teeth, pulled, then licked it, slowly letting go. He then roamed his hands down the sides of her face, out and over and back in following the curvy line of her shoulders, her ribcage, her sweet small waist and those round flared hips. Fuck, he needed her naked and in a bed, sprawled out so he could see every inch of her luscious body before he took her. He let out a frustrated growl, cursed his new-found sensitivities, and found the lever to jack the seat back up.

He gave her one more kiss and waited for her to be the one to pull out of it because even though his conscience was kicking his ass right now, he couldn't be that good as to leave the taste of those plump lips. She pulled back when she must have felt his jaw stop working so feverishly against hers.

Her dark brown eyes pierced him. "You stopped."

"Earlier you asked me not to make you any promises. Remember that?" he said.

She nodded yes.

"I decided I do want one from you," he said and touched her lips with his finger.

"Okay," she said.

"Promise you'll forgive me for making you wait until we get back to the house to finish this. I need you in a bed, Dani. Stretched out under me." Thunder boomed loudly. "And there's that too. Another storm's about to break." Plus he'd seen a security car drive through the lot a couple of times now and would be all kinds of pissed if he got arrested again for public indecency. Shit, Mom would love that. Although moving to Nashville to escape that kind of embarrassment might be her only choice. Nah, not worth it. Of course now the thought of having sex with Dani outdoors slayed his last shreds of sanity. But it would have to be someplace private.

A loud breath came gusting out from her mouth. "I guess there has to be an end to this crazy night." She blinked several times and zipped her top back up. "But you know I can't go back with you to do that. I'm sorry."

No, no, no, no, no, he silently muttered. *Stop saying no to me, woman,* was all he could think although he loved it just the same. "It's going to be a very good ending you'll be missing." He thought of his abandoned house again. There was no good reason he wasn't buckling her up and driving her there right now. *No you idiot. There are a million good reasons.* He just couldn't come up with one with his body and mind humming and zeroed in on her right now.

All Dani did was look down.

She wasn't playing with him. The truth she couldn't deny of wanting him sat on the warm tops of her cheeks. "I'm sure it would be," she said. "But I think if we've proven one thing today, it's that you and I can't keep our hands off each other."

At that, Stefan recognized regret like he'd never known. He could push her, but he wasn't going to do that. "That is very true. Can't blame a guy for trying."

Her hand went to his. "I love your Mom, Stefan." Dani's simple, loyal statement made him as happy as it frustrated him. It must have showed. "Her house," she started.

"Her rules," Stefan finished. It was something he'd grown up hearing and a guarantee his mom would have a rule against sexing up her helper.

"Am I still fired tomorrow?" she asked. "We could go out for that dinner." His body exploded with hope. But that didn't solve his most immediate problem. Stefan still wanted to get Dani back to his mom's house tonight where she'd be safe but his desire to fuck her was just as strong. He also wouldn't let her sit out here in her car which is what he'd pegged as her stubborn ass brilliant plan if he didn't back off. It sucked, but he had to make her believe he'd keep things platonic between them. Funny thing about that, companionable was exactly how sex had always been between him and his partners. Somehow he didn't think Dani would appreciate hearing that right now.

He took her hand and prepared to do something he'd never before done in his life as a man with a woman he clearly wanted six ways to Sunday. Curling her smaller hand in his, he kissed the tops of her knuckles and tried to ignore his dick. "You come back to my mom's, for good. I promise to respect you while we're under her roof. And tomorrow night, I'll take you out for the best dinner you've ever had."

He winked and loved the way she got all fidgety whenever he did that.

Knowing the truth of his actions, though, that sucked. He was no different than his dad. The man had pretended he wasn't leaving—told his mom everything was okay, just to string her along long enough to get her to finish her degree—then, he'd disappeared.

Yeah, Dad had done it with honorable intentions.

Could Stefan claim the same thing?

Not really sure with the way his honest desire to have Dani safe at Mom's kept getting hijacked by a vision of their two bodies connected, moving against each other, sharing. He blew out, hard and long at the mental image of their give and take.

Once he had Dani back at his mom's, could he be good like he'd just promised?

The motivation was there, heavy and real.

Stefan had to remind himself that he needed her taking care of his mom more than he needed her satisfying his hard-on.

Shit, anyone could do that. Someone, somewhere would step up to the plate if Dani didn't, and he'd let whoever it was in for that moment. Sex had been one of the greatest joys of his life, it didn't have to serve any other purpose just because he was into this girl. Right? Man, just thinking like that made him feel like shit. But she'd already proven she would bolt when she felt the situation called for it. He had to take this seriously.

What would any of this matter in two weeks when he left? Why did he care?

Why did he have to like this woman so much?

What sucked worse than any of this was knowing he had exactly what Dani wanted and exactly how bad she needed it. Her curiosity at what he'd feel like as her lover was written all over her pretty face. The eyes couldn't hide that shit. *If I don't take you here and now, you're gonna get away from me. Aren't you?* He watched her throat move when she swallowed.

Should he try one last time? He never tried this hard.

"Do we have a dinner deal?"

"Okay, deal." Her eyes lit up. "I want pizza. The good stuff. Mmmm, Mario's Hawaiian. That would be so good. I haven't had pizza in forever." This girl literally glowed as she made her request and now all he could think about was feeding her this damn pizza. He knew Mario's well. The owners had been friends with his parents back in the 80's when they'd first opened. It was easily the best in town.

WICKED FLOWER

God, you're killing me, sweetheart.

Chapter Twelve

She had no idea how they did it, but they'd managed to separate themselves and drive back to the house when Stefan pointed out the nighttime security detail patrolling the store lot. The second they pulled in to the driveway, Stefan hopped out of his car and came to her Buick's door, opening it and helping her out. And now he had her inside his Mercedes, not the neutral zone they'd agreed on otherwise known as Gina's house. Secretly, not being in there yet was fine with Dani. The houselights were off and she prayed Gina was asleep. She should be at this time of night, being the early riser she was.

Her son would be Dani's delicious death.

She sat there in the absolute luxury of his car, teetering on her metaphorical heels. Each time Dani pushed her senses back to where they belonged—which was the real world—the tight spots she and Stefan kept getting themselves into pushed back. First, Dani forced out a long breath and then the words that had better make it into his beautiful thick head followed.

"Inside that house, the best I can give you is friends. Nothing more than that can happen. Cannot. Happen, Stefan."

She hated tossing the ultimatum in his lap like that—what she wouldn't give to be in his lap—but it wasn't something she could afford to budge on. Dani pictured Gina's face and how it would twist and fall when she confessed, *I got myself pregnant by Thom and now I'm sleeping with your son.* No matter that she felt something with Stefan that had been missing with Thom and every other guy she'd dated.

"There are many kinds of friends, sweetheart." His voice was still sexy as ever, laced with that *I want to lick every inch of you* rawness. It hazed her fears, making them seem like everyday problems people figured out all the time when it was for something so right. The deep, thick sound vibrated through her every pore. Stefan Calderon wasn't through with her. Her heart and body cheered. He leaned closer to her and his long fingers easily circled her wrist. He made her feel feminine in a way none of her boyfriends ever had.

Damn him for not just agreeing. He was forcing her to spell out the rules, to be the bad guy. "As soon as we walk in that door, it's hello, how was your day, good evening," she said, her mind absent because of how his fingers traveled, playing with the fine hairs on her arms. Was this how he played his beloved bass?

He turned up his car's music and she guessed he must really like the classic Journey song because he quietly sang the first few words about loving, touching and squeezing. Her tummy squeezed double time but his singing voice left her dumbstruck and mesmerized. First chance she got, she was downloading some Sin Pointe music.

"So formalities, as soon as we go inside," he said and dragged his hand still further up her arm to her shoulder and then down her shirt to the top swell of her breast where his thumb rubbed over the curve harder with each stroke. Unsure whether he avoided her nipple on purpose or not, he hadn't touched the tender spot yet and she leaned forward into his touch. He stared at her and quirked his brow, making her insides sizzle and excite. "I want you, you're beautiful, let me see your body. Formalities." His hand fell to the whole of her breast and he ran one finger around it in a circle then squeezed from the underside. He leaned in and licked the bottom line of her jaw from her ear to her chin. Dani's sex trembled. She knew she should stop him. Her mind blanked on why. "I can keep going." His caress became doubly electrifying when the hand kneading her breast was joined by the other riding the curve of her waist, up and down. "Your taste drives me crazy, all I want is to be inside you, I want you in my bed, you're leaving me no choice but to take you out here…"

"Formalities and only in passing," she panted, barely able to get that out. "Are, are there more?" she said, aware he'd just made her stutter.

"My formalities or yours?" His eyes danced and shone like fiery hot black ice.

"Mine. As long as I'm working for you, we have to keep it platonic." Not a shred of backbone supported her breathy words. "Yours," she conceded.

Finally, his thumb found its way to the hard tip of her breast and pressed and circled. She almost forgot she was fully clothed because his touch stripped her bare. When cool air blew against her hot skin and his even hotter fingers searched and pressed along her hip, she knew he'd taken the liberty to venture under her clothes. Her head fell to the very edge of his soft leather headrest and all she could think of was yes.

"Look at me." The darks of his eyes killed her resistance the second she obeyed him. Stefan's hungry look said he'd gone into possessive mode and that he knew he had her. The night outside felt darker. The car space inside felt deeper and warmer, all based on that look on his face. "Platonic," he said, never blinking and not allowing her to either.

"Yes, it means friendly. Nonsexual. Neighborly."

"I know what it means. I simply fail to see the point." Her breath nearly caught when he skimmed a finger inside her panties. His fingers trapped inside her cotton undies still managed to spread wide, asking without words for a couple inches of maneuvering room. Aching with need for this man's touch, she complied and parted her thighs just enough for him as she sat on his leather seat. "You're so wet, you're so pretty." His fingers played a sensuous game of slide up and down her opening until they dipped deeply inside her. She was so overcome with how good it felt that she missed when he brought his fingers up to his lips. "Your taste drives me insane." He rubbed the tip of his finger against his tongue and then touched it to her lips.

Vaguely, she spoke from somewhere outside of her mind. "You said that twice."

Stefan's tongue slid over her lips while his fingers trailed back inside her panties and returned to their play between her wet folds. She couldn't stop her back from arching. "That's because before I only wondered and now I know for sure. Your taste is exquisite, sweetheart. Your pussy's so wet, you fucking own me right now."

Was she dreaming? Was he really saying these things to her or was it some X-rated song on his radio? His rough thumb found the hard nub again peaking from the top of her sex and her tummy felt like it rolled. Intense, pleasure-filled tingles pushed her hips forward. The solid strong hand he used to bring her this insane pleasure met her pussy's thrust and pushed back. Her eyes squeezed shut, her jaw fell open and she ground her forehead into his shoulder. His fingers beat against her flesh for several minutes, hard and loud, giving sound to her juices and his thrusting. "Dani, if you could feel what I'm feeling right now … Come in my hand, baby …

you're so slick. One of these days you're going to let me tongue you down there. Aren't you? Say yes, Dani."

"Ye-yes," Dani moaned into his shoulder as her mind fought against the pleasure about to explode throughout her body. One of these days. He'd said one of these days like there would be more in the future. The things he said to her worked like a magic eraser over her frazzled brain. Oh God, she was so close. All she wanted, all she could think about was the trembling and how good it was going to feel once the jumble of nerves punched through her clit and washed over her. "Stefan." Her voice shook because at the uttering of his name, her body pulsed and her orgasm broke fast and strong, like a wave taking her deep under the water.

"Yeah Dani, there you go baby."

"Thank you…"

"That was my fucking utmost pleasure." He pulled gently at the back of her hair, bringing her head from his shoulder so that their faces met. He kissed her long and slow.

She just sat there, knowing her end of the kiss must feel lazy to him but her body was still coming down from the high. Her body continued to clench a couple seconds apart. Her heart thumped, helping remind her to breathe, even though the breaths she took were from inside his mouth.

"Mm, and you said I couldn't make you come," he whispered into her ear and continued kissing her ear.

And then she felt it.

The squeeze that felt like it came from higher up, nowhere near her vagina. Dani stilled instantly. Stefan's kiss stopped. "What is it?" he asked.

Dani didn't want to move yet. She waited, perfectly still, to see if the squeezing thing she'd felt a few weeks before when she'd masturbated and climaxed would do it again. Her pregnancy books said it was normal but she still wanted to check with her OB because it didn't feel normal to her. A few seconds later, her womb squeezed again. She sucked in a breath.

"Dani, talk to me."

She held her hand to her heart, waiting for another contraction because that's what she feared these were, some sort of orgasm induced contractions, but it didn't happen. Why had she forgotten, been so careless?

The shit scared her straight, for real this time. *Dear God, I'm sorry.* Her thoughts were all panic and fuzz.

"I need to go inside, Stefan."

Shame washed through her and she didn't know what else to say. She'd known, had that feeling before. All she wanted right now was to get to her bed and lie down flat on her back and pray.

"Okay," he said. "Did I hurt you? Your baby?"

"I don't think so. I-I don't know. I can't have any more orgasms. They give me contractions."

His face paled and his brow crinkled. "God I'm so sorry. I didn't know that's what you meant." He looked down at his lap. "What can I do?" he asked, shielding his eyes from her.

"I just need to get inside and lay down."

"Okay. Can you walk?"

"Yes."

Slowly, his head came back up and his eyes were moist. "Dani, are you in pain? I can't tell. Your face, it looks like you're hurting. Please tell me if I hurt you."

"No, no pain. Just a weird feeling toward the end."

"Do I need to take you to the hospital? I'll drive you."

"No, I think it stopped now. I just want to go inside."

His breath came out hard and loud. "I'll be right behind you."

How did she tell him that was her biggest fear right now?

Inside the still quiet and dark house, she thought of what she needed to say to him as she sat on the toilet, wiping and checking the toilet paper to make sure there was no spotting. Praying. There wasn't any. No cramping either. Dani's head slumped heavily. "Oh God, thank you. I promise I won't let that happen again. I'm so sorry, baby."

Still freaked out, she breathed and made her decision. One she had to stick to this time. To keep them both sane and safe, she couldn't lose control like that again with Stefan.

She nearly bumped into him standing outside the bathroom door, hovering.

"Everything okay?"

"Yes."

As he walked with her to her room, she turned and stopped so that he didn't come in any further. Her hand pushed into his chest and she waited until he stopped trying to move forward.

"I'll stay with you. Just to make sure you're okay."

His look was serious. The slight crooked part of his nose deepened his frown and told her the truth. She knew he was worried and being sincere. But no, she could not let him do that.

"Stefan? What you did for me tonight was, um, I don't even know the word. But it was wonderful. But I forgot something that I can never forget again. I have a little person to look out for. I'm no fool. I know I'll be doing it on my own which is why I have to take sole responsibility for all my actions starting now." She kept the rest to herself but it hummed through her mind all the same. Stefan wasn't a keeper because he had to leave in two weeks. And sadly, she understood. She also knew that if she gave in to him again, she'd lose her heart.

Maybe somewhere deep inside, she was happy he'd found a way to break the rules tonight. It just couldn't happen again.

"I need you to help me remember the rules. As long as we're together in this house, we have to be just friends, or stay away from each other. I'm sorry, I'm just not strong enough to do it on my own. If you can't make me that promise, then I really do have to find somewhere else to stay until you go."

Silence fell between them for a few seconds. Did it have anything to do with the reminder of his short visit? His mouth twisted but he took her hand in his and kissed the tops of her knuckles then put her hand back on her belly where he'd found it.

"Done," he said.

Just. Like. That.

She could have cried, and ended the day the same damn way she'd started it.

****

Friends. Her kind, not his. Maybe Will could tell him how the fuck that worked. Because all that taste had done was leave him needing more. It was going to be a long two weeks. He had no choice but to be good. Even if it killed him.

Watching her walk away to her bedroom, all he wanted was to lay down at her side and make sure she was okay. That he really hadn't hurt her or her baby. He closed his eyes when she closed her door. It had been a long crazy ass day.

Stefan shook his head and went downstairs then made his way outside and stood on the back patio.

A couple minutes later, Will joined him.

"Hey brother," Will said and sat down on Mom's picnic table.

"Can't sleep?" Stefan asked. "Too much Swayze?"

Will just snorted. "So what's up? We good to go?"

Stefan thought about it good and hard. "I think I just fucked up pretty badly, man."

It was the absolute truth and he hadn't come here to do that again.

Chapter Thirteen

The stormy days were wreaking havoc on Mrs. C's joints. Multiple days of wacky barometric pressure and Gina could barely get down the stairs on her own. Stefan had picked a bad day to ask for quality time alone with his mom but he was down to the last week of his visit. Dani pushed one side of the lacy white curtain hanging over the kitchen sink window open and praised the sunlight. At least it wasn't dreary outside today.

Inside was a different story.

Dani could tell the boys were about ready to bust out of their skin if they were stuck indoors one more day. The sun and fresh air would be good for Mrs. C too.

Stefan was playing by her rules.

Unfortunately, fortunately. She hadn't pegged him for having that kind of control but he did.

She'd gotten her dinner, anyway. Every night, they ate at the same table surrounded by Will and Gina. Watching each other.

It was what she'd asked for, after all.

They did their best not to bump shoulders passing through the upstairs hall. And that was a narrow hall when you added the larger than life men of Sin Pointe to it. She'd downloaded their most popular album, one called "Play", but hadn't had the guts to listen to it yet. Whenever they did pass, Stefan always gave way and let her go by first. It wasn't too bad except for when it was him heading to the bathroom for his shower or the times he asked her to step aside and let him be the one to help his mom down the stairs. He was trying so hard, in so many ways and it was the most beautiful yet difficult thing for her to have to sit back and watch. Those near-collisions were excruciating.

She'd seen a lot more of Will Cordero.

The man's shoulders and arms were the most defined she'd ever laid eyes on. Not that she wanted to be noticing those things about Will when Stefan sent him to help her move heavy stuff around the house, but if she didn't know better, she'd swear Stefan was pushing them together. Case in point, she and Will were going shopping today to give Stefan some of that alone time he wanted with his mom. Who was she to question that? Trying to be nice, Dani offered to use the day to go visit her baby sister. Stefan had never looked more relieved to her than in the seconds after she made that offer.

Her heart sank but she understood. She was fighting the same urgent call he was.

She looked out back, through the kitchen window, to see Will and Stefan standing in the middle of the overgrown yard, talking. Thanks to the recent rain, the grass was a good six inches too high and Dani had yet to bust out the lawnmower from its winter hibernation. Will had an extension cord in his hand and she lost sight of him when he walked away for a moment. But his hair made her smile. The mohawk was pulled into a knot at the back of his head. He wore an aqua blue muscle shirt with a picture of a bear on the front. The tank was without sleeves or sides. His ribs showed through because he was thinner than Stefan but the man's killer arms looked lethal. She took in Stefan. Wearing black for a change, he stood there in a clingy athletic t-shirt and matching pants. In white, he looked tan and massive. In the black, she could see his lengths. Legs, arms, torso. Dani closed her eyes.

****

The rain could stay in the fucking sky.

With it falling every day, Mom's lawn was grass on crack and shooting up everywhere. Today was nice for a change. Stefan didn't feel nice, but Dani was going to spend the day with her sister so his stress-level should be cut in half.

If he thought about Dani one more time, fuck.

At least she would be somewhere safe today. With her at her sister's, he could walk to the kitchen without bumping into her. Stefan took a rake and catapulted it up and over Will, past Mom's garden. It bounced off a large tree and nearly bludgeoned Will in the back.

Will ducked just in time. "Dude? What the fuck?" he asked.

"Yeah? What?" Stefan waited for Will to go plug his end of the cord into the socket on the side of Mom's house so Stefan could start mowing. He needed something to do with his hands before he went crazy or accidentally killed his best friend. Thank God it wasn't raining.

"You look like you're about to go Chuck Norris on your mom's lawn. Like if I leave right now, I'm gonna come back to not just a mowed lawn but fricking no more trees, nothing."

That's about how he felt. "I'm not gonna chop down her trees. There's way too many." Or else maybe he would. Luckily Mom's house butted up to the forest and Stefan knew he wouldn't make much of a dent if he went all lumberjack. Knowing Dani was inside that house jacked up his pulse like it did every minute of every day.

Will walked back up the slope of the yard where Stefan stood, watching Dani inside at the sink. "So I'm gonna take off with Dani today. She bribed me with Taggert's. You sure that's cool?"

"Why the fuck wouldn't it be?"

"Uh, because you're being a dick. And I know why. Want my advice?"

Only because it was Will. "You're gonna tell me anyway."

"Make good on taking Dani out to dinner."

Stefan wished he would have said no to Will's advice. "I can't. We're being 'just friends'."

"Bulletin, shithead. *That's* what friends do. They go out for meals together. You owe her that much."

"No, no, no. You misunderstand. Dani's idea of friends isn't the same as mine. I know I sound like an asshole, but the only place she and I can be around each other is here at the house, under Mom's watchful eye." He'd nearly hurt her baby with those contractions. Thoughts of Amanda crept in. The day she'd told him she'd lost their baby and then his parents screaming at him that it was his fault for all the stress he'd caused Amanda. Stefan gritted his teeth and tried to block out the yelling and the lies. No, he'd been nothing but supportive.

Will put his hands on his hips and looked like he'd just spent too much time with one of Jaxon's kids. "Look, I know I blow you off all the time when it comes to this stuff. And no way in hell do I want you lecturing me about this shit in return. So don't even think about it. But you're gonna be so pissed if you leave here next week and don't take that girl out."

Stefan wiped sweat off his forehead, forgetting what the sun felt like, and swore to shave his beard off when he was done mowing. All because he knew Will was right. Could he admit as much to his friend? "She'll say no." Just like his mom with the house. Just like

Amanda when he'd offered to quit school and work full time to support the baby they'd made.

"I'll talk to her today on our date," said Will.

Stefan wanted to pile drive Will for that one but didn't because that's just how they kept it real. "Fucking, don't Will."

"Stop being a baby. If it gets your mopey ass off my Swayze stash, it's worth it. You should probably take this opportunity to talk to your mom while we're gone. Come on, man. Do I have to think of everything?"

Stefan knew he was just being a smartass, but yeah, Will had done this relationship stuff before. Stefan didn't have a clue and for the record, he wasn't calling this a relationship. All he knew was he wanted to be with Dani. Dani wanted to be with him. But she'd chosen not to let that happen and for good reason. He wouldn't admit it out loud right now, but Will had no idea how needed he was.

Stefan watched Dani standing there at the kitchen sink. She was probably finishing up the breakfast dishes and getting stuff ready for his mom like she did every day, no matter how tired her body was, how upset her stomach might be, or how much shit she probably had on her mind. The whole time, she'd kept a smile on her face and even cracked jokes with Will. She'd fit in so well with the girls. Tris and Lily would get a real kick out of her. Jaxon and Ben would worship the ground she walked on for Dani's amazing ability to blow Stefan off. The fact he was even having those thoughts … He couldn't keep telling himself all it meant was that he wanted her for here and now.

He did owe her a dinner. Mario's pizza, he remembered. A peace offering maybe?

Stefan squeezed the electric mower's trigger bar until it roared and vibrated under his hands. And he'd yet to check in on his empty house. He closed his eyes for a second and hoped like hell she didn't shoot him down when he asked her to join him tonight because Will was right, if he didn't do it, he was a pussy. He let the mower die for a second.

"How do I do just dinner with her?" he asked Will, dropping as much of the asshole from his voice as he could.

Will stood next to him with his arms folded over his chest, both of them staring toward Dani in the kitchen window. "You got it bad, brother. Don't you? The fact you're even asking me that."

"You have no idea. I can't believe I fucking let this happen."

"Well, you can either fight it all night, or you can accept it and let nature take its course," Will said then looked at him and waited a second while he chewed his cheek. He closed his eyes then opened them again and Stefan knew he'd been remembering Honey. "The way you *just have dinner* with a girl is easy, man. When it's the right girl, you do whatever you can not to fuck it up. If all she can give you is dinner, then that's all you ask her for. In that moment, it'll be enough, if it's the right girl. You're just gonna have to trust me on that."

Stefan almost let Will go, aware that had taken a lot out of his friend by the hollow look on his face.

"How can she be the right girl? We just met." Stefan frowned.

"I knew Honey was it within minutes, brother." Will cleared his throat. "Hey, I gotta go. Your girl is waiting on me for our date."

"Fuck you." Stefan gave him a helpful shove toward the back porch door of the house. "Take care of our girl, or I'll kick your ass."

Will just nodded his head and ducked inside. Stefan watched him meet up with Dani by the sink. He closed his eyes and thought about the first time he'd seen Dani at that pump.

"Oh shit." It hadn't taken minutes, it had been seconds. He had to figure this shit out.

****

When Dani opened her eyes, Will was inside, standing before her. A funny look pulled at his face.

"Hey, ready to go shopping?" he asked.

"Oh, um yeah sure. I thought you were about to mow and that we'd go after." That had been an interesting exchange to watch between the guys out back. Men interacted with each other on a whole nother level she didn't understand. She wished she knew what had been said but their body language had fascinated her. Along with the flying objects and shoving.

"Nah. Stefan's got it. Let's go."

She put the last plate in the dish drainer to dry. "Oh, okay," she said, trying to come back from the whiplash in her mind. "Let's go."

Will just nodded and walked through the living room to the foyer by the front door. Apparently he was in such a hurry to leave, he wasn't concerned with much else.

Dani glanced behind her, still able to see Stefan through the large, back glass door opening to the back yard.

He yanked at a bright orange cord so hard and fast it looked to have bit him in the ribs. Then he kicked the ground he stood on so rigidly he sent clumps of dirt and grass flying. Was he pissed she was going somewhere alone with Will? Hadn't he just insisted the night before when she'd brought it up? Men, she'd never understand them apparently. Well, whatever. They'd gotten through one week. Just one more to go, she thought and squeezed fingers to her palms.

"Come on," said Will, his hand on her forearm. "We should go."

Will obviously knew something was up between them. She felt pretty damn pathetic.

Dani wasn't sure Will knew exactly what he'd signed up for, aside from his obvious excitement about Taggert's. Once they were in her car, she brought him up to speed.

"Hey, I hope you're really okay going with me today. Taggert's and my kid sister's place probably aren't on your bucket list so thanks." Now that Dani was accepting her paycheck again, she could afford to buy Daisy a new blender and toaster, as long as they were discount store brand and not fit for a gourmet cooking show.

"Yeah, um, no problem. How far away are these wondrous places?" Will asked.

She smiled. "About thirty minutes."

"Cool. Gives us time to talk."

Oh boy. Will had been a man of few words this week. What did he want to talk about? There was only one thing she could think of and that was the disaster she liked to call throwing herself at Stefan twice that first day. She also wondered now if Stefan had kept her secret. Had he told Will she was pregnant? Just by looking, you couldn't really tell she was four months along when she was dressed. Naked was another story as she'd seen this morning getting dressed. Pants were now a no-no so she'd had to switch to one of the few loose dresses she owned. "Sure," she said, but her stomach tossed.

Nervous about letting him start the conversation, Dani blurted out, "So you're sure you don't mind going to my sister's with me? I know I roped you in with the

Taggert's part." Dani shook her head, wondering how in the world Daisy survived on her own some days but was happy her sister led the life she wanted to live. Plus thinking about Daisy's issues took her mind off the Calderons.

Will tapped his thumbs against his cargo shorts pockets.

Dani twiddled her thumbs on top of the steering wheel.

Thank God he answered her, and in a sort of sweet way too that settled some of her jitters.

"Are we going to a Super Taggert's?" he asked and she swore he made a very deliberate point to look at her with an easy face when he did so.

"Super Taggert's all the way," she was able to say with a smile.

"I love those ones."

"Hmm, you know you didn't strike me as one of their biggest fans."

"What can I say? They sell this soap, I swear it really is magical. Turns an ordinary shower into a peppermint sauna. I can never find it anywhere else. And the dollar bin deals, I'm always finding stuff there."

So he was a man of few words except for when it came to soap and good deals. "The dollar bin deals rock," she said a little too enthusiastically. The silly talk made her like Will even more but also left her even more curious than she'd been before. He'd been nothing but kind since showing up with Stefan. Although he did keep to himself and only spoke to when spoken to first.

His next question surprised her. "So Daisy must be your *baby* sister." He emphasized baby.

"Oh you can't even imagine. How did you ever guess?"

"Emergency appliance run. Classic."

"You sound like you speak from experience."

He didn't have another quick comeback and when he was quiet a few seconds too long, Dani looked over at him to see if he was scowling or worse, hurt, by what she'd said. "Sorry, it just sounded like you…"

He nodded, the kind that wasn't for her but like he was acknowledging something to himself. "Baby sister-in-law," he said quietly. "Mother's Day, six years ago. Morning of." He put his hand up to the side of his head like he was on a phone call and speaking into his outstretched, non-tattooed thumb. She noted again how Will's tats stopped at his wrists like crisp neat sleeves. She wondered why but was too engrossed in this miniature revelation by Mr. Will Cordero. She smiled, encouraging him to continue. "I get a call. 'Will, I completely blanked about today. Need you to pick up my mom's gift. Honey's not answering'." His brows raised like he was unsettled at something he'd said. Then he blinked. Dani couldn't peel her eyes from his endearing face and the fuzzy, nearly bald sides of his head. "She'd had the forethought to turn in her mom's favorite pair of suede boots to be re-soled and made like new but had totally spaced on picking them up. I'm like, 'okay, no problem, Heather.' So then I ask what's wrong with her car. One guess what she tells me."

Dani knew instantly. "Out of gas."

"Exactly. So then I'm like, 'tell me the ticket number and I'll swing by and get it, no worries.' I'd be late for a few band things but no biggie. She's lost the claim ticket. Tells me her mom needs them for a special dinner that night. That the boots were their father's Mother's Day gift to her twenty years ago. She has to have these boots for that night."

"Oh man, next I bet you're gonna tell me they were at some place in BFE."

Will just nodded and a gigantic smile turned him into that man-child she'd seen beating the Mercedes dashboard at the truck stop and shoving around with Stefan. "Specialty shop. Fifty miles on the other side of Los Angeles. Freaking Dodgers game going on, due to let out the same time my dumb ass is driving to pick up these boots." He still grinned, even though the details sounded gruesome. Dani had never been but had heard of LA traffic.

"But I bet you went."

He nodded again. "If she called me right now, needing something, I'd find a way."

"And all this you'd do for an in-law. Lucky girl."

He frowned this time and turned to her when he said, "Lucky me. She'll uh, she'll always be family. So I uh, I'm sorry for the long ass story, but I get it. Why we're picking up the stuff for your sister."

Dani didn't know what to say. She'd wondered lots of things about Will. One of them being if he was single, married, girlfriended, boyfriended. Apparently he'd been married and spoke of the woman, Honey, and her family with so much love, Dani knew in the pit of her stomach the two hadn't split up. She glanced at his hand, no ring. But she'd wager there hadn't been a divorce. Life had to have taken this Honey from him. She wouldn't hound him over it. But maybe he'd be okay answering something about Stefan.

"Hey Will?"

"Yeah?" He rubbed his right hand through his strip of hair, tugging as he went and ending at the knot. "What do you want to know about Stefan?" He grinned.

Shit, he'd called her bluff, expertly she might add. "Nothing. I wasn't gonna ask you that. About him, I mean."

"Never been married. No kids. No significant other."

She tried to stop him even though she'd let him throw out these fragmented details about the man without end if she could. They were presently far enough away that she couldn't go running after Stefan like a desperate little puppy. "You don't have to tell me all this. I respect his privacy." She knew she just threw that out there for posterity. Trying to sound better than those who would pry into his private life even though she was curious to the point of salivation, especially after their mutual avoidance of each other. Only one more week and he'd be gone. The thought was as agonizing as it was a relief.

Will just tilted his head in her direction and smiled another soft smile. "Six-One. Hundred-ninety pounds. Oh, excellent smoothie maker, by the way." Did he just laugh?

"You're teasing me, aren't you? And this whole time I've been taking you for the nice one," she exclaimed.

"Yeah, well everything I said is true, but I'm just messing with you. Seriously, we can talk about Stefan, if you want. That was just my way of breaking the ice. I don't get out much."

"Will, you're just about the coolest guy I've ever met." She meant it. But talking about Stefan with Will, while it might be tempting, was entirely too nerve-wracking. Probably because she had yet to find out if Stefan had been the type to kiss and tell.

"Code for you're too nice of a girl to pry. That's cool. If you change your mind, I can be bribed with midnight trips to Taggert's. Just sayin'."

She laughed. "You wouldn't really divulge his secrets, would you? Isn't there some type of guy code you'd be breaking?"

"There is." He winked. "Like I said, if you change your mind." And then he added, "He's being an idiot avoiding you." He tilted his head and looked at her differently than he had when they'd been joking just now. What was that about? Will continued before she had the chance to worry anymore. "Which is why I'm really glad he plans to take you to dinner tonight. You can't say no because I need some quality time with Mrs. C."

A thousand emotions choked down any chance of even one word making its way out. Will must not know she was the one who'd insisted on the distance in the first place which meant Stefan hadn't complained about her to his friend. Stefan was only doing her bidding. Doing it well. Too well. He wasn't an idiot for it. He was … decent.

But with Will's admission, was there really anything else she needed to ask? With the little bit of time they had left? The thought that Stefan still wanted to take her to dinner and had told his friend both excited and broke her heart. What else could come of it?

She found her voice and spit out the first non-Stefan related thing that came to mind. "I think you're gonna get a real kick out of Daisy. You remind me a lot of her. She's cute and can talk to just about anyone, anywhere, about anything."

His drumming fingers stilled over his cargo shorts. It was only when they pulled into the Super Taggert's parking lot that he smiled again, and let go of the chunk of mohawk he'd fisted in his hand. Dani noted his reaction to her two-second stint as cupid and vowed not to ever go there again. But she couldn't help but suffer a little heartbreak for the kind man who for the strangest reason, she could totally see as being the big brother she'd never had. He adjusted his glasses and smiled. So cute.

"We're here," she said with a shot of overdone joy.

"Let's shop," Will said back, apparently over their awkward bit about Daisy. "I know exactly where home appliances are. Come on. Let's take care of that baby sister of yours."

Geez, how was she going to say goodbye to him too? She'd have to save up and go to a Sin Pointe concert on this tour. "Hey Will, do you guys ever come to Pittsburgh?"

"Who? Me and Stefan?"

She pinched him, and was so happy when he didn't frown or flinch. "You know who I mean. Your band."

He stepped alongside her so that they walked almost shoulder to shoulder but his hands were tucked deep into his shorts pockets. "Pittsburgh is on the schedule. I'm just not sure of the date. You're gonna come see us play, aren't you?"

"Maybe, I'd like to. I've never been. We'll see."

"Well, I happen to know that if you show up, there will be tickets with your name on them. Cool?"

"Cool," she said, amazed at how much better she felt knowing that this wasn't it. She had something fun to look forward to. She nearly slipped and said something about being very pregnant or having her baby in tow at the time of the show but held it in just in time.

Dani followed behind Will who indeed knew exactly where to go. She had to smile at the back of his tank top as she doubled her strides to keep up with him. *Save a drum, bang a drummer.* So he was adorable and had no idea. Daisy was gonna eat that up. Will would be lucky if he made it out alive. But at those thoughts, her mind went right back to Stefan, and this dinner he had planned. She'd gotten exactly what she asked for all week

143

with him avoiding her and now … she blew out. The more he stayed away, the more she wished he'd never leave. More accurately, the more she wished they didn't have to be apart. She realized it didn't matter where that was.

"Will, do you think I'm dressed okay for this dinner tonight?"

He smiled and it dazzled her because it was so real and genuine. His blue eyes settled on her like a brother's would. "You're exactly perfect, just the way you are."

"You're all right, too, Will Cordero."

"That's what they say, anyway." Another smile. "Come on, let's go get our Taggert's on."

Chapter Fourteen

Dani knocked on the door. When Katy Perry answered because the music streamed out so loud that she and Will could have sung along, Will stepped up. Were they really going to break out into a "Peacock" duet right here on Daisy's second story apartment door? It was so hard not to hum the words to that song but what would be even funnier would be to hear Will sing the chorus.

"Let me," he said, shuffling the red toaster he'd helped her pick out over to his left arm so that he could—holy cow—beat the heck out of her sister's apartment door. "Sorry, was that loud?"

He had to know his own strength. "Um, yeah, just a little." Dani made a "tiny bit" symbol with her finger and thumb.

But Will's pounding did the trick because a second later, there was Daisy. She'd blackened her already jet black hair with a midnight wash and stood there in a terry cloth shorts romper, the one Dani loved because the turquoise did something to lighten up all the dark stuff her baby sister tried to do to herself. Whether it was overdone or not though, she could never deny how much Daisy's thick, black liquid-lined cat eyes reminded her of their mom's senior graduation picture. It had looked beautiful on Mom in the Sixties and just as jaw-dropping on Daisy today.

Dani went to make her introduction of Will when she noticed him hedging back from front and center to nearly behind her. He licked his lips several times, more like he was stressed and not gearing up for sexy-time.

145

Dani was about to offer him some of the cool new balm they'd bought but he cleared his throat and raised his eyebrows just when Daisy stuck out her hand, grabbed him before he'd completely retreated to Dani's back and planted a kiss on his cheek.

"Hi, I'm Daisy. I love your hair, by the way. Hi Dani." Daisy smiled and touched the ends of Will's mohawk that were pulled back in that ponytail-knot hybrid. She was like this with everyone, Dani knew, but poor Will looked like he'd just been mugged. "Come on in. Sorry for the mess. Oh, is that for me?" she asked once she'd literally stood behind Will and urged him inside with a hand to the small of his back. "Oh, that's a great shirt," she gushed.

Oh God. Will, the last person on the planet she'd think as capable of murder, was going to kill her. She figured Daisy would take Will in and treat him like she treated everyone she met, but this was clearly more than he was comfortable with. How did he handle being the object of all the Sin Pointe fans' affections? Surely he'd starred in many of their dreams with the killer arms and sexy smart glasses.

"So," she piped in before Daisy had Will blushing or worse, escaping the small and yes, messy apartment. "That is indeed for you. And this is my friend, Will. He helped pick it out."

Dani looked at them both. It would be hard to tell if Daisy was affected because outgoing was just her nature. Along with touchy-feely and free-spirited. Will, on the other hand, could double as the poster-boy for affected if the stiff smile he hadn't let slip in the past five minutes was any indication.

"Oh my god, I love it. Thank you guys!" Daisy nearly shouted over the music and took special care to unhinge the toaster box from Will's fingers. "I love red. Don't you, Will?"

"Um, yeah, it's great. I'm glad you like it," he said quietly, bashful almost.

Dani knew then and there that she needed to have a quick word with Daisy. Out of earshot of poor Will. She went over to her sister, grabbed her in a hug and whispered into her ear. "I need to talk to you in another room."

"Okay," Daisy said and led them to the bedroom where the three girls managed to sleep somehow. "Be right back," she offered Will whose chin dipped but pressed smile never faltered.

"He's cute. And really sweet," said Daisy, fingering Dani's much more conservative neckline. "Did he really pick out that toaster for me?"

"Yes, he did. And the blender that's in the bag he still hasn't set down yet. They're a matching set."

"Oh my God! Where did you find him and why do you have him? What about Thom? Did you two break up? He was nice but…"

"Daisy. Please. Focus. Will is a friend of a friend. Actually…"

"You know who he kind of reminds me of?" Daisy said, interrupting.

But she wasn't a huge Sin Pointe fan and as far as Dani knew, either hadn't cared or was just too young to remember that Stefan was actually a family friend of theirs, removed and remote as the connection had become over the years. The young could be flippant that way, especially her twenty year old sister who fled the house at eighteen when she graduated, the same year their mom had died. "Who?" Dani asked, curious.

Instead of answering, Daisy ran and picked up a catalogue from the hammock strung between two walls that was her sister's bed. "This guy." She pointed at a male model wearing skinny jeans and a grey t-shirt. His hair was the same shade of light brown as Will's. "Isn't he gorgeous? I love his tattoos. But he looks so depressed."

"The model or Will?"

"Hmm, the model. I have to get a better look at Will now. I think I scared him."

"I think you did too." Dani started to finish what she'd been ready to share earlier. That Will was a friend of Stefan's who was Gina's son and currently staying with her. But she decided against that, suddenly protective of Will's privacy and remembering the heartbreaking reaction he'd had in the car ride here. Even though she could see Daisy getting lots of laughs out of Will. "Let's go a little easy on him. I think he's shy."

Daisy's face lit up and Dani knew she'd said exactly the wrong thing. "Oh my God, that's so sweet. Is he single? Please tell me he's single."

Oh geez. She couldn't ignore Daisy because Daisy would just go out and ask Will flat out herself. "Yes, I believe he is currently single. But hey, before you go out there and ask him to marry you, I need to tell you something. It's serious."

"Oh-kay. I'm listening." Daisy adjusted the piles of black curls atop her head and then put her hands on her hips. The serious pose, as serious as she could be barefooted. But Dani couldn't help but smile at the white and black manicure of Daisy's fingers and toes. "Come on, tell me already."

"What, or you're afraid Will will get away?" She had to tease her baby sister.

"Maybe. No. Come on, you said it was serious. Is Gina okay? Wait, is Thom okay? Tell me he didn't get hurt over there," Daisy asked, reminding Dani that Daisy was young but not completely wrapped up in herself. Her kid sister had a huge heart which was why she'd moved out when Mom died. It would have hurt Daisy too much to stick around. Dani was just happy Daisy didn't remember losing their dad. Since Daisy was three years old, it had always been just the girls and it hurt that Dani couldn't share the pregnancy news with her. Not until she told Mrs. C first. Daisy's heart was big but so was her mouth.

"Mrs. C is fine. And, so is Thom. Look, this is really embarrassing and I'm only telling you because I'd rather get this over with now and I know you'd get it out of me eventually."

"If Gina and Thom are okay, what's wrong?"

Yeah, that was pretty pathetic. Even buoyant Daisy had deduced the smallness of Dani's world and reach. She blew out an over-the-top breath and sat down on of all things, a bean bag. It was pink so it must belong to one of her sister's roommates. "Thom broke up with me and he did it in an email. Which hurt, but I'm over it and I wanted you to know so that when he comes home, you don't assume we're still together." Daisy was one of those with a knack for running into people in the craziest places and striking up the craziest conversations. Dani would be mortified should that happen with Thom and his acquaintances.

"He dumped you?" she screeched. "In an email?" She somehow managed to screech that part even louder.

"Shh."

Too late. To Dani's surprise, Will popped his head in the room. Daisy started for him but Dani shot her a look that said to stand down. So Daisy didn't grab his hand and tug him in further, but tempered it down to going and standing beside him in the doorway, close enough to hold hands if they were to accidentally collide. Will blinked.

"I heard screaming. I got worried. Also, some dude is at the door asking for you, Daisy." He said her sister's name so quietly. "And I got a phone call, Dani. For you. Um, so, yeah."

Daisy's eyebrows lifted and the doe-like brown depths of her eyes took Will in for the whole room to see. Surely if Dani had seen that, Will couldn't have missed it. "Hold on, I'll go say hi." Daisy left the room quickly. Will actually smiled, a little less stiff this time.

"I'm sorry," Dani mouthed to him. "She's a handful. I might have forgotten to mention that."

"Nah, she's fine. Just young." He winked with great tact, and Dani loved him all the more. "So, Stefan called. He's gonna swing by here later and pick you up."

"For that dinner?" She sucked in too much air. "Are you gonna come too?" She asked, a little too fast.

Will's hand was on her shoulder in that very second. "He said not to rush your visit with your sister. And no pizza dinner for me. When he gets here, if you don't mind, I'll drive your car back to the house for my date with Mrs. C. You don't mind riding with Stefan, right?" He didn't get to finish, if there was more, because Daisy tugged him by the elbow out of her room and the two disappeared. Dani didn't follow. She needed a minute. All she could hear was Daisy's excitement bouncing off the apartment walls. To answer Will's question, the thought of riding alone with Stefan in his Mercedes did what all thoughts of Stefan did to her. First came the thrill, then came the fear. Then the wish that he was just a guy and she was just a girl and all this other crap didn't exist between them.

"These are perfect! Thank you so much! This one's gonna go here and this one's gonna go over here." Daisy's voice boomed happily and reached down the hall.

Then it got real quiet and the next thing she heard was Will's voice, deeper than she'd ever heard it. "Um, you're welcome. You're, um, very welcome."

Something had happened and whatever it was warmed Dani's heart, even from Daisy's bedroom. She knew Will wouldn't stand a chance. No one ever did. To have that kind of effect on someone. Distantly, the thought snuck up on her that Daisy's carefree lifestyle would allow her to pick up and leave if someone like Will asked.

What Dani would give for a cup of that. She'd use every last ounce on Stefan Calderon which is why she knew better than to wish for it. The night he'd said done, he'd meant it and turned off his feelings for her. Feelings she knew he had. She'd been so stupid to insist they couldn't be close which is why his dinner invitation had her twisted, all inside and out.

Had she been so dumb as to have missed what this dinner could very well be about? Was Stefan just being nice and telling her goodbye like every other guy she'd ever fallen for? Maybe now that he'd had a reprieve with her being out of the house, he'd found it was easier. Telling her over pizza in a public place was almost as safe as cutting ties over an email. Would he turn on that cocky playfulness and let her down easy so she barely even felt his rejection?

Dani stood in Daisy's bedroom doorway and looked carefully toward the small kitchen, holding in her nerves the best she could. There they stood. Daisy tried out several different locations and plugs for her new appliances. She flitted from one side of Will to the other, picking up random pieces of fruit, tossing them into the blender, and gathering dirty cups then washing them quickly in the sink and filling them with her concoction.

Will just stood there mesmerized.

What did mesmerized look like on a guy? The same way Stefan had looked at her when she'd boldly told him to prove it in the stall. Their eyes got bright. And they tried so damn hard not to smile that a heart-stealing grin slipped out in its place. That's what she saw on Will right now and what she missed on Stefan.

Dani fell back into Daisy's room. She rubbed her belly, not feeling well at all. She tried not to freak out over the fact that Stefan was coming here to pick her up but couldn't keep the hold over her emotions.

For a few minutes, Dani thought about the whirlwind of the past week. How things felt so surreal, so wrong and so right at times, often within minutes of each other.

Timing was a tricky little thing.

Stefan rolling into town on the day Thom dumped her was the hardest to understand.

Will, who Stefan swore would have nothing to do with another woman for as long as he lived, was out there being charmed by her baby sister. The awkward silences and his stuttering short answers said as much. It had taken all of five minutes.

Dani had technically known Stefan her whole life yet in reality, they were strangers. Their reunion had been a short one but after the past week, she now felt like she really had known him her whole life. And he wasn't a selfish jerk. Not in the least.

Yes, time was tricky.

Suddenly a tremor of fear caused her to suck in a deep breath. What if time ran out before she put on her big girl panties and did the right thing concerning her baby's father?

The unpredictability of time seized her thoughts. She pulled out her phone to compose an email and wiped the screen with her shirt, clearing fingerprints and cheek oil from the phone's face. Dani took another deep breath and began typing. If she was going to face Stefan, the real Stefan because they'd be alone, she needed to face Thom first.

Hi Thom,

Sorry it's taken me a few days to get back to you. I hope you're doing okay, staying safe. Wanted you to know that I was surprised by your email but I understand. Won't lie, I was hurt, but I'm glad you were a man about it and told me. The reason I know how hard it must have been for you to do that is because this is one of the hardest things I've ever had to write. I guess it's my turn to be a woman and let you know that, I'm pregnant. Didn't want to tell you while you're deployed because I worried about distracting you. But the truth is, you deserve to know, now. I'm looking forward to meeting your sweetheart one of these days. From the bottom of my heart, if you love her then she must be a wonderful person. We'll talk more when you get back.

Take care and be safe. Oh and Thom, thank you.
~Dani

She thought about it for a minute and then hit send. The pink bean bag on the floor caught her weight as she sank down into it. The thought of a broad chest covered in white with a guitar strapped across it comforted her head as it thudded heavily against the bedroom wall.

Maybe men could be super heroes after all. More importantly, maybe women could be too.

"Stefan, please go easy on me tonight," she whispered to the empty room and rubbed her belly. She closed her eyes and rested, welcoming the soft bits of laughter she heard filling her sister's small kitchen. Stefan had been a good friend to her. If tonight was an early goodbye, Dani was at least thankful he'd respected her wishes. Respected her. If he was capable of nothing else for whatever reason, his respect did more for her than he could ever know.

She spent a few minutes stalking her phone's inbox for a response from Thom.

Chapter Fifteen

"Mom?" Stefan poked his head outside and found her sitting in her rocking chair. "Hey Mom, how are you feeling?" Stefan sat in the chair next to hers and it rocked back with his weight.

"Oh, better now. The yard looks wonderful. Thank you."

"Sure, no problem."

Stefan looked at his watch. He'd told Will he'd drive out and meet them around this time but it had been a rough day. Mom's dizzy spells had scared him but not as much as trying to take her blood pressure. He'd squeezed the damn cuff on too tight and she'd let out a yelp. "You're sure you're feeling better now? Are you dizzy at all?" he asked.

"I'm fine. It happens from time to time. It's the blood pressure. It'll even out. I'll be fine. Why don't you and Will go do something in town? Have some fun."

Downtown Moonlight wasn't exactly the kind of place he and Will would find fun. Besides he wouldn't want to scare any of the folks gathering at the fire department for bingo. It was too warm to cover up his tattoos and Will's shaved sides of his head. "That's okay."

This next part was what he'd been putting off, not wanting to add any more stress to his mom's already stressed day. But he needed her to know why Will would be coming back to the house alone and part of accepting there was something going on with Dani meant manning up with Mom. He reminded himself he was almost forty years old and a full grown man many years over.

"I actually made some dinner plans but I don't want to leave you alone for very long. And uh, I want to check on the house." In a moment of craziness, he'd packed an overnight bag for Dani. Depending on how dinner went, she might need it. He had no idea how she'd react to being told about relocating with him to Nashville. Of course in his mind it went that she was thrilled and they spent the night together at his empty house.

"Oh, okay. That's probably a good idea. Don't worry about me. I'll be fine. Come to think of it, why don't you meet up with Daniela and Will? I know you probably don't like bingo but there's some midnight bowling thing the younger kids in town are doing nowadays."

"Mom, I'm too old for that."

"Maybe so. Well, if I could still hold a bowling ball, I'd try it."

One day he'd love to take her bowling. From the truest place in his heart, he finally let the words out. "Hey Mom, my dinner plans tonight include Dani. Daniela," he corrected. His mom's face remained calm.

"And Will?" she asked.

Stefan cleared his throat and sat forward, toward the edge of his rocker. "Will is gonna come back here and stay with you. He's not much of a night owl. Dinner will be just me and Daniela. I'm taking her out for pizza. She said she's craving Mario's."

Why did he feel so goddamned nervous? Something he said struck a note with his mom, he just had no idea what. He was just glad it wasn't scorn that crossed her face.

"Okay. Well, I think she will appreciate a meal out that she doesn't have to cook. It's a nice gesture to thank her for all her hard work. She could use some friends closer to her age than me."

Mom didn't have to say much more to him. He heard that loud and clear. "Yes, I agree," was all he could say.

But then out of nowhere, she said, "Be careful, son. She has a lot going on right now, more than you might be aware of, and I love her like my own daughter."

Stefan just nodded, pretty damn sure his mom knew a lot more than Dani realized. Gina Calderon had always been a perceptive woman, excluding the shit with Amanda. Which meant his dumbass had probably been pretty easy to read all week too where Dani was concerned.

He was about to get up and leave when she put her hand on his elbow. "Will you be taking Daniela to your house?"

His neck tensed and he had the immediate need to laugh nervously or swallow deeply. "I'm not sure. Maybe." He went ahead and tried to swallow naturally.

Mom just nodded now. He couldn't read what if anything that meant and kissed her on the cheek. She didn't pull away but remained stiff. "Mom, let me walk you inside before I go, please."

She stood and let him take her arm. "Be careful," she repeated and followed him inside.

Stefan checked his watch, it was way past five which was when Dani normally ate dinner. But he'd decided the beard had to go so he stood at the bathroom mirror and stroke by stroke, watched the black hairs rinse down the drain. Feeling more like himself, he grabbed the bag he'd packed for Dani and climbed into his car. The entire drive to her sister's apartments, the words "Be careful" beat at him over and over. How the hell did he do that? He'd better figure it out, fast. He popped a piece of cinnamon gum in his mouth and drove, feeling the power of his car surge through his body. He ran his hand through his hair and then over his smooth jaw, deciding whether to ask Dani to give this girlfriend-boyfriend thing a shot before or after he asked her to move to Nashville.

****

Last minute and with Will waiting out front with her sister, Dani sorted through a few items of clothing Daisy had laying around on the hammock bed, desperate to look better than she currently did for her dinner with Stefan. For whatever he had to tell her.

None of this stuff would fit.

All too small in the boobs, hips, thighs, butt and now belly departments. No way did she need Sugar splayed across her butt, with rhinestones. She tossed the thin sweats aside. Her maxi dress would have to suffice. Dani tiptoed across the carpet to the bathroom, where Daisy and Cass's stray dark hairs and a few of Jen's blonde ones twirled around every size of curling iron known to man. Dani picked up a hot pink push-up bra and hung it on the doorknob, at least getting it off the floor. She left the towels there because she was afraid to step on what might lay underneath but her nerves and need to clean forced her to scoop them up. She straightened the small bathroom as best she could, wiping at flecks of bronzer that dotted the sink counter and then made her way out to the living room.

Dani honestly had no idea what the girls did with their days. Did they work? Someone had to, to afford this place, small as it was. Daisy hadn't said much about classes she might be taking or hours she might be working. Which reminded Dani she needed to keep better tabs on her baby sis.

But that being said, she knew she was stalling.

Hers and Will's visit with Daisy had come to an end. Stefan had called Will to say he was on his way nearly twenty minutes ago.

When she walked to the kitchen to say goodbye, she found that Daisy had already maneuvered Will to the outside stairwell and was still chatting him up. Dani decided to leave Daisy a note on the refrigerator note board, which she found was missing it's magnets on the back and laid on the counter instead. She smiled when she saw Will's number written on it with a smiley face and spikes for hair. Daisy had drawn a daisy next to it and a heart. Oh boy.

She didn't know what, if anything, might be brewing between them. Knowing what she did of Will, it was probably one-sided. Daisy's side. But whatever it was, she prayed for mercy for the man and secretly hoped something would come of it.

As she gathered up her bag to go, her phone rang. The clinic. She'd been meaning to call them and confirm her upcoming appointment since *that* day.

When I get home, she thought.

Dani gathered her bag and the thing of calcium chews she'd bought at Taggert's with Will and finished the note to Daisy.

Sis, I love you. Call if you need anything. She wrote the last word in all caps. And then followed by an X and an O, she finished with, *For a rainy day*. She left an envelope of cash, not much but enough for a tank of gas and a fast food run for her and the girls, on the counter next to the note board.

Dani stepped outside and found that Daisy had now walked Will downstairs. She was practically standing on the man's toes. *Daisy, Daisy, Daisy.*

Dani enjoyed the nearly perfect nothingness that greeted her as she made her way down as well. No humidity, no strangling heat, just warmth. No rain. A gentle breeze accompanied her the whole way. She was in the middle of praying dinner wouldn't be a disaster or end with her being humiliated just as his gleaming white convertible pulled up.

And gone was her teddy bear Superman because in his place sat the man she'd seen on the cover of that magazine, minus the spikey hair and eyeliner. No doubt about it, this was the real Stefan Calderon. She'd been wondering when he was gonna show up. Holy shit, her knees nearly locked up on her.

Chapter Sixteen

"Thanks for spending the day with us, Will. And thanks for putting up with Daisy."

He hugged Dani and went to shake Daisy's hand but yeah, her sister wasn't letting him get away with that. Daisy lifted up onto her tiptoes and pulled him down for a hug. He just nodded bashfully and stepped back as soon as Daisy let go but he did toss her sister a kind wave goodbye. Then he left them to join Stefan who stood by his Mercedes.

"Dani, why didn't you tell me you had a hot date with—" her sister started to say.

"Zip it. Not going there right now," Dani said out of self-preservation.

"Fine but I want to hear all about him. If not tomorrow morning, the next day at the latest. I can't believe you didn't tell me who—"

She flashed her sister another warning to zip her lips while she watched Will and Stefan and tried to guess when she should make her way over there. When the guys slapped each other on the back, Will came back to her and she handed her car keys over to him. He nodded and eventually ducked into the driver seat and pulled out of the driveway.

"Okay hon, we'll talk soon. I love you and I had a good time with you today, even if you did spend the entire time assaulting that poor man."

Daisy just smiled. "I really like him."

Dani shook her head and hugged her sister goodbye.

Stefan stood by the passenger side door, waiting for her. Geez, you'd think she was either walking down the aisle for her wedding or death row by the choppy steps she took.

Completely unexpected, he leaned in and kissed her on the cheek before he opened the door and waited for her to sit down. "So that's your baby sister. She's cute," he said.

"Oh, you have no idea. Will probably hates me right now."

"Now that I see her, I'd have thought so too but he seemed okay," Stefan said as he sat down in his own seat and started up the Mercedes engine. "Were you playing cupid? He hates that shit. Speaking from personal experience."

The nerves rolling around her tummy were still there but nowhere near where they'd been five minutes ago. As long as she remembered not to stare too long at her first glimpse of his drop dead beautiful face without the beard, she might be okay after all. "Scouts honor I was not playing cupid. I even told Daisy to back off."

"Yeah sure you did."

"No really. She's probably got four or five boyfriends right now and I'm pretty sure one of them showed up today. Daisy's just Daisy. She loves guys, especially cute, sweet ones like Will."

Stefan checked his phone's GPS and turned onto the state highway. The wind did its best to blow her hair right off her head but she'd been prepared and pulled it back with her thickest band, knowing who was picking her up and his propensity to ride topless. She grinned at that and he saw her and responded. She held the ends of her ponytail and enjoyed the air hitting her face.

"So, other than torturing Will, how was your day?" he asked her as they drove the familiar streets that would take them back to Moonlight.

"It was nice." She had to acclimate to being in this type of situation with him. It felt strange after their week of pleasantries. "Obviously, Will was a great sport. And even with Daisy being Daisy, I forgot how infectious her energy is. Mine was running low and feeding off her for a while was good."

"Great. That's great." But she noticed his face turn down. There was no beard to hide his chin and jaw which looked tense.

"How was your day?" she asked, still stiff and awkward and wondering if it was her fault that they seemed stuck on pleasantries. She'd grown to expect and appreciate his humor but her grand idea had stripped him of it. But there was no way she could have that kind of power over a man. Especially one like him. The thought simmered through her spastic mind until his hands tightened over his steering wheel.

"It was okay."

That was way too short of an answer. "How's your mom?"

His sideways glance, very uncharacteristic of him, had her worried.

"Stefan? Was everything okay with your mom?" she asked as they drove. He took a familiar Moonlight exit and drove them through the quiet streets that would lead to the older section of town.

"It was fine."

She'd thought he'd be an excellent liar. Turned out he sucked at it. They drove on in silence and she kept her mouth shut until twenty minutes later when they pulled into Mario's parking lot. A couple other cars were parked there too but Sunday night wasn't a big eating out night for most in these parts. Folks traditionally stayed home and prepped for the work and school week. That was probably good considering Stefan's unpredictable mood and his lack of a beard. Clean shaven, he stood out. Literally, stood out about as much as if the real Superman had come strutting down Moonlight's streets in full on red and blue costume and cape. Something about his smooth, chiseled face was just as dazzling as his fancy car and the million dollar grin she wished he'd flash now. There was nowhere to hide his emotions without the beard. She frowned trying to figure out what was going on.

"We're here. Let's go inside."

He didn't feel real. Didn't sound real. Something was messing with his dark, thick beautiful head. She hadn't needed to know him longer than the one week to pick up on that. But she followed him inside, trying not to gawk and be dazzled too much when even through his obvious funk, he opened her door and led her inside the restaurant first.

"Have a seat anywhere you'd like. I'll bring water," said the young man acting as host. Stefan led her past several empty booths and settled on a table in the very back. He pulled out her chair and then took his own seat. Her phone startled her with a text from Daisy so she put it on silent.

She sipped her water and watched him ignore his. "I don't mean to push you on this, but how was your day with your mom, Stefan? I only ask because I've had some rough days with her but I've also seen her bounce back."

A gust of air rushed from his mouth. That he was frustrated was clear.

"I don't know how you do it, Dani."

But just then the waiter came by to take their order. She hadn't looked at the menu but didn't need to.

Already her mouth started watering at the thought of her favorite Mario's pizza.

"For the lady?" asked the waiter.

"I'll have the Hawaiian please."

"Personal size?"

She was going to say yes even though she could have easily scarfed down at least a medium all by herself when Stefan spoke up. "Bring us a large. I'm having the same. And I'll have whatever you've got on tap."

"Yes, sir. And for the lady to drink?"

"Nothing on tap for me. I'm fine with water." Her hand naturally fell to her stomach and she rubbed it. It was the first time she'd acknowledged in a public place other than her OB checkups that she was pregnant. Stefan watched her carefully although his eyes looked so tired she nearly reached over and rubbed his brow for him.

"Oh hon, what happened?" she asked as soon as the waiter left. "Come on, it's me."

A buzz came from her phone but she ignored it. Daisy would keep this up all night. Dani watched as he blew out and rubbed his jaw like he really just wanted the pizza to get there. Why? He'd invited her here and didn't seem to be kicking her to the curb. But when the waiter returned with a tall glass of beer, Stefan took a long drink and then she started getting her answer.

"She was dizzy all morning. We checked her blood pressure. I didn't know how tight to squeeze the damn cuff. I wanted to drive her to the emergency room to get it checked by a professional but she's so stubborn. Wouldn't go. I squeezed that damn thing on so tight, I saw her wince."

"Hey, I've done that too. Her arms are too small for the adult cuff but not quite right for the kiddy one."

"Yeah, well I bruised her skin. I saw the marks..."

Stefan's eyes darkened and then he looked away. Something was not right. "Hey, what are you not telling me?"

"I saw the marks because I had to help her into the shower this afternoon. She needed a shower in the middle of the day because while I was messing around in the backyard, she got dizzy and fell in the mud. All the damn rain lately. Fuck, I felt like total shit that I let that happen."

"Stefan, hey, I know this might not make you feel any better right now, but I've had worse days with her. Okay? In the grand scheme of things, yes it was tough, but she's gonna be fine."

"She could have broken a bone, Dani."

"Then it's a good thing she landed in the mud." She hoped he'd smile at that.

It nearly worked but he kept blinking his eyes. "She uh, she used her last Depends today. I think you need to add that to your shopping list. And her teeth were giving her problems. Something about the stuff that's supposed to keep them stuck in place. She could barely eat anything I made. Fuck, Dani. It was a tough fucking day. I was gonna call you and say we should eat another night."

But he hadn't. So either he wanted to be here having a meal with her or he needed to be here to cut the ties for good.

His eyes started to shine and she didn't know what she'd do if they teared up all the way. He rubbed at them like he was soothing a tension headache but she could guess the truth.

"Hey," she said, completely unprepared for him like this. She reached out and without thinking, grabbed his hand and held it. "It's okay." He let her hold it but not for long. That was the strangest feeling of all when he pulled away. She didn't know how they were going to get through this meal. Not now that she'd seen this side of him and all she wanted was to comfort the man. There was no teasing in him. Everything he'd had inside, all that playful joy she loved watching, today had wrung him clean of it. The man sitting across from her was all that was left.

****

Half an hour later and she was full. Stefan could tell because she leaned back in her seat like she was stretching to make room for the food to go down. Mario's pizza was as good as he remembered. Stefan was still exhausted. But the food in his stomach and the beer and her company had helped. They had the place to themselves. They could talk, now that he wasn't so on edge.

"Hey, sorry for the Eeyore imitation earlier. I guess all the stuff with my mom just got to me. But I'm glad you came tonight."

"Me too. And you don't have to blow off how hard today was. I wouldn't lie to you about your mom, though. She's gonna be fine. In fact, seeing how good she looks tomorrow will probably mess with your head more than today did. It's just one of those things. You get used to it. It gets easier."

Her phone must have buzzed again because every time he heard the vibration, she patted her dress pocket. He almost wished she would just answer it but the fact she ignored it for him flattered him.

Stefan felt like shit for being so grumpy through the pizza portion of their meal. He decided to shake it off and enjoy the rest of their night. He had a lot to get to.

"So what are we having for dessert?" he asked. When she kept her head bowed low, he knew she was hiding a smile because he could still see her cheeks bunch up at the tops.

"I shouldn't … screw it. Cannoli, please. What about you?" she said.

That's right. She had the sweet tooth and he did not. "I'm not really a sugar guy." Her face fell. "But I'll have a bite of yours."

"Okay," she said and held him with a look in her eyes that said all this polite date-like stuff was just as awkward to her as it was to him.

The waiter took their cannoli order and disappeared.

"Hey, I haven't had the chance to compliment you on your new look," she said.

Stefan rubbed his jaw between his fingers and thumb. He preferred the feel of his skin over the whiskers and the thicker they'd gotten, the itchier. He was glad it was gone and happy she wanted to give him a compliment over it.

"Oh yeah, you like?"

Her head dipped. She must have heard him try to be himself for her just now. "I do. You look completely different though. I'm surprised you shaved it off. I thought it was your vacation disguise."

"It was but turns out yard work makes a guy sweat which makes a beard itch like hell. So good different?" Falling back into the easy playful way they'd talked those first days started coming back and rolling off his tongue. It didn't hurt so much to take a breath.

"Handsome different."

"Handsome? I was looking for something more like hot."

She bit the bottom of her lip, failing to suppress the smile. "That too."

"I like your new look too. It's hot. I'm not a wimp like you. I'll say it. Sexy hot."

She looked down at her dress and tugged her windblown ponytail. She didn't say anything because she obviously thought he was lying. But the long summer dress clung to her body while managing to look comfortable. He could see all her curves which was all that mattered. He wouldn't tell her right now, but her baby bump showed. "But if you'd rather, I'll just say you look very nice tonight, Dani."

A soft, comforting smile opened Dani's cheeks. "Thank you. Daisy found it for me in one of her roommates' piles of clothes."

The waiter showed up with her cannoli and her smile broke loose, wider than he'd seen in a while. He could watch her dote on Mom for hours and could bet that if he didn't have her out of the house, that's exactly what she'd be doing right now. She cut her cannoli down the middle and offered a half to him.

"Here you go."

He hesitated because he only wanted a very small bite but she held it out to him in her fingers. Well, if she was offering, he was taking. That had been the deal he'd secretly made their first day. Stefan leaned in and bit from the one end as she held it. A big bite that nearly nipped her fingertips. She obviously hadn't been ready for that because the flaky crust crumbled and cracked under his bite. They each tried to scoop up what was left but his half was a lost cause.

"Sorry," she said.

"No need, that was good."

She'd hand fed him. He'd known from the first minutes of the grape licorice experience that being hand fed by her would be exquisite. It was better. He licked his fingers and wiped powdered sugar from his face from the cannoli explosion.

"Here, you missed some," she said and wiped her thumb against the corner of his mouth. He caught her hand in his at the wrist, wanting to lick the sugar from her finger.

Realizing he startled her, he let go. She went back to eating her half, having none of the troubles he'd just experienced.

"Hey, so I was thinking today and realized I know very little about you. Other than the basics like your favorite pizza place and the fact you don't like my band." She tried to chew her bite quickly like she wanted to refute his teasing but he didn't want her rushing and her mouth was full. "Just teasing you. Slow down, enjoy your dessert." It looked so good on her. He'd wait until she was done to repay the favor and wipe her powdered sugar away. Or better yet, what he really wanted to do and lick it off.

Fuck, he'd done so good all night not to go there. Now he was there. Stefan guessed there was no avoiding the way he wanted her. But after Will's chat, there were still other things he found he really did want to learn about Dani.

"Like I said, I think we need to even up the playing field. You've read that magazine interview about me. So now it's my turn to ask some burning questions."

"Oh gosh," she said between bites and sips of water. "Really?" Her face scrunched up.

"Yep. Okay, so I'll go easy on you at first." She probably thought he was about to ask what her favorite sexual position was but he'd thought about these on the drive over and intended to get to know her better because yeah, he liked this girl a lot. Of course he'd do a little teasing too since she always smiled whenever he did that.

"I guess I'm curious to know what you'd be doing if you weren't taking care of my mom." Never had cared to know that about anyone else but he'd spent hours wondering that this past week watching her work.

"Oh, that's not what I was expecting…" She trailed off.

"I want to get to know you, Dani," he said from that place he was still getting used to talking from. It beat hard, waiting to hear all about her.

"Well, I'd be doing the same thing, just in another home or a clinic somewhere."

"Really?"

"Yeah, don't sound so shocked, but I was going to school to be a nurse when my mom got sick." She kept a straight face but the pain of losing her mom had to be fresh still.

"Did you graduate?" His hands wanted to touch hers while she talked but he grabbed the glass of water the waiter had brought instead. He was being good and touching her right now would be a distraction. What she had to say was important to him.

"No. Taking care of my mom made it hard."

"Can I ask what she had? My mom let me know when she passed. I'm sorry I don't know more than that."

"It's okay. She battled cancer for a good few years but the last year it just took over and it was tough."

"God Dani, I'm so sorry, sweetheart."

"It was tough seeing her body go through everything it did but I think the reason she lived a year longer than any of her doctors predicted was because she stayed positive until the end."

He could see that she got some of that from her mom. But he'd gotten a two week glimpse of his own mom's fight against cancer and Dani had done it for two years straight. And now she was doing it with his mom, although not exactly at that same level. Fuck, he prayed his mom didn't get sick again. That she'd battled her battles and now would live the rest of her life as healthy as possible. He wanted to give her the best of everything.

"So you didn't go back to school after?"

"No, I thought about it but then Mrs. C asked me to move in and…"

"And what? Come on, it's me."

"Well, working as her caregiver allows me to do what I love which is help people and, it pays well." She shook her head at that like she couldn't believe she'd just said it out loud.

"Come on, you know you want to laugh with me right now. You brought that up all on your own. I never would have gone there." He held his hands up in innocence and yes, after a second and her blushing that turned him on, they laughed together.

It was an amazing feeling. He gave up on not touching her and snuck her hand into his. She told him about Daisy leaving home at eighteen to go be one of the girls and how happy she was about it. Dani's plans to return to nursing school someday made him happiest. She was awesome at it and owed it to herself to get her license. He thought several times about gaging how she'd feel about working in the state of Tennessee but didn't mention it out loud. But she'd be a sure hire at the children's hospital in Nashville. Sin Pointe had already played at a couple benefits for them and he could see Dani really making an impact there. When he asked her to move, he wanted options. That was one thing he'd learned about women. They liked those.

He'd be leaving the waiter a giant tip for letting them stay at their table so long. He checked his watch and two hours had passed since they'd been seated.

"So would you say you're more scared or excited to be a mom in, how long until you're due?" he asked, curious after the fresh view of her little swollen belly.

"Five more months to go and I think the word you're looking for is terrified."

They both laughed. "I can't even imagine. I mean, you've got a person growing in there."

"You're not helping soothe that whole terror I just mentioned."

He chuckled. "Sorry, it's just so cool and weird."

"It is very weird. But it's been happening since the beginning of time so I'm thinking I'm gonna survive. We'll see."

"You're gonna be a great mom, Dani."

"Have you ever thought about having kids?"

Okay, that was not on the list of things he'd thought to talk about tonight. But shit, he wasn't gonna shy away now. "I almost did, sweetheart. Back in high school." Stefan looked around the restaurant, apparently he still did that whenever he was about to speak about Amanda and her family in public. The Coopers could still live in Moonlight.

"Really? Can you tell me about it?" Her features rose like she wasn't sure if it was okay to ask him that.

He didn't want to talk about it, but he would. Nothing should be off limits if they were going to try dating. "Got my fourteen year old girlfriend pregnant when I was sixteen."
"Oh shit."

"Yeah, big oh shit. But I was ready to quit school and get a full time job to support her and the baby."

"Gosh, at sixteen. You were just a baby yourself. What happened?"

"Unfortunately, I'll never know for sure. I think Amanda was scared and told her parents that I was refusing to help her."

"Stefan, did she have an abortion?"

"I don't think so. She told me she lost it. That's about when her parents called mine and let them know what a horrible son they had raised."

"Why did they say that? That's just cruel. It takes two."

"Some sixteen year old kid gets their daughter pregnant. She's crying all the time, stressed out. They obviously believed I'd said I was having nothing to do with it and all that stress I'd caused made her lose it. I don't blame them. If I had a daughter, I'd be pissed too."

"What did your parents think?"

"What any mother would think getting a call like that. That all the hard work she'd put in raising her son the right way had been for nothing. Unfortunately, that was around the same time my dad left. I have no idea how my mom got through that year."

"Stefan..."

"Hey, it is what it is. And uh, I'm glad you brought it up. There's something I should have told you the first day I got here." Apparently he was going with dropping the Nashville bomb on her first and if she took that well enough, he'd ask her to go out with him.

"Okay..."

"Dani, I want to be the son my mom has deserved these last twenty years that I've been gone from her life. Not just want, I have to do better. The truth is I don't know how much longer she'll be around." He'd taken a minute on the long drive from Nashville to think about moms. Out of all his close friends, only he and Marion still had theirs. Trista, Lily, Jaxon, Lucky, all had lost their mothers.

"That's a good thing, Stefan, and this visit means so much to your mom. I can tell you two still have some stuff to iron out, but I'm not lying when I say Gina has been so much more at peace this week you've been here."

"Well, the only way I can see making that happen is by moving her to Nashville with me. Sweetheart, I'm going to ask her before I leave. I know I should have told you that before but I'm telling you now."

Her fingers settled on top of the table and her eyebrows stayed hiked. "Wow, that, that is a surprise. Wh—when did you decide that?"

Her stuttering worried him. "Once I got here and saw her for myself but I've been thinking about it ever since the plans for the next tour started coming together. I don't know how many more of these tours we're gonna do. That stuff will always take me away but with Mom living at home with me, I'll see her so much more. I'll be able to do so much more for her. It's not just about sending her money anymore for me, Dani."

He had no idea how she was going to respond. She sat there with her mouth caught like she was about to say something. "Um, of course. No, that's exactly what you should do," she said sounding like she wanted to mean it.

"It's one of the reasons I wanted you to come to dinner tonight. I needed you to know my plans because they will affect you too."

She still didn't look like she knew what to say. There would be a hole in the maroon table cloth if she kept rubbing at it like that.

"Sweetheart, dinner wasn't just about me telling you about my plans for Mom."

"No?"

It wasn't much but at least she'd said something.

"No. It's why I asked you here tonight. I had to tell you so you could make arrangements to…"

Dani grabbed her side pocket like it was on her last nerve. The way she whipped it out and looked at the screen this time instead of just ignoring the loud buzz stopped him. Several blinks later, she pushed up from the table.

"I'm, I'm sorry. Let me go see what this is about. I'll be back."

Shit. That wasn't good. Was she bolting on him again? But no, he told himself she was just going to the bathroom. She was pregnant after all.

Dani excused herself to the bathroom, and watching her walk away so determined brought his body to life again. He'd just learned that he could push those feelings to the back of his mind rather than let them own his every action and thought around her. Not saying it was easy. But he could do it.

Stefan used her bathroom phone break to text Will and check on his mom.

Stefan: Everything okay at the house?

It took a couple seconds but Will texted back.

Will: Mom says I make the best mac n cheese. How's dinner going?

Stefan: Good. Thinking about asking her.

Will: Girlfriend or Nashville?

Stefan: Getting there. Both. Fuck. Not my area of expertise.

Will: Stop thinking. Just ask.

Stefan: Go check on Mom. I gotta go.

He sat there waiting, looking around the small dining area. The last time he'd been here had been ages ago. He looked for the jukebox by the entrance but found it had been moved back near the bathrooms. Stefan went to check it out and was shocked to see a Sin Pointe song, albeit one from the nineties, but still. Did he pop a quarter in and grace the staff and the one other couple dining with "Play?" What the hell? This one's for you, Moonlight, he thought and pushed down hard on the play button. He loved those knobby old ancient buttons.

Classic Sin Pointe made him smile. He loved this one.

"I've got you how I need you. Don't cry, don't hide. I just want to play with your emotions for the night."

How many times had he sung that to the crowds? Stefan let the verses play on their own here in the restaurant but chimed in for the chorus. Jaxon had a special way with words, that was for sure. It had been Stefan's honor to sing his friend's songs the past two decades. Back when this one had come out, he'd felt like Jaxon had written the songs with both of them in mind. But the latest lyrics of his Aussie mate's seemed way more directed at Stefan. Jaxon of course denied it.

Stefan closed his eyes and blocked out the next song that auto-played on the juke box.

Silently while he waited for Dani to come back out, Stefan hummed his favorite new Sin Pointe song, one they'd recorded just a couple months back and would soon be singing to the masses, in his head.

"You kiss me like a stranger, but you hurt me like a friend. Every time I look at you, I'm lost back at the end. You ask me not to change too much, but I've hurt so many in this skin. This skin that you love to touch. You love this skin, I need your touch."

Damn. It was good and the reason they hadn't decided to hang it up yet. The deal was always as long as the songs kept coming to Jaxon, they'd keep at it. Apparently love had only unleashed more of Jaxon's brilliance. Fire burned in his chest when he thought of singing *Touch* for Dani. It fit. If she stayed with him tonight, he would sing it just for her.

A flash of orange and navy blue stripes came slowly out of the women's restroom and stopped in the doorway when she saw him. Stefan knew in that moment that it was time to ask her to consider moving to Nashville and being his girlfriend. He noticed Dani's hair was neater, no more flyaways around her hairline and the waves in her long black ponytail were smoothed and shiny liked she'd wet her whole head. Maybe that's what had taken her so long. He left the juke box to meet up with her and hold hands back to their table but her palms were damp and clammy. When she looked up at him, he knew something had happened in the bathroom and it pissed him off not knowing what. She inched back inside and tried to close the door before he made it in. Good thing he was a hundred times physically stronger than her.

****

Never in a million years had she thought the constant phone alerts were from Thom. She'd assumed Daisy. Dani had splashed so much water onto her face after listening to his voicemail that she'd had to take down her hair and finger comb all the shorter wet strands stuck to her forehead. He'd found a way to call her and she'd ignored him. Before she had a chance to organize another thought, Stefan was only inches away.

Thom's voicemail had left her shaken. But now Stefan was holding her clammy hands and pushing her back into the ladies' room.

"What are you doing?" she asked, frazzled at having heard Thom's voice and now seeing Stefan's intensity flare in those deep, dark eyes.

"I didn't get to finish at the table. We're alone in here. So let me finish now."

"Well, yes we're alone but that's beside the point." She watched him lock the door behind them.

"Unlock that." Yes she was on the defensive. No she didn't want him to spell the rest out here in private. He was about to tell her that she was being affected by his decision and would need to find a new job. A new place to live.

"No. Not until you hear the rest of what I was gonna say."

Her brain hurt.

"No need. You brought me here tonight to let me know I need to find a new job. It's my fault for yet again being so stupid as to hope..." She shut her hand over her mouth.

"Spit it out. Hope what?" His brows formed into stiff arches.

"No. Nothing." The room felt like it was spinning. Thom's voice telling her he was sorry. He was stunned. He didn't know what to say. But that he would help her anyway he could. And that they would figure everything out when he came home in two months on his mid-tour leave. Like any of that was what she'd wanted from him. No, she only wanted him to know he would be a father.

"You hoped what, Dani?"

"I don't know," her voice sounded hollow echoing back in her ears as she tried to be in the room with Stefan who she could feel was being affected by her shock.

"Well I'll say it then because I was about to get to this before you bolted on me again."

"Don't play with me, Stefan. I support you wanting to be with your mom. Maybe, maybe you should just take me back to my sister's."

"With you acting like this, I should take you back there." She tried for the door but he stood in front of it blocking her. "But not yet."

"I can't do this. Please just let me out. I can't think straight."

Stefan's hands cupped each side of her face and she wanted to fight out of his grasp but he was too strong and he wasn't relenting.

"I don't know what just got into you but you will listen to me, Dani. Stop fighting me."

She hadn't realized she'd been fighting him so hard and relaxed her muscles if for no other reason than for her baby. Her heart hammered and she felt like she'd been tipped upside down and shaken. Her world was again spinning the wrong way. Now she was losing her job, her home and the closest thing she had to a mom but getting her baby's father back. "Why didn't you just call and tell me over the phone?" A crack splintered her heart. She was losing Stefan. Really losing him and all ties that would have brought him back to Moonlight every now and then to visit her.

****

"Because, you stubborn woman. You're totally wrong about what I'm about to say. If I wasn't so…" But the bewildered look on her face stopped him short of telling her he was hung up on her and that was the only reason he was in there fighting her in the fucking bathroom. Shit.

"What?" she barely got out. "What? I don't…"

He took a minute to remove his hands from her wrists and rub his face and hair. When he did that, she rubbed her wrists too.

"Fuck, did I hurt you?"

"No," she whimpered out.

"Good. Do you promise to stand there and be quiet and let me finish?" he asked, trying with everything he had to be tender.

But before he could say another word, she said, "Stefan, that was Thom calling me. He left a voicemail. He wants to see me when he comes home in two months on mid-tour leave."

He felt his face sink and his lips didn't close. The fuck? Thom wanted to see her? Fuck Thom. His eyes darted around the bathroom ceiling, aware he was having the wrong reaction but unable to accept what he was hearing. He blinked so many times he had to concentrate on making himself stop and his throat had never felt so dry. *He's her baby's father. He deserves a chance.* For that look on her face, the one telling him she couldn't possibly process what was going on because it was too much in that one moment, he kissed her forehead and then forced himself to take a step back. "That's good news, sweetheart. That's a good thing."

But the words of his heart stuck in his throat.

Dani, I brought you here tonight because I want you to consider moving to Nashville and I want you to do that as my girlfriend. He thought them but would not say them. Not now. He wouldn't put her in that position. Not on the chance that he *might* be ready to be a boyfriend. That just wasn't a good enough reason. He took her hand and led her out to his car then drove her back to Daisy's. She didn't argue. Good thing he'd packed her that bag.

Chapter Seventeen

Two days later…

"I think it's time to get Dani back here. Your nurse skills have surprised me, but you need help. We need help," Will said as he started the lawn mower back up and hiked it further up the hill of Mom's back yard. More rain, more grass on crack. Will let it die again. The motor chortled a loud groaning sound then Will shouted from the top. "I'm glad we're here to do the yard work and I kind of like being a handyman, but I think your mom needs a lady to help with the lady stuff. We suck at that."

It was true.

Stefan yawned, then hoofed it up the hill to retrieve a rake and eyeball Will who stood there, waiting.

"Not calling her. You know why," Stefan said and grabbed the rake.

"You're making a mistake," called Will after him.

Stefan just flipped him off as he went over to clean out some leaves from Mom's flower pots. He couldn't bring himself to fuck with Dani's life anymore and he'd told Will why. It was time to drop it.

He'd just gone to get the weed whacker and start on some edging when Mom's house phone started ringing. If she was up, he'd learned that she would get to it rather quickly and if her balance was off, she risked stumbling. If she didn't, and the sun was out, she was probably down in the laundry room, in the sound proof basement. Another thing he'd noted about Mom being alone. That should never happen. She could fall down there and no one would hear a thing. Luckily he'd been there when it happened yesterday. Stefan dropped the whacker with a thud and jogged inside.

"Hello," he said, out of breath from sprinting down the hill and slamming inside the house's back door. Irritated, he picked up.

"Yes, I need to speak to…"

"Oh, I've got it, Son."

Mom must have picked up one of the other house lines. Stefan heard the caller next.

"May I please speak with Daniela Foster?"

"Oh, she isn't home right now but you can leave a message with me. This is Mrs. Calderon," his mom said. Stefan just listened, unable to hang up because it was about Dani. He put his hand over the mouth piece and tried not to breathe loudly. Pathetic.

"Sorry, I actually can't disclose that information, Mrs. Calderon. But if you could please have her call this number back, that would be great. The number is 878-555-0100. She can ask for Sherri."

"Okay, thank you. I'll give her the message."

Everyone hung up.

Stefan wished Benny was there. He'd find out who that number belonged to. Same way as Benny had tracked down Honey's address back when Will's bright idea had been to hide her away from the band and pretend he wasn't married. He'd done it in the name of shielding Honey from the ugly side of their band's fame but eventually, life kicked everyone's ass. Stefan understood Will's motives so much better now.

Stefan glanced out the window and saw Will with headphones in, making nice neat lines in his mom's lawn. He ducked into the living room and opened the laptop he'd bought Mom, then did a Google search on the phone number, hoping it was really that easy. Holy shit. It was. No wonder fans seemed to catch him in the most inconvenient places these days. Fucking technology.

The number belonged to a women's clinic. Had to be where Dani got her checkups done.

Was Dani okay? Was her baby okay? Why had the clinic called and spoken so cryptically? He'd never forgive himself if something happened to either of them on account of his stubbornness. This would hurt, but he had to call her and pass along the message.

Stefan wiped at the sweat that beaded on his forehead. He scrolled to her cell number on his phone and waited for her to answer.

"Stefan?"

Fuck he still liked that she had his number programmed in her phone. Didn't matter though.

"Hey, are you screening your calls because the women's clinic just called for you on the house phone. My mom took the message. A lady named Sherri wants you to call her."

The line was so quiet he couldn't be sure she hadn't hung up before he'd gotten that last part out. "Dani? You there?"

"You know I haven't told her yet," she practically whispered.

He should cuss her out for that but hell, Stefan knew all about not wanting to disappoint his mom. "Yeah, I know." Did he tell Dani his mom might already know? No because he wasn't sure. "The lady was very discreet and only left a name and number."

"But she must have said she was from the clinic."

Oh, that. Fuck.

"No, that was me. I, fuck, I Googled the number she gave. Sorry. I was trying to help. I'm the only one who knows it was the clinic."

"All right, thanks for the message. So, have you talked to your mom about Nashville yet? I'm only asking because I'm coming back today. Out of clothes and I need to sleep in my own bed. I don't want to accidentally say anything if you haven't yet."

"No, didn't wanna stress her out any worse." And more than anything, he did not want to discuss it with Dani. Shit, he might not even ask Mom at this point. Knowing that Dani wouldn't come, how did he separate them?

He heard Dani blow out and then a car ignition started. She was coming back now?

Stefan knew what he had to do. No heart allowed.

"Drive safe, sexy," he said, stripping down to the only thing he could give her for the remaining days he had here. Play.

He hung up and then sat down and yawned. Shit he was beat. It was tiring work doing everything for someone else. Mentally, physically, emotionally. He could fall asleep, right now…

Chapter Eighteen

The next day...

Dani walked into the living room, tired but too worn out for sleep. As was her nightly custom, she made her rounds, making sure all the doors were locked and all the appliances unplugged. Mrs. C's string of rough days aside, it was nice to be home. Not avoiding Stefan as much as they'd done before under the same roof was like a fresh coat of paint in an old house.

Sure he teased her, but something had changed with him the night of Thom's voicemail. Stefan seemed to be trying really hard to be nice to everyone but if she knew any better, she'd say it was because he was avoiding things they'd discussed at their dinner date. His plans of taking his mom. As far as she knew, he hadn't asked Gina and she wondered why. Whenever she got him alone, he didn't run but he pulled away, like he wasn't really there with her. It was very frustrating because she wanted to come up with a plan. Now that the idea had settled in, she'd begun to think that taking his mom to Nashville was a good idea and if he could wait until she had a chance to talk to Thom in person, that she and Gina could then make the move together. Dani had no plans of staying with Thom. She didn't love him like that and he had someone. She'd always let him be part of their baby's life but it didn't mean she had to stay in Moonlight. Now if Stefan would just hear her out.

Dani's eyelids had never felt heavier either. It had been another long day. The kind she wouldn't wish on any mother and son. One had seen too much, the other had revealed too much. With the both of them trying to be strong for each other, it had worn everyone out. Even Will who uncharacteristically had one of his legs slung up over the back of Gina's couch, seemed too tired to keep with his manners. His shorts were undone and his shirt was pulled up exposing his belly and more tattoos. The trademark pair of black rimmed glasses lay on the coffee table, just barely clinging to the edge.

Dani saved them from falling, scooting them to safety, and left Will where he lay and crept quietly up the stairs. She checked in on Gina who was asleep. Then she made her way to Stefan's door. It wasn't closed and she wondered if he'd left it that way on purpose. It wasn't the easiest thing to be sharing space with each other again. Dani knew that was the least of his worries after today. The anguish she'd seen him try to hide after Gina's stumble on the stairs nearly buckled Dani's knees. He'd probably crashed and forgotten to pull the door closed. She gave it a gentle push, wishing things were easier between them. Dinner at Mario's had seemed like the gateway to that but now things were weird. What she'd give to have his wicked, playful beautiful ways back again.

She peered around, focusing on where she knew furniture to be and tried to familiarize herself without the benefit of a light. Unsure if Stefan was on the air mattress or the bed, Dani took careful steps into the room. She squinted and once her eyes adjusted, she could see that he wasn't there at all. Where had he gone?

She checked her room and then Gina's more closely in case he'd crashed at his mom's bedside, worried she'd roll out of bed during the night. But no Stefan.

She went downstairs and when she crossed into the kitchen, she noticed movement from the back porch which she hadn't seen before. The porch light was off but aptly enough, moonlight shone down on Stefan as he sat in one of the rockers.

Quietly, she opened the back porch door and went outside to check on him. Her heart broke for the worry he'd kept hidden today. If things hadn't been so non-stop, she would have reminded him again how she sometimes bruised Gina too because her skin was just at that stage where that happened more easily now. But every little thing that could happen had. Just like the other day when he'd been here with Gina on his own and she and Will had gone to Daisy's. Dani felt horrible for making him believe Mrs. C would bounce back and be good as new. The frown he'd gotten when she showed him the special place in the pantry where a months' worth of protein shakes was stocked made her cringe now. But liquid nutrition was better than nothing.

Was it really a good idea for her to be here, with her heart breaking for him so strongly? They still had their agreement in place. It was sort of going unspoken, but while under Gina's roof, they were still holding to being nothing more than friends. And not the kinds with benefits.

So why was she deliberately searching him out?

She couldn't stop thinking about him and how around his mom, Stefan was a beautiful and dutiful creature. Who was she to limit him to pleasantries in his own home? But he'd done it, because she'd asked. A thought nudged her. Stefan didn't strike her as the type of man to cower to anyone's demands.

Dani could watch this moonlit porch and the shadow of him resting peacefully in the rocker, without needing for anything. Poor baby. Having to watch his mom unable to eat and not having the experience of knowing it was just a passing thing that really would get better. Dani's fingers ached to take his curls and move them here and there, off his forehead so she could … plant a kiss there. *Sleeping Superman*. Watching Stefan deal with it all today, his helpless looks marring that handsome face, had left Dani heartbroken. Her energy spent, she could close her eyes and fall asleep standing and be dead to the world for the next twenty-four hours.

If he wasn't lying right there.

Should she wake him up though to sleep inside? Not yet, he looked too peaceful and the night was a perfect temperature. She sat down in the rocker beside him, wanting some of that peace too.

"Mom?" she heard him say. He sat up so fast. Her hand flew to steady him before he fell out of it and her heart trampled over itself when she saw his brow crinkled in a tight squint.

"Um, no. Sorry, it's me. I didn't mean to wake you up." All the times she'd seen him in those white shirts he favored so much, and the way they fit him so well, leaving little to the imagination. She was overwhelmed now at the sight of his bare chest combined with the exhaustion that had him fumbling with the chair pillow with those tattooed hands.

"Is my mom okay?" he asked, obviously disoriented.

"Hey, looks like you fell asleep out here. And yes, I just checked and she's asleep." His face relaxed. "Sorry I woke you. I'll go back inside now."

"No," he grumbled out.

She swallowed.

"I should go," she said. A bird called from one of the surrounding forest trees.

She watched him hold one of the quilts from the couch and wished she could cuddle up with him right now.

He seemed to have gotten his whereabouts straightened back out and his hand came out from under the small pillow folded behind his head. He rubbed his chest like he'd forgotten she hadn't seen him like this before. Or maybe he just hadn't expected her to have a reaction under their platonic clause. Neither she nor Stefan would ever win an award for diplomacy. They both sucked at sticking to agreements.

But all her eyes were capable of in that moment was following his hand and the colorful ink that coated his arms and shoulders. He rubbed his bare chest back and forth, split down the middle with two firm and equal sides of broad muscle. There was golden tanned skin. And there was the coating of black hairs over each side of his perfectly chiseled, tattoo free chest. Her gaze dipped to where the ink picked back up at his side, over his ribs. Something wicked looking wound down into his lounge pants. Why did he keep rubbing at his chest like that? So oblivious that her body and soul were turning to mush and fire all at once with each of his strokes.

"I shouldn't have come out. I'm sorry. I'll let you sleep. It's a nice night out for that."

A moment later, catching her just as she'd have been out of his sight, he responded with a softer voice, still deep, like dark honey dripping from barbed wire.

"Don't."

She hovered there, feeling the sting of what he didn't say. *Stay with me, Dani. I need you tonight.* Maybe it was only what she wanted to hear. He'd done a stellar job of keeping things neighborly. That was his super power. Inhuman amounts of self-control.

"Don't leave?" she asked for clarification. He could have easily meant don't come out here again.

"Turn around. Look at me."

His voice gave her no choice but to obey.

But what she saw broke her heart all over again. His hands weren't rubbing through his chest hair anymore, they were at his temples, trailing down his nose and wiping under his eyes. And then they were folded, just like his arms, over his smooth abs. His rugged beauty slapped her senses awake. Dani stopped herself from crawling up his body and cradling his head in her arms. It would have been tricky in the rocker but she had no doubts he could have held her steady.

He studied her, she felt like a sneaky little lab rat, playing with her life and his.

"Don't what, Stefan?"

"Isn't it obvious?" His eyes turned shiny and she nearly ran to his side because she knew what that meant.

He pulled his lips in together and inhaled through his nose. She did the same and took in the scent of nature cooled by the night. Still sweet but more delicate. He shook his head like he was aggravated.

"I'm trying real hard to do what I'm supposed to. For you, your baby, my mom. Fuck, it's hard, sweetheart. Harder than I thought."

He rubbed at his eyes several times and cleared his throat. She expected to see bruises under his eyes when he finally pulled his hands away but he'd done a good job of avoiding those the past few days somehow. Still, he looked dead tired.

If he wasn't who he was, she'd have rolled onto that chair alongside him without a second thought. Something God-given about Stefan was exactly that inviting. Unfortunately, there was nothing either of them could do about the obstacle of whose roof they were under. Or the fact that she carried a child, by another man. Strangely enough, that hadn't seemed to bother Stefan until the night at Mario's.

If he'd talk to her about it, she could clear things up.

Dani pulled her rocker closer to him and sat down, not wanting to upset him but desperate to make things better for him.

"I can't sleep inside. I'm going crazy in there."

"I understand. Lucky it's such a nice night." They could talk. She could tell him about her plan to wait for Thom's return and then the best way to transition Gina to Nashville. "Wanna talk?"

"I suck at talking and I feel like shit. Believe it or not, I don't want to be an asshole to you."

At that, she sat stiffly with her back against the chair and her arms tucked to her sides. She crossed her legs at the ankles. With their chairs lined up side by side, her feet stopped right around where his knees started. "You're great at talking. Maybe not about anything serious. You and Will both. Great at getting laughs."

"You like Will a lot, don't you."

"Who doesn't like Will?" she said.

He nodded, still looking tired beyond his years, which she'd figured to be thirty-eight, give or take a few months, she supposed he could be thirty-nine already. Apparently Dani was too tired to sleep as her brain seemed stuck on autopilot with Stefan its only passenger. She wished he didn't seem so distant.

"Wanna know a secret about your buddy?" she asked, hoping to entice him away from his worry over Gina.

"If you've got one of those on Will, I've really pushed the two of you together way more than I should have." He rubbed his arms. "Oh shit, here, have the blanket," he said and started to strip it from his body to hand her.

"No please you keep it. I'm hot from running around inside." No she wasn't but she'd catch fire if he took that blanket off himself right now.

She watched Stefan's brow crinkle like his head was hurting. Studying his features was doing nothing good for her pulse.

"I think Will and my sister had a real moment the other day at her apartment," she shared. "You saw them, right?'

Stefan's one eyebrow hiked up. "You didn't see anything. Will doesn't have *moments* with women. Not anymore."

Aside from the need to point out he'd just called her a liar, Dani didn't want to agitate him anymore. She knew something Stefan didn't but would keep it to herself. She thought Will may have picked up one of those fancy Keurig coffee makers, in red, at another of their Taggert's trips. Her guess was the next time she visited Daisy, it'd be on the counter. Stefan would apparently never believe that though. Why was it so hard for him to believe Will might like Daisy back? It saddened her that the reason could be he didn't believe in love. Lust and pleasure? Relocating his mom's entire household? Yes. But those weren't necessarily permanent things.

"All I'm saying is Will's a great catch. And now I'm going inside."

Stefan let out a loud breath and fanned the blanket away from his body like he was hot and uncomfortable.

Her traitorous eyes followed his movement.

The hairs that blanketed his chest so expertly disappeared, giving way to a smooth and outlined set of abs, although not so ripped she could count them. The dark hairs picked back up just below his belly button. There was no trail but a soft dark patch, shadowing the space above his lounge pants. Black and soft looking, the pants and his body's fur captivated her. She remembered his offer to hold her the night of her contraction scare and wished he'd invite her again. Dani's throat burned and she had to make herself look down at her socks to keep from staring and imagining and aching.

"I wish I could tell you why I know that about Will, sweetheart."

So easily he slipped into his super hero suit.

"Bro code?" she got out.

A sleepy grin broke through his pain at that. "Yeah, something like that."

"You love him." Dani could see it every time the two overgrown boys were together.

"I do, like a brother. I'd be nothing without Will Cordero."

Dani sensed there was so much more behind what he'd shared. She longed to ask him. "What makes the two of you so close, if you don't mind me asking?" She scooted back into the comfort of the second rocker chair since he'd been the one to keep their conversation going.

In the cutest way she'd ever seen, his eyelids slid closed and his head began bobbing. God, to be that confident. If their roles were reversed, she didn't know if she could be as trusting, letting him watch her in a moment like this. His brow furrowed but not in a frown. He'd found some inner groove and looked like he might have forgotten she'd asked him a question.

But then he opened his eyes and found her again. "Know much about the inner workings of a band?"

Did she? "Not a clue, sadly."

He warmed. "Well, if you've ever found yourself listening to a song and you just settle into that deep, comfortable head bobbing groove, that's because the bass player and the drummer are feeling each other. We call it the pocket. Without Will, it'd be impossible for me to be able to play bass and sing. And that's just musically. Let me tell you, that guy right there, he's the most forgiving mother fucker I know."

Stefan sat up straighter, pulling his legs to his chest and wrapping his arms around his knees. She couldn't help but smile.

"What's that pretty smile for? Hmm?" he asked.

Dani's face immediately flushed.

"It's a bit late for blushing," he said with a hint of his usual teasing. She doubted he wanted to tease her but he probably couldn't turn it off completely. That one phrase he'd shocked her with in the stall would never leave her and she knew that's what he hinted at. She'd be eighty years old and using a walker and still hear the perfect, deep vibrating timber of his voice whispering what he wanted to do to her.

"I was just about to say you're a good teacher and then you throw mother effer in there for good measure. Always keeping people on their toes, you are, Mr. Calderon."

She couldn't tell how he'd taken that and then he tugged on his lounge pants, straightening them and pulling them to where he must be more comfortable. They just hung there on his hips. Her eyes popped too wide and she accidentally let a "Shit" spill out.

"Aren't you the interesting one tonight?" he said. She'd have called it his usual teasing but his every word and action tonight barely covered the tired pain so evident in his voice, his hands. He rubbed at his hip bone and then raised it to do the same to his forehead. "What?"

"I just half expected everything you own to be white. PJ's included."

That got her a more genuine smile although still heavy with his exhaustion and worry. "White pajama bottoms would not be appropriate for me at Mom's. At least not with you around."

"Why not?" she asked.

"Really?" He closed his eyes for a slow second and flexed his toes.

"Consider me clueless. I've rarely seen you in anything but white around here. Why would pajama pants be such a jump to make?"

She was so thankful that even though she felt severely below intelligence levels right now, that they were talking about something as mundane as the color of his clothes.

"You know how hard it is to hide an erection in white cotton?"

Oh shit. She hadn't thought about that. At all. And now she really was a blushing fool.

"Oh."

"Yeah, big Oh," he said and let his legs fall into a more relaxed position on the chair. Still didn't look like he'd found a comfortable position. "Hey, not trying to be a dick, but you should probably go back inside, Dani." His eyes darkened.

"Okay." But Dani couldn't help but find just the right angle of peripheral vision to check him out now. Yes, there. The front of his soft pants betrayed nothing inappropriate below. Just a natural male bump that signified he had his man parts. Her heart somersaulted. Her belly spasmed but that had nothing to do with Stefan's glorious body laid out beside her. She casually tried to act like she hadn't just scoped out his crotch. "I didn't mean to disturb you."

"Wait," he said. "I'm fighting it, Dani." His voice came out low and then finally, because it felt like it had been ages, he touched her. Just a single falling ringlet of her hair but in that one gesture, she had that proof again, even if it felt like he was trying to keep it from her.

His jaw worked. Her insides turned to hot goo.

"I don't know what to say. Thank you? I'm sorry?" she asked.

"You don't have to say anything. But since you're not leaving, it would be nice if you told me what you're doing out here with me."

What else could she say? "I know today was tough for you to see. I wanted to make sure you were okay. And to tell you that I promise your mom doesn't have many of these days but when they hit, they hit hard."

"But she'll bounce back. You said you've been through this with her before."

"Yes, Hon—"

He stopped her with two fingers covering her lips.

"Never been called that by a younger woman. It's nice when you do it."

"It was a slip. But I'm glad you're okay with it," she said. "Stefan, your mom will be okay. I'm not just saying that. Even though I did say that before."

"If you tell me this shit will pass and she'll be better soon, I guess I have to believe you."

There was so much more she should have focused on but Dani couldn't help but wonder how many women Stefan had loved and how young and how old? She decided to put some insane number in her head so if and when she ever found out the actual amount, it would sound absurdly low. Silently, she calculated in her factors while he smoothed her lock of curl between his fingers and focused on nothing else but the back and forth action for a few moments.

He was thirty-eight-ish. He'd been in his band for something like twenty years. He was drop dead gorgeous, single and rich. He not only played bass guitar but also was the lead singer. His body could melt the polar ice caps. At least what she'd seen of it. And, he would hook up with a woman just about anywhere. Shit. His number had to be astronomical. Before she assigned his, she thought about hers. Eight. Nine if she counted Stefan. They hadn't actually slept together but what they had done was more sensual and erotic than all the others combined.

Her eye caught how completely absorbed he looked in the petting of her one lock of hair. If she didn't know better, she'd think music was about to flow from her head, with the look on his face like the one in the magazine picture of him with his beloved guitar. Quickly, so as not to fall completely fairy tale in love with this man who at every turn found new ways to taunt and confuse her, she mentally blurted out, five hundred. But realized that he could have done that in a handful of years. One thousand. That's what she'd keep telling herself.

Funny though, she wasn't disgusted by the outrageous number.

"What in the world are you thinking about right now?" he asked her, and finally let her long curl go back to the others.

"Math?" she said, wondering if he'd take that and chalk the oddness up to the fact she was also dead tired.

"Is that a question?" he asked.

She just shook her head. Tell him, Dani's conscience egged her on. "Did you know you have a way of making me feel like I'm the only girl in the world? I bet you make everyone feel that way." It was the reason his thousands of previous lovers didn't send her running right now with her tail between her legs. And why there was no way she and Thom could ever be together. Or she and any other guy. No one made her feel the way Stefan did.

He scratched behind his ear and just shrugged.

"Hey, thanks for the talk. It helped. I feel less like shit now," he said rather than acknowledging her compliment.

"But still not great?" she asked.

"I'm fine, Dani. Go." Slowly, he downed his chin toward his bare chest.

He needed to get some rest and she should do the same. Gina was an early riser. Four-thirty would be there soon. She guessed he really was sleeping out here tonight.

"Why don't you stay asleep in the morning? I'll get up with your mom," Dani offered him.

"Hey..." Stefan sat up. He looked away for a moment then came back to her. "You shouldn't have come out here ... but I'm glad you did."

Dani stood, her hand a little shaky, like she couldn't possibly have heard him right.

"I know." Her cheeks bunched because she was overcome with emotions. She wouldn't miss the crazy mood swings pregnancy brought along and took a few steps away from him.

Before she got too far, his voice called her to a stop. "So anymore word from Thom? He doing okay?" Stefan's eyes were still tired but he looked genuinely interested in a distant kind of way again.

Maybe he wasn't really ready for her to go either, but talking to him about Thom threatened to cloud over the warmth she got from just being near Stefan. "He hasn't called or emailed again. I don't expect him to. It's not like that."

"Not like what?"

"We're on friendly terms but we're not close like that. Remember? He's got someone who loves him." Her lip quivered. No matter how much she tried to stop it, nothing helped. She couldn't talk to Thom like she could with Stefan. "How horrible does that sound? I didn't realize until I just said it. But it's true."

"Hey." His chocolate eyes under that crinkled dark brow held no secrets right now. Just the same plain, raw need she felt inside too. "Come here."

Dani stayed put, wiping sudden, unexpected tears away.

"Come back over here. Sit down with me," he said.

In a trance, caught between what they should do and the need she felt every single time she was in his presence, Dani hovered over his chair.

He took the quilt he'd already pulled back earlier into his hand and held it up like he was waiting for her to join him so he could then cover them both with it.

To him, it would appear she was just standing there, ignoring him. But really she was trying to figure out who he was. She'd seen so many different sides to him in the matter of ten days. Hours ago, even minutes earlier, he'd been distant. Now he wanted her to lay with him on the chair.

"Shit. I can see it all over your face. You wish I was someone else," he said.

He dropped the blanket. It fell to cover his lower half. He started to roll over, away from her but stopped. Like this was her very last chance. Their very last chance.

To answer him, she didn't wish for that. She just wanted this to be real so badly. She wanted to be his proof, the person who calmed and soothed him tonight. Who told him it would be okay without needing the words. Dani's gut twisted when she realized then that she wanted a real relationship with him.

Well, that was impossible.

"Fuck, Dani. There's nothing I can do about who I am. I won't beg for this. I just wanted to hold you."

Incredibly hesitant, she joined him lying as straight as she could at his side. She pointed her toes straight downward so they didn't poke him.

"This ain't gonna work." He pulled himself up and stood then brought her to her feet as well, holding the rocker's pillow and the quilt. He led her by the hand over to a soft patch of grass where he sat. "Join me?" She adjusted to the odd feeling of laying down on the ground outside as he pulled the soft quilt up and over them. Technically, they weren't under Gina's roof and the implications of that and this made her woozy. A legion of goose bumps took their places on every inch of her skin. Stefan's smell had permeated the pillow, the quilt, her hair. It was so warm and deep, like everything else about him and it made her blood hum. He placed one chaste kiss on her cheek. "Told you, I just want to hold you."

She fidgeted some more.

Her baby bump showed under the blanket and she smoothed over the top of it.

She turned her face to the right to see him and paid for it instantly. If his look didn't say how bad he wanted her...

"How far along are you again, exactly?" he asked, a genuine mark of curiosity lit his face. Dani studied the handsomeness of his slightly crooked nose but his absolutely perfect full lips for a second and then returned to staring at the ceiling of stars above them.

"Eighteen weeks."

"So that's what? Four months?"

"A little over."

Dani couldn't help but touch her stomach. Although she knew she had to stay aware that this tender of a moment would only make things harder for her and the quizzical man lying a foot away in the morning. Even if it was just holding, as he'd said.

A roll of indescribable motion tumbled low in her belly. She always gasped when the baby did that. It hadn't gotten old since two weeks ago when she'd felt it for the first time.

"You seem happy about your baby. I admire that, Dani."

"I have a lot to be happy about," she said. Some might think she was crazy to come to that conclusion, but she couldn't think any other way. The little guy was on his way. Dani was so anxious about her ultrasound appointment in the morning when she would confirm whether he was indeed a little guy or gal.

"Stefan, are we still operating under that promise we made?"

He brought his hands up and clasped them above his head. His armpits smelled like spicy, rustic heaven and the black hairs fascinated her. What was it about his body hair that set off every one of her man-loving hormones? That there wasn't too much, just the perfect amount to outline his muscles and look soft to the touch?

His biceps flexed and called to Dani to kiss them.

"It feels like we've made a few of those damn things. Are you speaking about the one where we don't sleep together under the same roof? Because I don't think I can stay awake much longer. So you can count that one shot to hell," he said. "But then again, we're outside."

"Broken on a technicality then," she said back as he yawned and she saw that his teeth weren't perfect but they were a nice pearly white in the moonlight. Of course they would be white.

"You know, back to what I was saying earlier about you being happy with your baby, not everyone would see things as positively as you do," he said then yawned.

"You refer to things most would be ashamed of. Like getting knocked up by someone who doesn't even love me."

"Some people would be ashamed of that. But—" Dani cut him off, unbelieving.

"If I wanted to be judged, I'd go to confession, Stefan."

"What about the last week, the truck stop, my mom ... makes you think you can say that to me and have me take you seriously? You should consider letting me finish what I'm saying sometimes," he finally let out.

Cracks surfaced in their mutual promise.

Every time she thought he'd close his eyes to blink or shut down, he didn't. With solid, eyes wide open, he seemed to want to challenge her. "Go to sleep." He maintained his stare.

Dani let out a breath and patted her part of the quilt over her stomach again.

"Sorry," he said. "I'm just tired. I'd never judge you. Thought you would know that by now."

"It's been a long day for us both. And I do know that. I'm tired too," she said and shimmied down into the cushion of the soft ground.

"A second ago, something happened. What was it? A kick?" he asked.

Dani hesitated but this was the man she wanted to be sharing these moments with. It shattered her heart into a million pieces to allow herself to think that thought. "A tumble. It was more like a tumble," she said low.

"May I?" Stefan moved his hand toward her hip.
"Why?"

"You must really think I'm some sort of leper."

She hated that she'd made him feel that way.

No, they both knew she didn't think that of him. Neither of them should remind the other of how they knew. That didn't stop the images. The gold, ember-like flecks she'd seen as he kissed her barreled in first. The peak of his tongue before she'd felt it in her mouth. This tender version of him asking to touch her stomach.

The baby rolled again. She gasped. Stefan's hand hovered over hers.

She took it and pressed it down over her skin.

"That's something special, Dani." He took his hand away then did like she had before and looked up at the sky. She felt like she had missed something and wondered if somewhere deep inside, Stefan might be thinking about the baby he'd made and lost so sadly.

"Anything you need to get off your chest?" she asked.

He looked at her and a half grin gave him that naughty air she'd missed the last few days.

She wanted him to share something serious. If for nothing else than to even them up.

"No, I prefer taking things off your chest, sweetheart." He was terrible. "Your Thom is a lucky man. You're going to make an excellent mom for his baby." And despicably tender again. She'd never win with Stefan.

"Thanks." There were too many details and the simple answer told him everything he needed to know of her gratitude.

"Goodnight."

Should she ask out loud the question that popped into her mind just then? For all she knew, he'd been the guy in a situation like hers. How could he not with all those lovers over the years?

"Stefan, aside from your Amanda, would I be naïve to think you've never had another woman tell you she was pregnant?"

He blinked.

Her eyes grew wide.

He just nodded.

"Tell me please."

She felt his fingers roll over the top of her hand and then he gave it a gentle squeeze.

"What's your real question, sweetheart? Hmm?" He yawned and she felt one coming on too.

In as unjudging a voice as she could manage, she asked him. "As an adult man, has anyone ever told you that you got them pregnant, Stefan?"

He rolled onto his side so that he faced her but Dani stayed on her back, taking deep breaths of the nighttime air but trying to keep it unnoticeable. It was so stupid, but she wished her baby was his. He'd never believe her but she thought he'd make a very good daddy.

****

Looking at Dani now, he couldn't lie to her. He had to tell the truth. It was all they had for the next few days until he left.

"Sure, there have been a few."

"Oh."

"But it's not possible. I try not to be a dick about it. I offer to be tested, just as a formality."

"How can you be so sure?"

"I haven't slept with a woman without protection since I was sixteen. Not one single time."

Dani's face nearly went white. She probably didn't believe him, but it was true. He'd learned his lesson and it had cost him too much.

"But condoms don't stop all pregnancies."

205

"That's a wives' tale, Dani. They work just fine when you're not trying to get pregnant. Otherwise…"

"Otherwise you'd have kids running all over the place?"

Shit. Yes, but he should have put that out there with some tact.

"I am genuinely sorry if that offends you. I've been very active sexually for a long time. You should know that. But I always used protection."

"And your more recent activity?" she asked. He'd give her credit for hanging in there with him, dead tired as they both were. Not to mention he didn't know a female on the planet who wanted to hear her man had until very recently slept with hundreds of women. Fuck. Her man, he thought. Huge ass slip for him to make. Stefan drew in a deep breath to douse the pain that slip had just caused him and prayed he didn't get slapped.

"Not as active," he said.

She looked like her brain was playing a mean game of table tennis and he knew he'd have to elaborate.

"It's been a month since I was with someone." He felt the need to clarify that it had been just sex. Nothing close to all this confusing ass shit Dani was doing to his insides. But what she said next did him in for good where she was concerned.

"I guess that's not so bad. Hell, I slept with someone four months ago and I got myself knocked up. Sometimes sex is just sex. Until a baby comes along."

Oh, his heart was so screwed. Hell yeah he wanted to be her man. But he'd already sworn allegiance to the devil that he wouldn't put her in a bind. He knew her well enough that seeing Thom face to face was important. No way could she up and relocate to Nashville with him now.

Leaving her in a few days was going to suck.

Right now that he had Dani where he wanted her, he was calling it a night. She was stuck with him for the next few comatose hours.

"This doesn't mean what you think it means," he whispered across the foot of space separating them. And then that distance melted away as he rested his thigh over the tops of her legs, careful he hadn't landed it near her belly. He pulled the blanket up so it covered them both and took her hand in his. "If it did, you'd know it. Now, I *will* be good. Let's get some sleep." Crickets sounded nearby. He gave Dani the rocking chair pillow and let the grass be his.

****

They had to both be out of their minds balancing this line with absolutely no respect for how razor thin it was. Before she had time to wriggle out from his heavy thigh, he cleared his throat, low and subtly so she'd barely heard it. And then he began to hum, singing a word now and then.

His singing voice was the most gorgeous sound she'd ever heard. Dani closed her eyes tight to try and memorize it, taking the sound into her heart and holding it there.

The baby pushed. He must like it too.

Stefan moved his hand ever so lower and he rubbed at the kicking spot. His humming took on the distinct form of a lullaby.

Dani's heart lodged in her throat.

He was being terribly cruel and wonderful again.

She'd been prepared to wipe away his tears, listen to his fears about his mom, but he'd held the pain of it in, leaving her with nothing to do but lay in want, under his heavy thigh. Her dark Superman had returned and she knew that if there were any way possible, she'd give in to him. Dani started to feel like he'd never ask, but after today, seeing his true heart, she'd follow him to hell and back. But, he hadn't asked and she was still too gun-shy to invite herself for fear of being told no thanks.

Chapter Nineteen

Stefan woke up in the middle of the night with Dani snuggled close to his chest. Petting her arm and back gave him a calm he couldn't remember ever waking up with.

"I want to make love to you, Dani," he whispered near her ear. They still had a couple hours until they had to be awake. He wouldn't make things worse for her by getting feelings involved, but he'd share his body with her. They both deserved that much at this point.

She stirred and her eyes opened. Shit.

"I thought you were asleep." He kissed the top of her hair.

She turned her head until she faced him. They kissed the most natural, lovers' kiss. His heart pounded so loud he could hear it in his ears. Her lips were so soft. She moved her neck like it was stiff from how he'd had her tucked into him all night.

"Here, let me help you with that."

Stefan rubbed her neck and she wrapped her right arm around his back and began to massage him there and down his side, letting her hand rest on his hip before holding him in a hug again. He swallowed deeply. Fuck, why hadn't he come to her while she was out of her mind asleep before? God, he hoped she knew what she was doing. That this easiness between them wasn't just sleep induced on her part.

"Is that better?" he asked, finishing the neck rub, wanting like never before with anyone, to be tender with her.

"Yes, thank you." She snuggled into him and the softer her body felt against his, the harder his shot to life. "I want to make love with you too." She let her lips rest against his for a few seconds. "But, I can't. We can't. I'm sorry, Stefan."

What she'd just said.

It forced him to take a breath.

She'd gotten so far under his skin, hearing things like this built him up and tore him down like he was made of nothing because she was just too much.

"Aside from the other issues, will you be honest with me? Are you worried I'd hurt the baby?" He felt his brow crinkle with his question, fearing she'd say yes.

"Being completely honest? After all that's happened, the other issues don't seem as important. But that one, I don't think you'd hurt us on purpose, but yes," she said, shifting like she'd become uncomfortable. He didn't want to let her twist away from him but she'd hurt him with that.

"I promise I would be gentle, with both of you. I am capable of that." He hadn't been soft with a lover since he was sixteen, but with Dani, he would be again. He knew he would treat her with the utmost sensitivity, just like he'd done with Amanda all those years ago. Tenderness had become a foreign concept to him but there was no doubt, he'd do it for her.

"I know you would, Stefan."

She softened the blow.

They kissed and petted each other some more. His body stayed on constant alert. The second he sensed she'd let him, he would give it all to her. He didn't want to waste this miracle of them simply lying in bed, no games being played. Just the two of them, connecting. Her not pulling away and saying they couldn't. He couldn't leave her and not have at least this experience with her.

Steadily he petted her hands, her arms and back and her face and hair. He would show her he could be gentle. She might have just said otherwise, but he also believed she still felt very strongly about the other issues they'd had and he didn't want that stuff getting in the way of what they could share tonight.

"I want you to know that my personal feelings for you have nothing to do with the professional and greatly appreciated service you provide for my mom. Those two things are completely separate for me, Dani. I promise I would never let one affect the other. No matter what. You know staying away from you because of that has been killing me."

He realized just then that he'd admitted out loud he had feelings for Dani. She seemed at a loss for words to respond and so he just held her and rubbed her back some more, waiting.

"Stefan, I don't think I ever explained this properly to you. The other day when I told you I couldn't have an orgasm wasn't because I doubted your ability. It's because I'd had one recently…" His look must have changed because she amended her words, slowly. "I mean that I gave myself one a few weeks ago, and I didn't just feel the usual parts spasming. I felt my womb squeeze. It scared me then and it scared me again when it happened with you the other night. That's why I thought maybe I'd done something to my baby."

That explained a lot. Was she okay right now?

"Have you talked to your doctor?" he asked.

Didn't people have sex all the time when the woman was pregnant? Jaxon came to mind. The man craved pussy as much as Stefan. And he was sure Trista and Lucky, with the way they always looked so into each other, had to have kept up a healthy sex life even during pregnancy.

"I haven't asked. But I have my monthly check-up in the morning. I should ask then."

"You should," he said and caressed her jaw. Making love with her would be his parting gift. But it would be more for him because he knew he'd treasure the experience forever.

She looked at him earnestly while he continued holding her one hand and pressing her fingertips to his. "Stefan, all that other stuff, I hope you understand that wasn't me just being a bitch. I really wish your mom was independently wealthy and that you had nothing to do with paying me. I mean, I know it's not gonna matter now, when she moves."

Fuck. He did not want to talk about this with her. "I've never once thought of you as a bitch for feeling that way." He stopped short of telling her he'd figured a way to fix that issue because it was moot now. Mom had always told him she'd rather pay for her home health nurse with her own money. He'd always just been too stubborn and insisted he do it. Now he knew his idiocy had cost them right from the jump. "I might not ask her to move. To be honest, Dani, I don't want to get into it right now. Too tired, okay?"

He felt her shoulders shrug tucked into his side.

She reached up and kissed his chin which turned him into a hot spaz. Fuck if his toes didn't curl. A shot of her taste splashed on his tongue like his favorite tequila. "Okay," she said and paused while she petted the dent in his chin. "But I do have one more question."

"What?" he said, distracted by what she was doing with her fingers and lips to his chin.

"Do you think you could be with me and stop before the climax this time? My climax I mean, not yours."

She asked so directly, he couldn't speak at first. It reminded him of the very first time she'd told him to prove it.

He took a long few seconds to think about his control and how he could see himself losing it with her. Sure, he'd probably gotten off over the years when his partner hadn't but picturing that with Dani was inconceivable, especially after having his hands inside her the other night and feeling what he could do for her. Every night he'd gone to bed the past week, he'd pictured the look on her face as he ate her pussy and cherished her gorgeous body with everything he had. He'd gone over what her mewls would sound like as she panted in his ear, begging him to stop and then for more, over and over. Even after deciding asking her for a relationship was out of the question, the fantasy always ended with her praise for how well he'd pleased her.

Never did he imagine her telling him to stop and actually mean it.

He had no expectations right now. The fact she was here still shocked him.

So he gave her an answer because she'd asked and he owed her something.

"You'd have to tell me when you were close so that I could." He pulled back and took a long look at her. She was serious but just as tormented as him. Fuck, there was no doubt in his mind. They were meant to be lovers. Not just for this week.

She smiled. "I don't know that I trust myself to be able to do that. Not after us in my car. Your car." A frown creased her pretty brow and she kissed him long on the lips. He hummed at her taste he'd been denied for too long. "Stefan, for now, how about this?"

Her hands rubbed his body up and down and she pulled his head to hers. Her hand moved over his ass. "What are we doing, sweetheart? Practicing our control, or playing with fire?"

"I trust you," she said.

Stefan was still processing the words he had to have conjured up when her hand came around to cup him. Damn, he'd been waiting nine long days to feel that again. He groaned into her hair and felt his balls fill, his cock harden and his pants tighten. His hips rolled into her grasp. They played back and forth, her squeezing him and him riding her hand until she suddenly stopped cold. Shit, maybe he had imagined it all.

Her one hand caught his as it shot to her belly, the other between her legs.

Something very real had just happened and his heart slammed against his chest. "Are you okay? Dani? The baby again?"

She blew out, swallowed and blinked. "That was close. I almost let go."

While he registered how good it felt to know she was okay—it had been a false alarm—it felt even better to know how easily he affected her. No question, they had a connection. What a waste, he thought. She wiggled out from their sideways embrace and scooted down on the grass. "Where are you going, sweetheart?" When she pulled him out of his pants, and her lips touched him, his eyes rolled back in his head. His head hit the lawn he'd mowed in order to keep his mind off this very thing.

He wanted her so much and had been thinking about this for too long. *All it can be is sex. Remember that.*

****

Dani's toes curled and her spine arched as she took him in. She closed her eyes, breathing and calming her heartbeat. It took her every bit of concentration, but she pushed the desire to let go and feel this with him as far into the background as she could.

The clean, musky scent of the hair encircling the base of his beautiful cock called to her nose and cheek. She ignored the call and laid her fingers over it, laying it flat so it couldn't tickle her nose and distract her from her mission.

His foot petted her side and gave her goose bumps.

She took that tempting foot into her hand and pushed it away. He made a sound of disapproval until she compromised and found his ankle. Dani began rubbing tiny circles, massaging her way around his foot while at the same time laying her first kisses at the inside of his thigh. His hips relaxed and she gently worked up from his ankle with her left hand. He kept his knee bent and his calf close enough for her to touch. She kneaded the ball of tense muscle between her thumb and fingers until it felt more pliable then traveled her way up to the back of his knee and then the top and down over his muscular thigh.

He let out a deep 'unh'.

Good. She hadn't known how he'd respond to her taking her time. To any of this, it was such a 180 of what she'd insisted on before. His repeated 'unh's' told her he appreciated it.

The soft blanket of hair covering his thigh did its best to call her own body to a swelling point but she resisted. With her left hand working his thick thigh she made sure to keep her belly lifted by supporting herself on her knees and right elbow. It limited what she could do with her right hand but found he must enjoy the way she used it to smooth the thick, wiry hairs surrounding his erection. When she splayed her fingers as wide as she could and drove her thumb down and under his balls, massaging more small circles along the edges of his tight flesh, his hips thrust up and she got a face full of Stefan's sex. He cursed which gave her a chance to regain her own control.

Dani went back to work, her hands still in their caressing places, Stefan's butt flat again on the ground. His hips had fallen more open too. She thought about glancing up, curious to see what he looked like when he was getting a blow job. Were his hands folded cockily behind his head? Did he like watching her face so close to his swollen cock? But just the thought of what he might look like right now added a tremble to her arms and she felt herself begin to warm. A tingle sprang to life inside her.

Stop, she thought, reprimanding herself. She couldn't think about what his pleasure looked like because that would in turn bring her so much sexual joy as a woman. She could only give him the pleasure. *Be like him,* she thought. Deliver her touches straight up. No thinking. Suck his cock with the muscles and walls of her mouth and tongue, not her heart. Let him come, finally, let him have that much before they parted.

Dani spread her knees and pivoted back for a better position. Her butt stuck out and the tip of her nose collided with his cock, but she didn't care. His hand couldn't have been up behind his head because in that same second, it was in her hair. Massaging her ear. His thumb stroked her temple.

She took the swollen tip of his cock into her mouth and once she had the first couple of inches of his thickness firmly inside, she took her right hand that had kept his hairs from tickling her nose and found his hand, pulling it away from her head. She guided his hand down and pressed it to the grass instead.

She pulled back, letting his cock slick with her saliva rest at the side of her face for a moment. "If you want this, you can't touch me, Stefan."

He grunted. She had to look up and see his face. Know that he understood her, that they were on the same page.

His eyes held her the second they locked on each other. A hard pain, but one that looked to be bringing him exquisite pleasure covered his face. Like his hand was inside a flame but what he was touching at the flame's center was the best feeling in the world. But she wasn't supposed to be caring about those details.

"I want you," he said.

"Shhh," she said with her lips playing at his sensitive tip. Already she tasted his salty leave leaking from it.

Dani dipped her head back to her task and ran her tongue down his shaft. Off to the side, she saw his hand move toward her and then he withdrew it, out of her sight. She assumed he must have gone ahead and locked his fingers behind his head because in the small space she allowed herself to glance around, Stefan's hands were nowhere to be found. God yes, he wanted this from her.

She shut out the sounds of the crickets and the occasional ruffling of tree leaves to maximize the rhythm of his breaths, especially on the exhale when they became throaty and laced with deep moans. Dani fitted him back into her mouth, overcome with the sensations of having this worldly man at her mercy. She felt every inch of his smooth, hot skin as she tried to take more of him in. She wanted this to be good for him, not comparable to any he'd had before. She wanted to feel him all the way to the back of her throat but needed air and a chance to swallow. She slowly came off of him for a breath and to prepare better now that she knew his thickness and how much she could take in at once.

Before diving back down on him, she used each hand to spread his legs open wider. They fell easily. She tried resting her elbows between his thighs but it was very uncomfortable as the tiny pebbles in the soil dug into her skin and she fidgeted. Breaking the rule she thought she'd made clear, his hands were on her and she nearly pushed them away until she realized he was bringing her elbows up to rest on the tops of his thighs. That was much more comfortable. She watched as he then clasped his hands behind his head, his abs contracted as he held his shoulder blades just slightly above the ground.

"Thank you," she murmured.

He just held his lips closed tightly and watched her.

Dani used her hands to stroke his cock while she swirled her tongue over the head. His hips lifted for a second and then came back down. She sucked his tip into her mouth harder now and he bucked again. When his butt came off the ground with that thrust, she slid her hands underneath to cup and support him. His ass was soft and smooth and she loved the feel of it in her hands. She felt him push down with his tight butt muscles this time instead of lifting up like he was pinning her there. She gave him another squeeze, accepting he probably liked a bit more control when he was with a woman.

"Oh fuck, Dani."

She would have teased him by asking what he was moaning about and what he wanted more of but that would only serve to turn her on. That could not happen. The dark vibration she got from his three simple words nearly brought her away from the steely focus she had to put in to this blow job in order not to have herself coming right along with him.

Focus, she told herself.

Aware she was only going to be able to deny her need for him for so much longer, she got serious. One hand fisted around him at the base of his long and thick cock. She didn't need to hold him up straight because he was so hard he did that on his own. She did hold him still so that her mouth wouldn't have to worry about doing it. With the other hand she intended to extend his pleasure, and decided to run it up the center of his stomach. His abdominal muscles contracted again under her fingers and she rubbed up and down, adding her fingernails to the mix. His entire lower section shuddered and again, his hips thrust up. But this was good. He didn't do it just once. His hips rose and lowered in a steady rhythm that coincided with his breathing. She relaxed her neck and throat, tried to forget how tight her lips felt with them stretched around his thick cock. Tried to block out that this thrusting was his body's natural rhythm, the one she'd have had all to herself if they'd been able to make love.

He moaned louder. She responded by bobbing her head in rhythm to his thrusts and breaths. So full of him, she felt when his cock expanded several times. His body had to be preparing to pump his semen out and she prayed she'd be able to stay for him, drinking him in and not pull away.

He didn't say her name again, just breathed loudly like he might be doing it through gritted teeth. Finally she heard a thud near where his head would be, like he'd thrown it back against the ground and one final grunt then the back of her throat was bathed in hot spurts of his cum. For a second she tried to stay calm and loose enough to swallow it down but she had to come off of him and breathe. Had to stop and forget and find her control.

She hadn't realized until now that her heart was racing.

Long, deep and slow breaths. That's what she needed.

"I don't know what to say, sweetheart." His voice so tender and low surprised her as he wiped at her chin where some of him had spilled. "I want to be inside you, so fucking badly right now."

She swallowed, his saltiness still on her, splashed on the sides of her mouth, under her tongue. She was about to remind him why he couldn't but that she appreciated the sentiment when he reached out with one long arm and scooped her to his chest. He kissed her in the next second. His tongue nudged her lips to open, not taking no for an answer, and then he devoured her mouth. She shouldn't but he wasn't having it any other way. Only for a few moments, she told herself. Without her needing to interfere and remind, he slowed and then placed one final closing kiss over her lips.

If he hadn't have stopped when he did just now, she'd have orgasmed. That quickly, simply from that kiss. "Don't go," he whispered into her ear.

"I have to," she said hurriedly to him. "Back inside. Your mom, she shouldn't find us together." Dani grabbed her forehead and was just about up on her feet when she realized something else she needed to do for him. "Stefan, there is one promise I want you to make me."

"What?"

"Take your mom to Nashville." She wanted him to have his mom, knowing his soul would never be whole until he felt he'd done right by Gina. She wanted this man's heart to heal, at any cost, so he'd be capable of giving it to someone someday. Dani would make her own way, somehow. "I've decided to go back to school. But I can't do that knowing your mom needs me here. Take her, Stefan. You'll be doing me a favor taking her with you." She wanted to walk back and cup his jaw but had to get to her own bed and talk herself down from this crazy ride. She felt the tingles with each step she took over the cool, solid ground. A tear leaked down her cheek.

Please let that have worked.
****

Stars.

That's what he'd seen just now. Felt them too. He laid his hand over his chest where it burned from the inside out at what she'd just said and done for him.

He hoped like hell it was true that she wanted to go back to school. He'd get Benny to help him keep tabs on her and her tuition would be paid for in full, secretly of course because she was a stubborn pain in the ass about that shit.

The problem was, he knew what Dani was really doing. Sacrificing her livelihood to make taking his mom away easier for him. In a way, it's what Dad had done to get Mom to finish school. Hell, maybe it's what Mom had done, kicking Stefan out, to get him away from a town that would always see him in a bad light. Sacrifice.

Stefan took a deep breath and rubbed between his legs with the blanket in hand. He then rolled over onto his side. Dog tired, he couldn't sleep now. Not after that.

He wanted inside her. All the way, everywhere. Fuck, in her heart, where he didn't belong. He couldn't fuck with her that way. She was gonna be a mom soon. But he couldn't stay away.

He doubled his pillow and cranked his neck until it fit comfortably enough that he could close his eyes and hope for sleep.

In the morning, he told himself. Dani had her appointment. She'd get her answers and that would resolve her worries about being with him. Just once before he left. He wanted to give himself to this woman, all the way, no stops, no holding back. He'd ring every last ounce out of her and fill her back up. She'd never forget. He'd never forget.

He pulled his lips in tight, holding his breath for as long as he could until a yawn forced the air out.

He also had his own phone call to make. He'd always trusted Trista and she'd be able to tell him how to be with Dani and not hurt her baby. Because after tonight, Stefan knew one thing for certain. He wanted to make love to Dani. He also knew she could now claim something no other woman had. She was his first love.

Chapter Twenty

At some point today, Dani was going to need a moment alone, when she wasn't driving and needing to pay attention to the road, or sitting at the pancake house stuffing her mouth with Will, Stefan and Gina, to look at her little black and white photo of *him*.

No matter how hard she tried, she couldn't contain the smile. Her little guy, he was so tiny. She was bursting to share the news from her checkup and she hadn't felt happy and bursting at the same time in a long time.

The four of them stood inside Moonlight's official rose gardens, talking about how the pancakes had tasted as good as they remembered and how fragrant the air always was here this time of year. Will, gracious as always, agreed, going on today's experience alone. Gina looked wonderful. Her color was healthy, rivaling the peach of one of their favorite rose bushes. Dani noted that she stood near Stefan but not on his arm. Her balance had held through the first two thirds of the gardens today.

"So everything went well at your appointment?" Dani asked Mrs. C, smiling. She'd been too hungry at brunch and too busy smelling all the new blooms to talk. "I'm sorry I couldn't go with you guys." Dani didn't make up a lie, but didn't share that she'd been at her own doctor's visit either. Stefan knew, that was enough.

Gina smiled back. The sun fell perfectly over her white blonde hair, adding shine to the short strands. But Dani knew what really stood behind Mrs. C's bright outlook. Her son, who gleamed like a brilliant knight standing amongst the green hills filled with rows of oranges, reds and lavenders, with his white button down cargo shirt, sexy dark jeans and flip-flops.

Dani realized then that he was the one other person she could share her first baby picture with.

Her chin dipped because she also had another bit of news he'd be interested in. That bit warmed her right alongside the straight shot of sunshine and the sweet smell of roses. Doctor Zuniga had reassured Dani that the spasms she'd felt from her orgasms were not the same as labor contractions. And since Dani appeared to be having a normal pregnancy, she'd been given the okay to have sex. The whole drive over to the pancake house, Dani had repeated Doctor Z's words, that sex was a natural and normal part of pregnancy and that intercourse wouldn't harm the baby who was protected inside her womb.

Should she have been rehearsing so fervently? Probably not. Stefan was leaving in a few days now and hopefully, taking his mom with him. She knew that. But connecting with him each day had brought her further away from all the issues she had about being with him and closer to wanting—no, needing—to continue what they'd started. She didn't want to live her life never having had that intimacy with him. It shouldn't have turned out this way, but together, they made sense. In a perfect world, she'd let herself want a relationship with Stefan.

How wickedly would he grin when she told him they could make love without a condom? The excitement at being able to gift him with that one small thing before he left rivaled the hummingbirds flitting around in the perennial garden. The scent of the honeysuckle dipped into her happy space again.

She stole a quick look at him, aware she couldn't stare long with his mom standing so close. She'd bet he was pretending not to notice her eyeing him but the tiniest uptilt at the corner of his mouth peeked through. Somehow, she'd get him alone today.

She was about to say they should all check out the new composting exhibit before wrapping up today's visit when Stefan's fingers brushed against hers.

He pinned her with a stare and she watched his eyes focus solely on her, blocking the rest of the rose garden visitors out. He then turned to face Gina.

"Mom, can we sit for a minute? The three of us need to talk. There's a bench right over there."

Gina's skin crinkled at the corners of her eyes so she shaded them with her hand. "Okay, yes, that's fine," she said, looking as surprised as Dani felt.

What was going on and why hadn't this come up while they sat inside at a table? Or once they'd returned home? In the brief second that she could manage it while Gina said hello to a family who'd recognized her, Dani whispered at Stefan. "What are you doing, Hon?"

"Something I should have already done."

Why did that make her so nervous for him? Gina continued talking to a family who Dani recognized as the Franks, giving her more time to understand Stefan and what he was doing.

"Okay. I get that. But are you sure you want me involved?" Didn't he remember she'd given him an easy out when it came to relocating his mom? All he had to do was explain that Dani was returning to school and couldn't care for Mrs. C at the same time. Surely Mrs. C would understand, be supportive even, and go with him. Just because Dani hadn't as much as looked at a class catalogue in five years.

"What I have to say to Mom affects you too."

Bull shit. His face said there was more.

"Stefan."

225

He scratched the side of his face like he missed his whiskers all of a sudden. "It's no big deal. Stop freaking out. I would have done this during brunch but I forgot how much the good people of Moonlight love their pancakes."

"So there were too many people inside Pop's?" But that made no sense. The man had to have lived half his life amongst crowds. Hadn't the magazine article listed Sin Pointe's first leg tour dates and how many shows already had SOLD OUT listed in all caps? She saw his glance cut to his foot as he shuffled it across the pavement. "Did someone recognize you at Pop's, Stefan?"

"Yeah," was all he said.

She wouldn't push. Especially not now that Gina had said her final goodbyes to the Frank family and walked back toward her, Stefan and a very quiet Will. It was amazing how such a petite, unassuming little woman like Gina Calderon could turn a grown man into a statue of himself.

Gina's face crumpled again as she re-took her place in their group but this time she stood near Will, facing Dani and Stefan. Dani could tell herself Gina was squinting because of the sun but she'd be lying. Shit. Well, looked like it was time to put on her big girl panties again and act like she was about to be a mom. Gina would understand. Wouldn't she?

****

"It's a beautiful day, huh Mrs. C?" Will said when his mom rejoined them. "Before we leave you'll have to help me pick out my first rose bush seeds."

"It is and I'm happy to, Will. Son, before we all chat, can I speak with you for a moment alone?"

Uh-oh. Stefan's gut tightened at the way Mom's hands were folded too perfectly, her fingers laced just so, like she was praying for him or something.

"Sure, Mom," he said and began to lead her to a shady area near some of the reddest roses he'd ever seen. He'd wanted to have Dani present so that when he laid out his plan to his mom, Dani would be held to the sly promise she'd made him of going back to school.

"Mrs. C?" Dani's voice stopped Stefan and he and his mom turned together.

"Yes dear?" said Mom.

Poor girl. All eyes were on her and he knew right away she'd never make it up on stage. You had to be able to turn that shit off and Dani clearly was wired to fidget in situations like this. What was she doing, anyway?

It hurt Stefan to watch her squirm like that. "Will, here." Stefan tossed him his old wallet. "Pick something out for Tris? I need to talk to Mom for a second." He looked to Dani and tried to reassure her that he'd do his best not to blow her cover. Nothing about her being pregnant or the fact she was messing around with him. Clearly Dani still wasn't ready for his mom to know.

Dani stepped closer to him but he brushed her off and mouthed, "Don't worry."

He waited while Dani and Will wandered inside the gift shop, out of ear shot.

What did he say? Where did he start? He had such little practice communicating with her lately. "Mom, I'm glad you're feeling better. I was worried the past couple of days."

She reached over and patted his arm. He guessed maybe she had the same problem with him. That was his fault too, he knew it. Something inside him needed that to change. To be better. He loved his mother so much. Had missed her, no matter what had happened in their past. He

227

needed not just to hear her tell him she was proud and loved him. He craved the feeling of those things. But then she spoke up. "Dani takes good care of me, son. You don't need to worry."

He could sense there was more, something else she wasn't saying. Maybe because of the way she held her chin up but let her eyes blink closed more than usual. He didn't know what to say so he let a truth slip. "She has impressed me. I trust her to take good care of you. I'm glad you have her, Mom."

"Me too. Son," his mom breathed in and out. "There is something I need to know." She paused and he stayed silent, stealing a glance toward the gift shop where Dani watched him like a hawk.

Back to his mom.

He felt like that sixteen year old again and this was the same conversation they'd had the day Amanda's mother had called and told Mom what he'd done. Seeing Amanda's older sister a few booths over during breakfast—one of those who hadn't changed in twenty years, not even her hair do—apparently married now and with kids, had given him instant anxiety.

At sixteen, Stefan hadn't known how to answer for himself, except to beg his mom to believe him when he promised he would take care of the baby. That he'd never told Amanda he wouldn't. She must have gotten scared and made it up. That's when Mom had told him what Amanda's mother had said. That there would be no baby. That Mom should be ashamed of her son for getting a fourteen year old girl pregnant and then causing her so much stress that she'd miscarried. Stefan's eyes felt raw but he was incapable of moving a finger right now. Mom's silence was hanging over him and whatever question she had kept him still. He didn't so much as blink.

"Can you tell me why Sherri from the Women's Clinic called for Dani yesterday?"

Oh shit, he hadn't planned on her throwing that out there. He couldn't tell her. That was Dani's decision to make. Even if he could talk about that, the thought of shaming his mom again crippled his brain. Even if it had nothing to do with him, he knew she'd most likely be disappointed in Dani.

His mom kept on. "You wouldn't remember this, but Sherri has been an obstetrical nurse at that clinic for going on forty years now. She's one of the very best Moonlight has ever seen. Sandra said she'd never have gotten through Dani's birth had it not been for Sherri's expertise. I saw her after Sandra passed and she still had that calming air about her. Her voice is so striking, so deep for a woman, but I suppose that's part of the soothing she brings to her patients. Which is why if Dani is being seen by her, she's in good hands." His mom's thin lips drew out in an air tight line and she patted her blouse with small but stern hands Stefan remembered from his youth. His mom had never spanked him. She hadn't needed to. Something about disappointing her had always been enough for him. It was the main reason he'd left home. To avoid shaming her again at all cost.

Stefan wished he could shoot back something clever like the fact that he was sure women went to clinics like that for all kinds of female issues, not just pregnancy. But his mom wasn't an idiot. No, she knew what was up.

And, he wasn't about to lie.

If he lied right now, that would prove all the horrible things he'd felt from neighbors, the Coopers, teachers, his own parents, were true. He was here to be different. Spending time with Mom and Dani had convinced him that he did want to be better, too. More importantly, it was possible.

Without a clue as to where to start, his only thought took him back to the very beginning. "Mom, I ran into Dani before I got to your house the first day of my visit. At the time I had no idea who she was but—"

He felt a soft hand lace with his fingers.

"I needed his help, Gina," said Dani, squeezing his hand. "I had a really bad day and we just happened to run into each other getting gas, right when I needed a friend." Dani looked up at him and he felt them fall down some invisible deep pit together. No, this wasn't part of his plan. He was supposed to tell his mom he wanted to take her to Nashville and that Dani supported the move because *she* was getting her ass back in school to finish her degree. And he was doing the right thing by leaving her alone to do that.

"Actually Mom, no need to rehash all that. All I need to know is if you're willing to move to Nashville with me? Since Dani intends on—"

Dani shot out, "No, what I have to say is important. I should have told you but things are complicated and I have had so much on my mind lately."

Mom looked at him and Dani like she was stuck between who she needed to address first.

Stefan felt the need to save Dani from going any further. She'd said plenty and had to know how much it meant to him. She didn't need to throw herself into the fire just to make things easier for him with his mom. And she wasn't wiggling out of what she'd promised him. "Mom, I'm the one who should have said something. It's my fault," he said, trying to win back the conversation from his little heart thief pain in the ass.

His mom stopped him. "Kids, I think I know what's going on. Son, Dani has a boyfriend. Okay, I know that. He is a soldier who is deployed right now. He's a good man. Thomas treats her well. Dani, you need and deserve that. With all you do for me, dear. And in turn, all she does for you, son." Mom's brow worried itself into a crinkle as she gave them her take on things. Her hand patted his forearm and then left him to squeeze Dani's fingers like Mom was asking him to fade away and hoped he hadn't already messed things up.

What could he say? He heard the warning in her voice and felt it in her hand. That Stefan should honor what Dani and the soldier had. But Mom didn't know the truth and it wasn't his place to share what had happened. Stefan was going to come off as a selfish prick, no matter what he said. He kept it short and simple. "I know, Mom." Not at all what they were supposed to be talking about, this detour had his head pounding.

What else was there to say? Stefan let out a breath and cleared his throat at the same time.

Apparently, there was more to say. He just never expected Dani to step up the way she did.

"Mrs. C … Gina, Thomas and I aren't together anymore." Dani's eyelashes fell and flashed back open. Stefan wanted to tell her she didn't have to do this. "He emailed to let me know he fell in love with someone else. Stefan isn't ruining anything for me. He's been the one person I've felt comfortable talking to about this. I don't know what I would have done without him."

Stefan barely had time to soak that all in because Mom's hands unclasped and she covered her eyes with one. To anyone else, it would look like she was shading herself from the sun but Stefan knew better. She probably couldn't stand the sight of him right now.

"Dani," Mom paused. "Is there anything else you need to tell me?"

That look would drag anyone's most well-kept secret out into the light. Stefan had joked about mom vision with his friends and their kids but this was no laughing matter.

Dani started clenching her fingers and Stefan took her closest hand into his. Mom saw it and breathed in so deep that the flowers of her silk blouse moved up and down like there was a machine under there pumping might through her small, thin frame. "I'm pregnant," said Dani.

"Son, what have you done?"

Holy fuck. His mom thought he was the reason for Dani's visit to the clinic. The funny thing about that, aside from it being impossible? He wished he was.

Dani started to explain but Stefan stopped her.

"No, Mom's right."

So much hurt welled up inside him that he didn't know what to do with it. Rage told him he was a pussy if he didn't stay there and fight for who he was, the real him, the one who cared about his mom, even though she'd just torn him down to nothing and hadn't even addressed him asking her to move to Nashville. Reality told him it wouldn't matter. That fucking emotion he hated to even admit he'd let drive him this week reminded him that he had to think of Dani and what was best for her.

"Dani, please go back inside with Will. Mom and I aren't done talking."

He could tell she didn't want to, but Dani complied as he knew she would.

"Mom, just so we're clear, I did not get Dani pregnant."

"I know that, son."

"Then why did you ask what I'd done?"

Mom took a moment to search his face. He couldn't tell, but was sure he saw some of that old pain come to the surface again. "Stefan, I can see you like Dani, and she clearly feels the same. But she just said so herself. She's having a child with Thomas."

"Thom, who dumped her in an email," he said curtly.

"I understand, son. But what do you think Thomas will do when she tells him? I assume she hasn't done that yet. I could be wrong I suppose."

"You are wrong, mom. Dani told him."

"He's a good man, Stefan. He'll do the right thing."

"The right thing? What is that, Mom?"

"I love Dani like a daughter. And you, you are my son, Stefan. My one and only child. Listen to me, please. I only say these things because I want to protect both you and Dani. I don't want either of your hearts to be broken."

His mom, better than anyone, knew what that felt like. But she didn't know everything Stefan's heart bled with when it came to Dani and how he wasn't even here to win Dani. In fact it was the opposite. He was trying to let her go. Like that stupid saying people in love always said about letting shit go so it could come back to you if it was meant to be. Fuck all those people. He breathed in to calm his ass down.

"What exactly are you saying, Mom?"

"Promise me you won't interfere until Dani has a chance to speak with Thomas in person. Let them settle whatever needs to be figured out when he comes home. Don't you see? If you don't allow them to do that, you risk leaving Dani and Thomas with too many uncertainties. Things she'll always wonder about between them. I say this because I love you, Stefan. I pray you never know that kind of heartache."

Stefan wiped at his mouth and cleared his throat, swallowed down a couple tears too. "I just want to take care of you both, Mom."

"I understand. You have to trust me on this. Give her the space and time she needs to come to terms with it all. Promise me, son."

"I shouldn't have come back. I promise, I won't be a problem."

"Stefan," Mom began. "About going to Nashville with you."

But with that, he waved Will over who stood outside of the gift shop with a plastic souvenir bag and Dani. Stefan needed out of there. Thank God Will was with him.

"It's okay, Mom. I'm a big boy. No need to say it." He left his mom's side after giving her a goodbye kiss on the cheek, effectively cutting off the part where she again told him no thanks.

"Hey, I'll ride home with them. Go cool off," said Will.

Stefan just nodded at his friend. He didn't let himself look at Dani.

Chapter Twenty-One

A little while later, Stefan pulled into his driveway. It had been years since he'd last been to this house. It used to make him smile, knowing he'd bought it for his mom. Even though she hadn't wanted it, he still felt good that it was here if she ever needed it.

The vision he'd had of ever walking inside, hand in hand with Dani, kicked his foolish ass good and hard.

He was standing at the front door, fishing for the key, when his phone rang. It was Trista. Stefan nearly let it go to voicemail but he couldn't do that to her. They didn't do that to each other. Too much bad scary shit they'd saved each other from over the years meant answering even when you felt like crap. He wouldn't let her worry and took her call.

"Hey Tris, can I call you back?"

"Sure. Five minutes?"

No, he'd meant like in a week or so but she wouldn't let him off so easily. He knew why. He'd mentioned needing her help in the message he'd left her and probably sounded like a whipped little desperate pussy when he'd done it. She wouldn't let that go.

Stefan cradled the cell between his ear and shoulder and finally finagled the door open.

"Five works. Bye, babe," he said and closed the door behind him, trying his best to sound like himself.

Inside, he hovered in the foyer, thinking long and hard.

He'd have to be dumb not to know Dani would try to contact him. Should he talk to Dani about what his mom had said, now that he could replay the conversation without the need to pound something? Try and convince her to give things with her baby's father a chance? Maybe this guy would have a change of heart when he came back and saw her swollen belly with his child inside. How different would Stefan's life had been if he'd had that chance with Amanda?

That shit pissed him off so bad.

He didn't need to call Tris back. His phone rang and it was her. He flipped on a light switch, glad to see property management had done its well-paid job of keeping the power on and accepted the call, even though Tris had jumped the gun and called early. He'd have done the same thing for her.

"Hey baby, what's wrong," Tris asked right from the jump. She knew him so well. "You said you needed help. I'm all ears." A baby, most likely her little Eddie, jabbered in the background. Trista cooed at him sweetly.

"It's not important, I can call back later," Stefan offered. Did he really need Tris to tell him it was safe to have sex with a pregnant lady? Dani had made it to her checkup this morning and with the way she'd been sneaking looks at him during their pancakes, his guess was that she'd asked the doc and been answered. Of course none of that mattered now.

"No, come on now. You know I'll get it out of you."

She was right. But things just didn't seem meant to be with him and Dani. Going in to all that over the phone with Tris made him want to scratch out his eyes. He could just pretend, maybe that would be easier. "I met someone," he said, amazed he'd admitted that out loud. "Tris? You there?"

"Sweetie! That's wonderful, sorry I just, was a little surprised is all. So tell me about this someone."

Trista used soft words to calm her baby after that burst of excitement she'd had for him. He could see her with the cute little pill bouncing on her hip, even in his rotten mood. Dani would be a good mom like Tris.

Where did he start? Admitting all this would hurt later when he had to tell Tris there would be no one coming back with his sorry ass. "Her name is Dani. Not that it matters now," he muttered and wiped his hand over his hair. He scratched at the stubble already growing back. That shit was coming off when he got off the phone.

"And when and where did you meet?"

Obviously she hadn't heard all of what he'd said. She cooed more for Eddie. He wanted to smile but didn't have it in him.

Trista didn't need to hear his pity party. What good would it do to bring her down? He'd keep up with the charade.

"Stef?"

Fuck, this was gonna hurt.

"She's an old family friend actually." He thought of the thing he cherished most about Dani. "And she's been taking care of my mom."

"Well, she must be pretty special for you to call just to tell me about her. You sure there's nothing else. You said you needed help."

"Oh, you know me. I just wanted to call and hear your gorgeous voice."

"Yeah, nice try. Stefan. Listen to me. You're a good man. I've always known that when you found the right girl she was gonna be very lucky and it was gonna knock you on your ass." Tris giggled warmly. He missed her. She'd been like a loving sister to him. Never judged him not once. Kicked his ass plenty of times but out of love. "Is this the 'I've been knocked on my ass, Tris, and

I don't know how to get back up' call I've been waiting to get from you? Is that the help you need?"

What could he say? That's exactly what this was. He just hadn't realized it in time. He'd been playing a game this whole time with Dani and now it was too late. He'd lost.

"Lucky is a lucky man, Tris."

"He is," she said. He could see her winking in his mind. "But that's the thing. I'm just as lucky as him. Without each other, we'd have self-destructed. But had we met when I wasn't ready, it never would have worked. You, of all people, know that's true."

He took a moment to let the reasons behind her words sink in. Remembering that night when he and Lucky had found her and Jaxon beaten and left like trash in the street bubbled to the top of his heart. He hated remembering that shit but he also never wanted to forget it. You had to protect the ones you loved. It's why he'd kept the number of people he loved to a minimum. All the time he spent away from home, it would kill him not to be there if he was needed. "I do. You're so fucking smart, Tris."

"I love you too, Stef. So this Dani, is she someone I might get to meet anytime soon? Jaxon was telling Lucky and me at dinner last night that tour rehearsals are just about to get started week after next. He was joking— at least I think he was joking—that he hadn't heard much from you and Will. That he was gonna have to go snatch you guys up and drag you back home. Have you asked your Dani to come to opening night? I'd love to meet her. I'm so glad the tour's kicking off in Nashville."

If she only knew how wanting that had driven him insane, because now there was no chance of it happening. "Not yet. I was still trying to figure that part out. Like I said, she takes care of my mom. So…" His mom who wouldn't be coming back with him either.

Before he could go any further, Tris chimed in. "You know, Lucky and I were just driving home the other day and there's a large ranch style house, it's pretty big, between us and the dress shop, that just went up for sale. It's got its own little running creek with the cutest little bridge. Lots of trees. Not too far from the studio. It made me think of you since I hear from Jaxon every other day that you still haven't gotten off your ass and bought a place yet. His words, not mine, sweetie. It's huge. Has to be at least five bedrooms. Guess what else?"

"What?" As long as he was torturing himself.

"It's white."

Stefan chuckled for the first time in a few days it seemed. She was persistent. "What do I need with such a big ass house, Tris? Huh?" he was mostly teasing her. He'd already planned to find a place big enough to fit at least him and Will. The dream of including his mom and Dani popped like he'd just shot a bubble with a mean ass sharp little needle. His head throbbed. Rubbing his temples did nothing.

"Well, a nice big house solves your lady problem. Mrs. Gina and Miss Dani."

She paused but not long enough for him to stutter through anything more coherent than, "Whoa."

"Don't whoa me. I'll text you the realtor's number. You do need a place, after all. In the meantime, I have one more question about this someone special."

"Okay, shoot." Why the hell not? His heart couldn't hurt any worse at this point and Tris was like the big sister he'd never had who found all kinds of crazy joy planning out his fairy tale life. Yeah, he'd pay like hell for it when they hung up but he'd give her this much.

"Does she make you happy, Stef?"

"Fuck. Yes she does." His heart may as well have flat lined. His fucking eyes thought he'd let them get away with tears but he wiped that shit away. "She doesn't close her eyes when we kiss."

Tris cooed quietly on the other end, this time he was sure it was for his pathetic, soppy ass and not her baby. Stefan knew exactly what her face would look like with that big ass smile and turquoise eyes. Yeah, it was no secret, he'd crushed on Tris back when she'd finally hit twenty and had been working for the band a few years. But both he and Jaxon had declared her off limits. No matter what. She was their adopted little sister. If Lucky ever broke her heart, Stefan would hurt him. Bad.

"Lucky doesn't either. They're not ashamed of us. No matter how much we've screwed up in the past. It's freaking precious."

"Tris, I want it to work with her. But there's more to it than me being happy." It was like he physically couldn't keep the damn truth to himself.

"I understand, Stef. I do. Trust me on this because I speak from experience. If it's meant to be, it doesn't matter how much the two of you, or the world for that matter, tries to fuck it up. Eventually, love gets us all, babe. Even your hot, horny little ass."

"I love you, Trista."

"I know. Glad you called, aren't ya?"

"Smart ass. I'll see you soon."

"Go get our girl. Bye, Hon."

They hung up. Stefan took a few minutes and a lazy stroll through the bottom level of the house to get a grip on all the shit the call with Tris had just stirred up. His mom's words were still stuck in the back of his mind, mostly because he cared about Dani and knew he wanted the best for her and her baby. But fuck if he didn't know with everything he was that he could be good for her. For them, he amended. He punched the wall. Property management had a hole to fix.

Chapter Twenty-Two

Dani was lost.

Will had sent her off with the address programmed into the GPS and the cryptic message that if Stefan screwed things up, to give him another chance. Actually Will had asked Dani to give Stefan several chances because he would most surely screw up more ways than one. Guy thing, he'd said and hugged her.

Finally, she pulled the Buick through a thick section of tree line and found the private driveway that led to the biggest home she'd ever seen. Mansion came to mind.

She parked alongside Stefan's Mercedes and walked up to the front door.

With as much Will Cordero as she could muster, she knocked loudly.

It took a minute, time she used to scope out the several A-frame levels and windows and garages of the home, but eventually the door opened.

"What are you doing here?" he asked.

Chance number one used and now onto number two. He wasn't going to make this easy but she was determined to get inside. Yes, to the house, but more importantly, his heart.

"The least you could say is 'Please come inside.'"

"No, the best thing I could say is go away, Dani."

Okay, so she had two choices here, if this was how he was going to play. She could either slam him with the L word which would surely leave him stunned enough to let her pass inside or she could go this route.

"You owe me dinner and amazing sex, Hon. I'm not leaving until I get both. Unless you're incapable of providing those things for a woman."

Bingo. He stepped out of the doorway and let her pass.

Yes, that had been a clever little intro of hers because Stefan wasn't the only one who knew how to get what he wanted when he really wanted his way. With the way he still stood there taking her in right now, her Superman, she envisioned at least a few more chances in his future. But she had to make sure they also took a moment to talk. Her little black and white print out was in her purse on the breakfast bar in the dining room. She'd probably need help getting back to it. First things first, pregnant lady and all.

"Stefan, am I close to a restroom?"

His jaw flexed and she found that the light stubble growing in was the hottest look she'd seen on him.

"Take your pick," he said. He sounded distracted.

The way he had yet to sit down on any of the luxurious furniture, Stefan seemed uncomfortable, too. Maybe he was still thinking about the rose garden fiasco. It had taken a couple hours of talking but apparently, she was in love with Stefan and when she talked about him, it was clear. She'd earned Gina's blessing to be here and some very good news that Dani couldn't wait to share with Stefan. After she peed.

Dani wandered around some more, thinking she'd found a bathroom only to be wrong. She continued checking doors while her bladder squeezed. Their morning had started out so scattered. Coming here to find Stefan felt right on the drive over. Landing at his doorstep to a stiffer than usual bad boy had given her doubts but who wouldn't have felt that way after the way

Gina had unintentionally hurt him? That was the other reason Dani had to be here. To share good news and to make sure Stefan knew he wasn't the bad guy. Bad boy, yes. Bad guy, no way.

How hard had it been to hold in the good news she'd received from her OB doctor? Incredibly so. Especially after last night where she'd not just broken her own rule but smashed it to pieces by going to him in the back yard. The thrill still sent little reminders throughout her body. She'd been letting thoughts of Stefan turn her insides to goo the whole way over here since she didn't have to fight his effect on her body anymore.

And now here they were at this castle. It was filled with elegant furniture but empty of life. Regardless, it was the most breathtaking home Dani had ever stepped foot in.

She and Stefan might make love here tonight. Her breath dropped out of her lungs.

Looking around, she couldn't believe this gorgeous home had gone unlived in for years. Wandering down a hallway not too far from the grand staircase, she began trying more doors.

That's when she heard him call up to her. "Come back to the stairs. It's on the other side, third door down. You went the wrong way at the top." His voice lacked its usual warmth but she'd just find a way to combat that.

"Thanks," she called down.

Clearly she'd gone the wrong way, in many ways, but that was the danger and wonder of Stefan. How appropriate that her favorite country song summed him up so perfectly. He was a real bad boy but such a good man. All Dani knew was that when she was around him, she smiled. She laughed. He challenged her like nobody's business but that was good. Her coming life change wasn't so scary when she pictured him involved. And it had nothing to do with the fact he could afford a house like this. *A spare house*, she corrected. If he'd only just let her in.

Holy cow. She pushed open what should be the bathroom door only to spot a fireplace. She backed out and tried the next door but that was a bedroom, furnished like the rest of the home with model quality décor. The bed was easily the size of all the beds at Gina's put together.

She tried the next door and that was an office. Painted dark and with sections of padded walls. What in the world?

His deep baritone voice caught her off guard when he was inches behind her, still more raw than warm but an instant shot of heat through her weary bones nonetheless.

"You passed it again," he said, hiking one eyebrow higher than the other like a kindergartner could have found it so why couldn't she. Then he laid his hand on her shoulder and turned her around. "Back here."

"Hold on, what in the world are the padded walls for in that one I just opened?"

His handsome face brightened, washing away some of that leery vibe coming off him. They took a few steps back and peered into the room in question together. "This is where I bring my innocent victims. What, your last boyfriend didn't have a sex chamber at his home?"

Dani's eyes popped wide. "Very funny. I uh, I assumed I was the first person you'd brought here." She wasn't letting him get away with this terrible teasing, glad his innate charm was back but aware it still felt like his heart wasn't exactly in it. "And, I didn't realize you were my boyfriend now."

Not thinking, she pulled part of her lip through her teeth and held it there. That was a dangerous word to attach to him, especially after this morning. But she'd taken Will's warning that Stefan wouldn't make it easy now that he was convinced he had to let her go to figure things out with Thom. She'd do whatever she could to keep that from happening. There were things to figure out which was why she would do the right thing and see Thom in person. To discuss things like the role he'd play in the baby's life. But that was it. She had to make Stefan see that. She felt none of the things for Thom that she felt for Stefan. Not one.

His look darkened and she wished she hadn't said anything. He'd been playful for a split second and now she couldn't judge his mood at all.

"You are. The first. And this is a home studio. The padding is for the sound. When I bought this place for Mom, I wanted one room where I could do music when I visited." A somber shadow fell back over him and he took on more of the dark Superman she'd felt so a part of when she'd been hurting so badly at the truck stop that morning. He'd brought her out of that, in a matter of minutes.

She sensed she needed to tread lightly on the subject of this house and his mom. "That's a really nice thought, Stefan. I talked to her before I came over here."

"Yep. Well, the bathroom is…" He passed over the subject and she didn't want to bring him back to it, but she couldn't help it.

"You bought this place for your mom. What happened?"
"She said no thank you. No big deal."

Clearly that wasn't true. His eyes said he was as baffled speaking about it now as he probably had been the day he'd offered it and had his gift rejected. "I'm sorry, Stefan. It is rather big. Maybe she just worried about being able to take care of this beautiful home on her own." Dani had to admit she was confused too. Whatever the reason for Gina's rejection of Stefan, she'd had a change of heart and Dani couldn't wait to tell him his mom would consider moving.

"I guess. Hey, I thought you needed to use the bathroom," he said, shoving his hands down into his pockets.

When she didn't move, he brought his hand out and skimmed the small of her back as he guided her to the door with the fireplace. He pushed the door open with his other hand and stretched it out, ushering her in. Yes she had to pee like a mad woman but she was more concerned about the hurt she saw on his handsome face and why he wasn't insisting on coming in with her. Bathrooms were kind of their thing. She must have been just as easy to read.

"Dani, do your business and then we'll talk." He smiled softly for her but it didn't reach his chocolate eyes.

"I do have some good news to share with you," she said.

"Okay."

Dani stepped inside, closed the door behind her and nearly passed out. Fireplace, double sinks, a Jacuzzi tub that took up one whole corner and spanned two walls. The shower was attached so you could walk right into it through a crystal clean glass door, straight from the tub. A white fluffy rug laid on the floor that looked more inviting than her bed and the outward facing walls where the tub was lined up weren't walls at all. They were giant windows that looked out into the wooded back yard. There wasn't another house anywhere in sight. The blinds were hiked all the way up. Dani set her purse on the ultra-clean floor at her feet, pulled her dress up and flopped onto the toilet, looking out at the amazing view, unbelieving. As she relieved her aching bladder, she felt him kick. She wished Stefan was in there with her so she could have let him feel it too.

****

Stefan was busy setting out the dinner he'd gone ahead and ordered in for them. It was early, but she had a healthy appetite and without a meal, he didn't know what he'd do. Even though he'd decided he had to back off, she still called to him. All the women who he'd thought had been drop dead gorgeous, none compared to her. He knew now that the call went deeper than looks and sex. Shit, he hadn't even been with Dani. Not really.

"Dinner's ready," he said, trying to keep himself in check when all he wanted was to stake his claim on her. Thom was a lucky man. And a dead man if he ever hurt her.

Dani walked in from the deck out back and his mouth watered. She was truly an amazing woman. He hadn't seen her wear pants in a while, not even her yellow stretchy track suit he was so fond of. Right now he could barely tear his gaze away from the halter dress she had on. The white was stunning on her, making her look even more tanned. Her black hair was only half pulled up, the rest fell in loose curls, over her shoulders.

"Here." He offered her a seat as he dried a serving dish he'd used but she held something in her hands that brought out the most exquisite smile he'd ever seen. "What's that?" he couldn't help but ask.

"It's a picture of my baby," she beamed and held it out to him. "You're the first person I wanted to show it to."

He stopped what he was doing, speechless. The plate he was holding crashed to the counter which knocked something else in its path into the sink. Dani's dark eyes popped wide when he met her halfway between the kitchen and deck and took the black and white photo into his hands. The print out was already wrinkled.

"I've probably taken it in and out of my purse about a million times already. I'll probably ruin it but I can't stop looking at it. He's so beautiful."

"He? You know it's a boy?"

"Yep. See there," she pointed to a blurry white shadow. Stefan couldn't believe he could actually make out fingers, toes, a nose. It was the creepiest yet the coolest thing he'd ever seen. It was impossible not to feel her joy.

"Your son," was all he could get out.

Now she was speechless and shook her head. When she did that, tears fell onto her cheeks.

Stefan held her tight in his arms. Knowing he had to let her go. Knowing he couldn't get in the way.

Dani's tears continued to fall so they just stood there in the kitchen. Finally Stefan had to say something.

"Dani, you're gonna be a wonderful mom. You love your baby so much, sweetheart." Could he say the rest? He had to. "Trust me, you don't want me around. Staying here, going back to school, for real, *that's* the right path for you. Not me."

"Don't say that," she said through sniffles.

"Come here, sit down." He helped her into the stool. "Hey, my mom was right to jump to the conclusion she did earlier. She was only going on the way I've acted my whole life."

"No, she just didn't understand. She thought somehow you'd gotten me pregnant and thought Thom and I were still together. She told me at the house that she loves you and will miss you when you go. And—"

"No Dani. Stop. When I go. It's what I do. I leave."

Just like his dad. No better. No worse. No different.

****

Wow. Had Will pegged this perfectly or what? Stefan was determined not to hear her. What hurt Dani most was how his confidence had been shattered by a ten minute conversation in a silly rose garden.

She didn't even remember that she'd just been crying and the wetness on her cheeks surprised her when she wiped a piece of hair from her face. "But you come back. And when you do, you bring the best laughs and joy with you. You bring yourself."

"No, don't do that. Don't make me out to be some good guy, Dani. It'll only hurt you in the end." He paused and then stabbed her with a look sharper than steel. "You sucked my cock good last night, but that doesn't mean you own me. I don't owe you anything."

Her face flamed with sheer anger. She nearly spit the word asshole right back in his face but remembered Will's warning. She could be just as stubborn. "Try again. I did suck your cock good and no, you don't owe me anything. But you will hear me out. You know who else leaves their loved ones behind? How about soldiers?"

"That's different and you know it."

"How so? They stay gone for months. Thom gets one two-week break half-way through his year-long tour. He comes home one time, Stefan. In an entire year. How is that different than what you do?"

Stefan looked like she'd shot him. He held his hands over his midsection and hunched over before he righted himself again.

"I don't know. It just is. I'm not laying my life on the line for anyone."

"But you're putting it on hold so you can make all those people who love your music happy." She wouldn't stop now. "I bet if you were with someone, you'd find a way to see that person, no matter how far away you were. And I bet that person would be thankful, and…" Her eyes welled up with tears again. "So very happy for each moment, no matter how short or how much time passed between visits. Or how big of a mean jerk you could be sometimes."

The amount of time he stayed with his head bowed down killed Dani. Losing him in a couple days hadn't hurt before because she realized she'd held out hope that things would work out between them. That her Superman would figure it out and fix it all. He'd invite his mom to Nashville and Dani too. All she needed was an invitation and his ability to wait two measly months for her to arrive.

"Stefan, look at me."

She waited patiently.

"I'll just hurt you, Dani. Don't you get it? I fucking love you and I'd hurt you."

Her breath tunneled around her lungs and her knees threatened to give out but she wouldn't stop until she'd convinced him he would not do that. Not if he … not if he loved her. The way she loved him back.

"Why do you keep saying that? Leaving, when it's your job, doesn't hurt the one you love."

Her mind was nearly useless after his use of the L word. Maybe he was trying to tell her he wouldn't be faithful.

"You don't understand me, Dani."

"Then help me out here. Are you saying you'd sleep around on the road? Is that some inevitable part of you being Stefan Calderon, bass player?"

Crap. He wasn't answering her.

"Fuck, I don't know. Maybe. I've never been tested like that."

"What the hell do you mean?"

Again he went silent. And this time he got up out of his stool and walked to the sink. As if they hadn't just been in an industrial sized conversation, he reached up and pulled a glass from a cupboard and filled it with water. He guzzled the entire thing down then filled it up and walked back over to her. He set the glass down in front of her, nudging her hand which she realized was in a tight fist.

"Fighting can't be good for the baby. Dinner's getting cold. Let's eat. Then maybe we'll talk more."

Maybe we'll talk more? Who did he think he was? Ending their discussion like that. But her chest had tightened and she knew he was right when she took in a deep breath and felt the built up tension leave and her body relax back to normal.

She hated that he was right. But if he thought she wouldn't fight for him, he was dead wrong. She took the glass of water, emptying it then handed it back to him.

"What did you get?"

She could play nice while they ate. He loved her.

Stefan brought their plates over. He sat down across from her and stabbed a peapod and a chunk of pink salmon, shaking his head as he bit the food from the fork and chewed. He stabbed another and another bite.

Whoever had made this man, had gotten so many things so very right. No matter that all those things combined made her absolutely crazy.

He loved her. He'd said so.

She chewed, and tried not to cry smile.

Chapter Twenty-Three

Stefan remembered never to order salmon again when he lived thirty miles from the closest restaurant willing to deliver. Or when a fight was pending with the woman he loved but couldn't keep, and the fish was going to set out for longer than he planned.

She looked like he'd treated her to a feast fit for royalty but it was just take out. Dani was taking such care with each bite. Shit, he hadn't been paying her enough. It was something he would fix. He could imagine her face when he told her he wanted to up her salary since he wasn't separating his mom and her. She'd probably spit fire and spear him with eye daggers. Well, he would never tell her. But the thought of doing things like that for her managed to make him hard. He adjusted himself below the table and watched her chew. As soon as she was done he'd send her home, hoping she would forget his declaration.

"That was good. Thank you. I was really hungry."

He was just glad she wasn't yelling, forcing him to talk about shit he'd be better off forgetting. He never should have said he loved her. It was a selfish move, but he couldn't take it back now.

"You're welcome."

The shorter his answers, the longer the looks she gave him.

When she finally got to her dessert, he was mesmerized as she pulled her fork out of her mouth for the last time and he imagined how lucky the berries were. Now was the time to send her home. Why bother fighting some more only to have to send her off anyway? He reminded himself that he couldn't keep her and he didn't want to have to explain why.

"Dani, you should go back home now."

"I knew you'd say that. And it's not happening. Not unless we go together."

Stubborn pain in his ass. Fuck, he didn't want her to leave.

"What are you doing, Dani?"

"I forgot my sister picked this out for me a few summers ago when we got sunburns and needed extra loose clothing. Luckily it fits."

Her rambling blew dangerous gusts over the fire already burning inside him.

"That's not what I asked you."

"But you like it?" she asked, killing him with her hiked shoulder.

Stefan stood up. He took two steps until he stood directly in front of her. "You know I fucking like it." He grabbed her hand and pulled it away from the strap where she nearly untied the halter top. "Get your ass home, now."

"Or else what, Stefan?"

"Don't play with me, Dani. This isn't a game."

"Oh, but I thought that's exactly what our whole time together has been. It's too bad, you know."

"What's too bad?" His jaw clenched so tight he barely got that out. What the hell was she thinking, baiting him like that?

"That you're so god damned afraid to win."

"I'm not afraid, sweetheart." But there was nothing sweet about the feelings welling up in him. The taste in his mouth was bitter as he thought about the shit keeping Dani from him. He kept her wrist in his fist and pushed her until her back met up with the wall. He'd been gentle so as not to hurt her. He pinned her wrists to the wall in both his hands and leaned down so that he spoke inches from her face. His lips ached to kiss her. "What the fuck is so hard for you to understand. I. Don't. Want. To. Hurt. You. The only way to keep that from happening is for you to go back to my mom's. Done. Finished. Not playing this shit with you, Dani." A thousand slaps would have felt better than having to speak to her that way.

"Let go of my wrists, Stefan."

Instantly, he obeyed her wish. At last, she'd seen his reason and was grabbing her purse to leave. But no, she only took it to put the baby picture from her dress pocket back inside. She took two steps toward the stairs.

"Dani," he said, tiring of not being able to just love her.

"If you're not afraid to win, prove it. Once and for all." She made her way up the stairs, one slow step at a time, and disappeared into the bathroom.

Fuck. He waited at the bottom, squeezing his eyes tight to block out the vision of her swishing, fine ass. If this was love, how the fuck had the world continued to populate? Because it was doing its best to kill him. No wonder Will couldn't go through this shit again. But Stefan also knew in that moment that there was no stopping it. If he went up those stairs, he wasn't coming back down until he made her his.

He bit back a curse and swallowed hard. Then he took the stairs, one at a time.

Chapter Twenty-Four

Stefan stepped inside the bathroom and pulled her closer to him by one lock of her shiny black hair. "Fine. Since you're being so stubborn. But you asked for this."

Right before her very wanton eyes, he stripped out of his clothes, without shame for standing there completely naked in front of her. For a few seconds, he didn't move or look directly at her. Which was different. Stefan always made strict eye contact, but not now. It reminded her that this hadn't been his idea.

Dani's eyes dropped with the sting but slowly she let herself take him in. His feet were planted there, a hip's width apart and it was the same stance she'd seen many times at the house. Him in front of the fridge, him out on the porch. The cocky pillar pose when he wasn't budging for anyone or anything. His legs were much longer than she realized but the same natural tan as his chest. As if that was what she was really focusing on. Before she could ogle his front any longer and how at rest, his penis hung almost to the middle of his thigh, he turned and stepped into the huge round tub, giving her the full view of his ass.

Inside, she made a sloppy aww sound.

Stefan had a bubble butt which made her smile because it was sexy as hell rounding out from his thighs. Two thick muscles framed either side of his back that was so broad, just looking at it left her feeling protected. His neck. The black hairs curling as they grew up his hairline trickled along the tattoos that sprang from his arms and connected in an arch over the top of his back.

Jet-made bubbles floated over the top of the water, hiding nothing from her view as he sat down and hung his arms cockily over the sides of the tub. The perk was her view of him right now. The drawback was that now she had to undress while he awaited and watched. Maybe he was counting on her not being able to follow through. She'd show him.

Dani pulled her long hair up into a makeshift bun and tied it around itself on top of her head then reached behind her neck to untie her dress's halter top. Once she did that, it fell loosely to the ground. He smiled more to himself than for her benefit, she was sure. She liked that about him. No shame, even though she'd bated him up here and he'd clearly preferred she just go home.

Next she stepped out of her sandals. Finally, his grin appeared, although only for a second. Yes, he must be aware she was wishing she had more to strip off but all that remained were her bra and panties.

An awareness came over Dani just then, just like it had that morning when the nurse had rubbed the ultrasound wand over her. When she looked down at her white cotton panties hugging her hips, she saw the bump of her belly sticking out. Like she had a kid-sized ball tucked under her skin. It was so hard not to get lost in the little man growing in there, now that she'd seen him. She didn't just feel bloated now. She felt like a mother.

Before she knew it, splashes sloshed around and the gorgeous, brooding man soaking in the tub stood toe to toe with her. Water gushed off Stefan's wonderfully large and shiver-inducing body and onto the floor but he didn't seem to care. His large feet were planted right by hers and his black hairs ran down his long legs in streams. Dani's hands now rested over her belly, mesmerized as she was, picturing her baby boy floating in there, happy. Asleep because he wasn't kicking her.

Unless she was hallucinating, she felt Stefan's arms wrap around her and pull her in for a hug she was so grateful for. His chest, God his chest. But what he was really doing was unclasping her bra. It fell to the floor by her dress. She'd taken too long and he wanted what he wanted. What she'd dangled in front of him at the front door. His wet, warm hands skimmed down her sides, making her shiver. She waited to feel her panties being torn off but what she felt were his hands covering hers over her belly.

His hands stayed over hers while he rested his chin on top of her head. A hiccup or a cry tried to escape her mouth but she held it in because she didn't want to ruin this moment. Yes, it was incredibly sexy but she'd never felt more cared for in all her life when his hands moved to her back and rubbed.

Vaguely, she remembered she still had her good news to share with him. But the power of this moment had claimed her. Stefan wanted her this way, he was so evidently turned on by her as she felt his every hard muscle and member slowly coming to life along her hip, making her shiver in response.

"Stefan, there's something I want to tell you. I don't have to say it right now, just please don't let me forget. You'll want to hear it. Two things."

"What?"

She wanted to scream that they could have sex, just to make it official but the look on his face said he'd already guessed. Was she that easy? Yeah, but she didn't care because she wasn't alone. This man hugging her to his hard hot body was easy too. There was no shame in being this way together. He'd never believe her that Gina had agreed to move. If she could remember to spit it out.

His lips moved over each other like he was smoothing lip balm over them.

"Come to Nashville with me." It was a low, dark whisper.

Her ears must have water in them. But no, in her fog she remembered she hadn't gotten in the tub yet.

Her voice left her the deeper his became.

"I want you to come. And my mom. I'll," he paused and kissed her shoulder. "I am buying a house and I want you both with me. I know it's wrong, and you have every right to say no, but that's what I want."

She couldn't move but felt a murmur leave her lips.

"Shh, don't answer me now. Let's get in the tub and you can tell me your good news." He laid a scorching trail of wet kisses up and down her throat. But the only coherent thought she could make was that he'd asked her! A thousand emotions must be hammering across her face. She couldn't leave with him in two days but in two months, he'd get both her and his mom. If he could wait. Unaware if she was supposed to speak or just free fall into the warmth of his invitation, she followed him into the tub.

****

That scrambled look she got. Fuck. Why had he thrown that out there?

"Stefan?" she asked. He wanted to stop her from saying the word NO before it fell off her sweet lips. But something told him he was going to have to hear this out. "That means so much to me." A tear dropped from her eye and he hadn't even seen it form. "More than you can ever know."

"But?" he said.

"Just that I can't go right away. But soon, two months." Her voice kicked up at the end like she doubted he'd wait for he. God, she was wrong.

"Really?" He was stunned and a huge part of him didn't believe he was hearing her right. Stefan cupped handfuls of her hair, wishing he could snap his fingers and make everything work how and when he wanted it. Not in two months, but now goddamit.

Trista's words rang in his ears. It felt like the world was fucking with him and he was not thrilled. But Dani was right. He knew she was. How fucking unfair was it that this Thom had broken her heart in an email yet the world would come crashing to an end before she even dreamed of not speaking with him face to face?

He heard her begin to cry, a steady stream of tears and hiccups. His arms were around her, holding her tight. He couldn't see her like this but he was the only one allowed to protect and surround her until she felt better.

"Hey, what's this all about, huh?" He had to make it stop.

"I hate saying no to you." Her voice hitched and the cries became wet. She sniffed.

Stefan caressed her back, her sides and her shoulders, realizing he had to be patient. That she was worth it. "I understood that to be a yes but not right now," he whispered the truth to her, not caring about the pain it caused him to have to share her in any capacity with any other man. Two months wasn't that long, he reminded himself. He could see them living a life, a fun life that meant something. One where he was happy most days. "There are places I want to take you. Fuck, I want you on tour with me, sweetheart." He ran his fingers through her hair and massaged her scalp that she let fall heavily into his hands. But he knew that was impossible. "If I could just get you to Nashville. Now." His hands roamed over her body, harder now, greedier. "But I can't take you away from my mom. There's still that." His nose nuzzled past all her hair so that he could suckle her neck.

She cried out a tiny moan, which he loved. "You didn't remind me. That was part of my good news," she said, her voice huskier than it had been before. What was she saying? "I talked to your mom. She says she's willing to give Tennessee a try if…" Her voice trailed off as she stretched her neck for him.

"If what?"

"If I am, she is. And if you're willing to wait and let me do what I have to do with Thom. Then she's on board."

Mom didn't want him to rush Dani and have it come back to bite him in the ass. Just like she'd said.

"She loves you. Like a daughter. She told me that." His mom was wise and Stefan could learn a thing or two from her.

His fingers hadn't felt enough of Dani's body and he adjusted so he could skim his hands down her thick, luscious thighs. God, her ass felt so good. He wanted to lay a kiss to her belly but he held back and stayed nibbling at the peach fuzz near her earlobe stealing glances down the front of her body, over her full breasts and between them to her swollen belly.

"Dani, how can I take you away from your life here? In what universe am I that worthy? So what, I'm a fucking musician? Are you sure?" She, a twenty something young woman had to be the one to have the unselfish thought of taking the time to do the right things. She was so much better than him. If he pushed too hard without making it clear what she was getting herself into with him, that's what he could see coming back to bite him in the ass. If he ever disappointed Dani like he'd done his mom, he'd never get over it. He'd be just like Will. Stuck. "This beautiful baby growing in your belly isn't mine. He belongs to a young man risking his life for our country." Dani twirled on him and kissed his

261

shoulder. She ran her hand up and touched the stubble growing back on his face. His abs shuddered when she started touching the ink running up his ribs on the side using the lightest touch of her fingertips.

"Stop it. You're stuck in your head. I want you stuck here with me. All these things you're worrying about, there's a fix for everything. We can figure it out. You took the biggest step when you invited me just now. That was huge and I know that." He felt her wiggle onto his thigh. Oh, fuck.

She made sense but he couldn't stop the thoughts from coming as they rubbed against each other. He found a new spot to kiss her and his cock jumped when he felt the goose bumps he'd just given her. Her hard nipples scraped against his chest and he groaned inside. Still, the world hadn't wanted Stefan to be a father to his own child and so that baby had died in Amanda's belly. Who the fuck was he to think he had any right to this man's baby?

His mom was right. Just like she'd been when she asked Stefan to move out on his eighteenth birthday. The whole town had thought he was a shameful, selfish asshole. He wasn't back then but he'd sure grown into one. In a bitter twist, he knew he was no different than his dad. Better or worse didn't matter. He'd strung Dani along just like Dad had done to Mom. To get what he wanted, he'd strung her along this whole visit with what? The promise of one great night of sex? Her nipples, dark and rosy, held his attention. And then he'd gone and asked her for something she should never do. To put her trust in him and join his crazy life.

"Saying yes, it makes you as selfish as me. I can't make you like me, Dani."

New tears welled up in her eyes and fell when she blinked.

"Hey, hey, shhhh. Don't cry. It's okay. I shouldn't have asked." He wiped away her new tears and kissed her cheekbone.

"You're taking it back and pulling away." Her face broke his heart. "If it's because I asked you to wait … Two months. Three max. That's all I'm asking you for," she said to him, killing him with that pained look and her shiny eyes. "I am willing to try this if you are. Are you, Stefan?" Her brows hiked up with her question.

Her hope gave him a glimmer of it too. But she needed someone who would be with her forever. A partner for life. Could he be that for her?

"I'll be on the road in two months. You'll have to get settled in all on your own. I won't have any time to help." She'd be so pregnant by then.

"Oh." Her face fell. He was such a dick.

"Sweetheart, I meant that of course I'll wait. I just wanted to be there, you know. I'm not a very patient man. And I don't like to share what's mine." Stefan took her face in his hands and kissed her nose, aware he was slowly committing to her. "I also can't lie to you. Dani, you deserve someone who wants to make love to you, and I do. But I also still want to fuck you, sweetheart. Does that sound like the kind of boyfriend you want? Huh? Tell me the truth."

"What about all we've been through in the last week makes you think you can say that to me? Huh?" Her forehead wrinkled with the honest question. He smoothed the lines with his thumbs and kissed each of her eyebrows, remembering when he'd used those words on her.

"You're right. Let me make it up to you." Stefan caressed the top swells of her hips and then slid her panties down and off. He helped her into the tub and reset the jets. They fired up but all he could see was the hour glass of a woman he was following after. He held her hand so she didn't slip and then scooted her down to sit between his legs. On her own, she scooted until her back melted into his chest. This felt so right. He wanted to try.

"Dani," he kissed the top and sides of her hair, she had so much of it and it smelled like coconut heaven. "The reason I couldn't answer you earlier, about being on tour."

"Yes?" Her hand floated over the water and found his. She caught it and laced their fingers together. "Why Stefan? What was going on there?"

"I haven't had a monogamous relationship since I was sixteen years old."

"Oh. Wow."

Their passion was still thick but he found talking to her while he touched her a major turn on. Even with the heaviness. He played with her hair both on top of her head and hidden between her legs.

"Yeah, and thanks by the way. Disturbing, right?"

"Sorry. No. It's just a long time to go without someone steady. Someone you can count on." Dani ran her fingers up and down his arms. "So what happened that scared you off relationships so badly? And lest I remind you my ass just got dumped via email so…"

"Message received, wise ass." But he loved her for it. "You've heard me talk about Amanda. She was fourteen, I was sixteen. We'd known each other since kindergarten. Small town stuff, you know how that goes." Dani shook her head that she did and crooked her head to look at him. Her gentle smile encouraged him to go on.

This was friendship. This was what he craved with her. This was what Will was talking about.

"How long did you and Amanda date?"

"She asked me to the Sadie Hawkins dance in seventh grade. Well, she was in seventh grade. I was already a freshman but I went because she was cute and her parents were friends with mine. We had a good time. I kissed her. She slapped me. But then about a year later I asked her out again."

"I bet she said yes. I bet she couldn't resist you."

"She did say yes. She also slept with me that first night."

"Well that's no surprise. Were you guys each other's firsts?"

"It was her first time but I'd already been with someone."

Stefan needed inside Dani. He wanted her riding him while the water sloshed wherever the hell it felt like it. He washed her skin with his hands, wetting where she was dry and watching the water run its way back down her body.

"Let me guess. Babysitter? Librarian?"

He maneuvered so that he lay back against the tub's edge and pulled her to him. "Babysitter. Come here. Sit on my stomach." She did and he realized he didn't like being in the bath water because he wanted to feel her wetness rubbing against his abs with no mistake of whether it was her or the water.

"Oh Hon, you know I'm only teasing, right?"

"I do and I like it. I have a friend, her name is Tris. She'd love that you call me that."

Dani smiled and he must have embarrassed her because her cheeks looked like the roses he'd spent all day drowning in. He could drown in her right now. "So what all happened with Amanda then? I've been curious but didn't want to pry." she asked him, skipping over what he'd shared about Tris and rubbing her hairs against his. He pressed down on her ass cheeks, guiding her and keeping her off his hard on for now. He realized Tris, Jaxon, Benny, they were his family and he wanted them all to know Dani. Yeah, he guessed he could see where that would make even his little firecracker a little nervous.

"We went steady that year. Like any other horny sixteen year old, I found ways for us to be together. I had heard from my buddy that as long as I always pulled out before I came that I wouldn't get her pregnant. It worked for a whole year but one night my stupidity caught up with me. I did get her pregnant. When she told me, I was scared shitless but I promised to help her anyway I could. I loved her as much as any sixteen year old dumb ass could."

"Did you have a job or anything? Did you guys tell your parents?" Her back arched when he toyed with her nipples and she continued to ride his stomach. Fuck, he needed to get them out of this tub.

"I got a job fast. My high school music teacher ran the Moonlight Emporium so he hired me to work on the weekends and during the summer, cleaning up and helping stock the instruments that came in for repair from the schools. It wasn't much but it was something."

"It sounds like you had a plan. A good one for such a young kid. So what happened?"

"I thought I was running things. I had a part-time job which I was willing to make full-time when I quit school, a girlfriend and a baby on the way. I felt like a man. Then one day Amanda came crying to me that she couldn't see me anymore. Said she hated me. Unfortunately, she yelled this during dinner with my parents at our house. Thinking back, I'm sure her parents found out she was pregnant and gave her crap about being with me. Shit, I might as well tell you now that my dad had been seeing someone else behind Mom's back and the whole town knew about it."

Dani's hot ass riding of his abs went still and she brought her knees up. "No way. Really?"

"Yeah. People didn't talk much because they liked my mom but I know they knew. They looked at me and dad like we were scum. Amanda's parents had to have hated that their baby girl got mixed up with a Calderon. Well, long story short, about a week later my parents had their answer to why Amanda had freaked out on me at dinner that night. Her mom called to tell my mom about the pregnancy, the miscarriage and that she should be ashamed of having me as her son."

"But I don't get it. You had a job. You stayed with Amanda."

That was it. He loved talking like this with her but he was done with the bath. "Come here, sweetheart. I'll tell you more but first you're going to have to come with me."

Stefan wrapped her in a jumbo towel and grabbed one for himself. The way her eyes watched him so intently kept his cock stiff. Rather than wrapping himself in the towel, he just dried himself off then left his on the floor. He led her to the studio butt naked and felt her eyes on him the whole way. His cock shot out in front of him, hard and ready to finally make its way inside her.

"Here we are."

"Your room with the padded walls," she said with a shy smile.

"None of that coy crap. I know you better than that."

"There's no bed."

"We don't need one."

He led her to the thick white rug next to a rack made for his basses. He laid down first on his back. "I want you to ride me again. That was so fucking hot. You had my cock so hard in the tub."

"Had?"

She took him in her hand which made her towel fall around them.

Then she lowered her head to take the head of his cock into her mouth. "I don't think so," he told her, pulling her up to his face. "You're not tricking me like that again. The only place my cock is hanging out tonight is inside you."

"Inside me where, Hon?"

"You know where." For some reason, he didn't want to say the P word. Never in his life had he not wanted to say the fucking P word. "In here." He inserted a couple of fingers inside her and watched her jaw fall unhitched.

Dani pulled him by the wrist until his fingers were outside of her. "You're not getting in there until you finish telling me about what we were talking about."

He chuckled. Had she forgotten where they'd left off too?

"That's gonna have to wait. You still haven't made good on one of your promises to me."

Her eyebrows pulled together and he loved watching her think so hard.

"Let me help you out."

Carefully, he wrapped his arm behind her neck and maneuvered them until she was the one on her back with open legs and spilling breasts. He kissed her nose and then licked his way down her sides with his tongue and lips, always with his eyes open and on her face, until he was there. The place he'd been desperate to taste since that first day.

"This."

He wanted his eyes locked on hers but at this angle, couldn't see her face for her baby bump. Stefan watched her hands instead as they fished the white shaggy rug. That was just as telling. He ran his tongue up the seam of her lips. Her grip loosened and then tightened again when he licked her with his full tongue. Her flesh stuck to him as he tongued her harder and deeper, adding his teeth. He kept his glance sideways on her hands and smiled when her fingers stretched so wide the tendons and bones of her hand showed.

"I want to suck you in and drink you," he said then blew over the moist pink skin of her pussy. There, he had his favorite word back.

So quick he couldn't follow, only chuckle, her hands left the rug and clapped both sides of his head. "Ouch," he said.

Immediately her fingers combed through his hair and she soothed and rubbed his head. "Sorry but you deserved that," she said and let out a sexy sigh.

"No I didn't." He smiled, knowing she couldn't see him doing it but confident she knew he was playing. He took a second and left her wetness to lay a kiss on the inside of her thigh that kept bumping the side of his head whenever he nibbled her. "But I liked it." He sucked the skin of her thigh in hard and kept at it until he knew he'd left a little mark on her. She squirmed some more and her hands fisted in his hair but the pain was the good kind and also reminded him how fucking hard he was for her.

Stefan nuzzled his way back to her sweet pussy. "Did I ever tell you about this girl who said I couldn't make her come?"

He heard her laugh. "I heard she—"

But when he thrust his shoulders up against the backs of her thighs, giving her legs no choice but to cradle his head and pushed his face so hard up against her pussy and growled, she went silent. Except for one little nearly orgasmic mewl. He then reached his arms around her hips and held her immobile at her sides while he engorged himself on her, sucking and kissing so hard and furiously like he'd been starving.

"Stefan—I"

There would be no answer for her now because he wasn't relenting. His tongue felt too good swirling inside her the deeper he went, the harder he pushed his face and the more he worked his mouth on her. Every time he swallowed, he knew he was taking bits of her inside him. After he was done, her pussy would smell like him and he would smell like her. *Don't you ever let anyone else in this spot, Dani, my spot.* He'd never cared about that with anyone else.

He could have gone on all night but after only a few more thrusts of his tongue, she began to climax. He let her hips buck wildly up into his face as he continued to hold her by the hips.

"I was wrong, so wrong," she cried out and fisted his hair so tight in her small hands.

He still couldn't talk because he knew it was coming and would not miss it. And finally he had it, not the virginal popping of a cherry but the heady womanly gushing when all her body knew to do in that split second was bundle up and explode. Different from the taste of the moisture that coated her outer folds, this little drop of pure sex burst onto his tongue. He relaxed and held still, letting it absorb into his taste buds. It wasn't sweet. He had no taste for that. This was Dani. That was the only way to describe it. People didn't try to describe salt any other way than to call it salty. It was the same with a woman's pleasure burst. He let his forehead fall against her soft mesh of short dark hairs and hugged her legs against the sides of his head while he came back down to planet earth.

"Ahem, so what were we talking about, sweetheart?" he whispered and kissed the mark he'd left on her inner thigh, branding her as his.

"Um, Amanda's parents…" Her neck stretched again. He continued caressing her with his fingers, aware she liked his rough touch, even though he was being gentle now. He was about to have his own orgasm just watching her enjoy his touch freely for the first time. He realized now how much she'd been holding back in at the truck stop.

"For the record, I've never talked this much during sex. You're amazing, sweetheart." Stefan was in no way done with her but didn't mind the breaks for sharing with her. It was stuff she needed to know. He kissed his way up her body. She searched for his hand until he squeezed hers in his. "But yeah, what parent in their right mind is going to trust a kid with their baby girl? I wouldn't have either. Amanda lost the baby. The last time I talked to her was about a month later. She told me things probably wouldn't have worked out. Shit, she was probably right but I never got the chance to prove her wrong."

"I'm so sorry," Dani said in that voice of hers that soothed him. The climax had relaxed her features and left her his favorite shade of flushed.

Talking about this shit, he knew he was getting a lot off his chest. He couldn't believe she was letting him go on and on about his past while he began to finger her again. He couldn't help it.

"Yeah well we were young," he said and maneuvered his ring finger in search of her asshole while continuing to rub circles at her very wet clit. She was so wet and his chest fired off knowing he'd gotten her that way.

Fuck, was she for real? He toyed with pushing his finger inside her ass and felt her wet lips still spasm and squeeze against his fingers. He was so close to orgasm but he couldn't let himself shoot off until he was buried deep inside her.

"Young. I guess. And your dad? Can you talk about that?" There was no guessing, she'd just panted that question out.

Stefan stopped. He had to finish off this conversation and then make real, explicit love to her. She looked at him and frowned when he pulled his fingers away from her openings. So slick and ready for more from him.

"Almost, sweetheart. Let me just finish this up and then no more talking. What else can I really say? Dad fell in love with someone who wasn't Mom." He petted her hair back from her face and gazed, yeah he gazed like the whipped little dick he was but he didn't care. "He actually told me he was leaving about a year before it happened. That he loved my mom but not that way anymore." Dani petted his face and his hair and the way she looked at him. Fuck. She cared about him. "But he told me straight up that he wasn't going to leave until Mom finished her college degree. That way she'd always have her education and would always be able to support me in case he fell off the face of the earth, I guess. It was so fucking strange to know that. I fucking had this countdown going. Like when kids used to make countdowns to Christmas."

"You were only seventeen and your dad made you deal with that crap? Unbelievable."

"Dani, I know it sounds crazy, but my whole life I've respected him for what he did. But yeah, it makes me wonder if I'm fucked up in the head. Or shit, in the heart."

"No. I don't think you are. I think your dad, like you said, cared about your mom but then fell out of love with her and rather than stay in a marriage without passion, chose to make a change. Stefan, if you were ever in a relationship and you stopped being crazy in love with that person, I hope you would do something about it. It would break my heart for you to be stuck in a situation like that. I wouldn't want that for you. Even if the other person in the relationship was me. Your dad wasn't a bad guy. And neither are you for loving him."

Just like that, his heart settled in his chest.

He was done playing the game.

He wiggled down into the comfort of the thick rug, then pulled her up on top of him. God, her breasts fell so naturally on either side of her chest, all real and all for him. He never wanted to touch another pair again. Hers were perfect and he wanted them in his mouth. Stefan slid her down his stomach and then lifted her up by the hips to settle her down on top of him when he remembered something very significant. "Sweetheart, I fucking almost forgot the condom."

She smiled so wide and bright that he nearly shot his seed into the crack of her ass where his erection currently sat a happy yet horny and desperate camper.

"What?" he asked, amazed by the brilliant smile gleaming from her right now. He held her face with his eyes as he helped her climb back down his body and then slowly perched herself over his rock hard yet still uncovered cock. "Hey, let me up. I meant it when I said I'd get a condom for you."

"Stefan." She said his name and he came that much closer to losing it. "I don't have much, but this one thing I can give you. You know you don't need a condom with me."

Fuck, he swallowed at the way she looked so vulnerable, offering him this gift. "Sweetheart, are you sure?"

"You can't get me pregnant and I trust when you said you've always covered up. I'm not worried about what you've done in the past." Her brown eyes always reminded him of a doe. Sometimes pissed and sometimes hysterical with laughter but always true. And fuck, she was right.

"Then ride me, sweetheart."

His hands released their tight hold keeping her up and she wiggled until her opening was lined up with his cock. He ground his molars when she slid down him, slowly allowing her body to stretch and fit him. "Fuck, I'm all the way in. You're so tight." He of all people appreciated why that was. She was a good girl and didn't share herself with just anyone.

"I'm not usually on top. Do you like this?"

She rode him in the cutest frog position. "I do. Very much," he said and couldn't help but smile. He'd bet her thighs were screaming but she took it like a woman. His woman. Their pleasure rose and broke together and when he came, she came. He squeezed her thighs, knowing she needed help soothing the burn.

She whispered and crawled like a slinky cat until his cock slid out of her and she straddled him, her knees hugging the sides of his ribs. A few moist drops, probably his cum but he hoped some of hers too, dripped from her pussy onto his stomach, making him ache to lick her belly clean. Her face was inches from his. Her elbows dug into his chest so she could keep herself propped up and he loved that she wasn't embarrassed to let her weight rest on him like this. "You don't ever have to wear another condom again. Not when we make love, and most definitely not when we fuck."

Her bottom lip tormented him tucked between her teeth. His heart thumped with pride and possession that this woman was his. They'd make it all work because he'd finally found the one he could be so very bad and so very good to.

"Sweetheart, you win."

Epilogue

Six months later, Pittsburgh, PA...

Dani's due date had long since come and gone. "Ugh, I don't feel sexy right now. How in the world can you stand to be around me? I feel like a gigantic baked potato with arms and legs. And the gas!"

"Hey, no fair complaining now. I told you there would be tons of sexual harassment involved when I re-hired you, Nurse Dani. And Benny passed this article he found online to me that my jizz has stuff in it that will help you start labor. My prostaglandins can help stimulate contractions," he said properly and rehearsed. "So come here. Now."

Ever telling her what to do. She smiled. "Those are some big words, Mr. Calderon. Big, intelligent words. You're so hot. What are you waiting for? Get over here and help a girl out."

"I thought you just said you didn't feel sexy."

"I don't. That's what's so unfair. I'm bloated but hornier than you, even."

"If I give you the best sex of your life right now, and it doesn't send you into labor, will you sit on the side of the stage while I play?"

How could she say no to that? Why mess with perfection? Gina was well enough that she and Dani had been able to travel to this week's Sin Pointe show in the big city. Pittsburgh was only twenty miles from Moonlight. Little Cord Calderon might just be born right here at the show which was fine with her. She just wanted the munchkin out of her belly. He had to be a giant by now.

Stefan killed her with a wicked grin.

Jaxon walked by just then. She should say strutted, in his black pants held together it seemed by zippers. He ran a hand through his dark blonde pompadour. He was one of Dani's favorites because every night when she and Stefan talked on the phone, Stefan would tell her the daddy trick Jaxon had taught him that day. "Hey sexy, you're needed for sound checky in ten minnies. If you see Will, tell him to get his ass on stage too. Oh fuck, hey, doll," he said to her and kissed her on the cheek. "Don't make my boy too late. And my Lily sends her love. Says she can't wait 'til you get to Bugscuffle."

Bugscuffle, Tennessee. The tiny town outside of Nashville where the bad boys of Sin Pointe and their former assistant now called home. And where soon, she would call home too.

"Aww, tell her thank you and that I can't wait to meet her. And your daughter. Maryella?"

"Yep, my Maryellie. Lily tells me she's been making little Cordy lots of baby clothes."

"Oh my goodness. That's so sweet."

"Yeah, she's a goody. Fuck, I almost forgot. Lily, Trissy, Hazel, they're throwing you a baby shower when you get moved in. You can't say no so don't even try. Right, mate?" He lifted his chin at Stefan who just smiled back.

Dani could listen to Jaxon speak in that rhymy Aussie voice of his for hours on end but the only man she ever wanted to hear sing was her Stefan. Just the thought of being here live at his show gave her a hot case of fan girl crush.

"I guess our prosta, what did you call it, Hon?"

"Prostaglandin."

"Right. Our prostaglandin semen exchange session is going to have to wait. Your boys need you. Go ahead and go. I'll go sit with Mom backstage and if I run into Will, I'll tell him he's been summoned."

Stefan looked mischievous. "I think I know where Will is. And if you'd have bet me money all those months ago when you said he was into your sister, you'd be a little richer right now."

"Really?" She didn't mean to squeal but next to her getting the boy, she would be over the moon if Will got the girl. Especially if it was her sister. "Hurry, tell me more. Then you have to go."

Stefan zipped his fingers across his lips.

"Don't even pull that bro-code crap on me. You're not supposed to be mean to your fiancée."

"All I'll say is that I may have seen his phone in the dressing room bathroom and it may have flashed an incoming call with your sister's name."

"Which means he would have manually had to enter it in!"

"Or your crazy sister could have snatched his phone from him and manually entered it herself. But yes, both ways, it's in there and calls have been made." He zipped a finger over his lips again. "That's all you're getting. Now I'll go snatch his ass out of the toilet and I'll see you soon."

His hand was still tentative whenever he rubbed her belly but he was getting better at allowing himself to accept that any day now, he'd be Cord's step-daddy. She felt his grin widen as he kissed her long and hard. "Okay, I've gotta go make some noise."

"Go get 'em, baby. I'll be right here waiting."

He saluted her from his heart and ran down the hall to the dressing room. All in tight white, he streaked away like only her Superman could. Her hero. Her good, her bad. Her everything.

Cord had run out of room to kick her much at this point so he butted up against her ribs and she found that stubborn little foot of his and gently pushed it back in under her rib. She took a super deep breath, held it and let it whistle out.

He was one lucky little man.

His father loved him enough to let the man who loved her raise him as his son. Thom was good, as she'd always known, and proved it during the short visit they'd had during his mid-tour leave. The best man though? Her Stefan. She'd shared Thom's acceptance of the situation over the phone that night and Stefan surprised her saying he'd like to meet Cord's father one day. To thank him.

Cord had so many loving homes just waiting to welcome him into the world, it nearly made Dani cry. Grandma Gina would be making their big move to Bugscuffle. Their new place wasn't too far from Auntie Trista and Uncle Lucky's house.

She clicked open her phone's photo album and scrolled through the pics Stefan had sent her of the nursery in their new house, just waiting for the little guy to be born so they could finally make the big move and be together. Stefan hadn't wanted her to risk any stress with a move during her pregnancy with him on the road and unable to be with her.

Whether they were here in Pittsburgh in the fancy hotel just minutes away from the hospital with Mommy and Daddy … and Uncle Will … and possibly Aunty Daisy—who knew?—Will could be hiding her baby sister in his dressing room as they spoke—no matter where they were, this little guy was being born into one amazing family. Dani couldn't wait to meet the entire gang in person.

Drums started up.

The bass joined in.

Keys, electric guitar and her man's deep honey voice brought the jam to life.

Her head started bobbing the second Stefan's bass fell into that perfect groove with Will's drums. He'd taught her that.

All she could think as she closed her eyes and felt the music crawl up from the floor into her toes and up her legs, was…

Mine.

Dani smiled. And yeah, she cried. Because she was nine months pregnant, her hormones were a real you know what, and whether she was a toad, a princess or a pumpkin, she was living her fairy tale life. Stefan Calderon was her wickedly cool happy ending.

****

Stefan stood there on stage, taking it all in. He was one lucky bastard. As he geared up to belt out "Touch", the thought that he kept locked in his brain every second of every day he had with Dani made his heart pound with fierce, wicked love…

If you cannot be good for yourself, be good for her.
Always be good for her.

—*Stefan Calderon*

The End

www.carlenelove.com

Evernight Publishing

www.evernightpublishing.com

www.ingramcontent.com/pod-product-compliance
Lightning Source LLC
Chambersburg PA
CBHW030238200626
46816CB00002BA/424